THE UNEXPECTED WIFE

THE THREE MRS. BOOK 1

JESS MICHAELS

To Mackenzie Walton, who is the most amazing editor and friend. Thank you for your excellent notes, which always make me sharper and better.

And for Michael. When this book comes out we will have quarantined together for almost a year. Thank you for making difficult situations better and for being the best company I could have asked for. I love you so much!!!

CHAPTER 1

Summer 1813

Owen Gregory liked a great deal about being an investigator, but there was one task that he despised above all others: telling a person that someone they loved was dead. There was often weeping and shouting and denying and even blaming involved, and those emotions would wash over him and almost stick, hanging there for days.

He was here in Twiddleport, a small village with a very silly name, to do exactly that. Tell a woman that her husband was dead. He had to tell her a great deal more and perhaps even worse than that, but he almost couldn't think about all of it at once or it got jumbled in his mind.

He shifted in his saddle and urged his horse, Lucius, a bit faster. The woman, Celeste Montgomery, had not been at the small, rather ramshackle home she and her late husband had let in town, so he had been directed to a cottage just outside Twiddleport where her parents lived. Based on the directions he'd been given, the home in the distance was the one he sought. He pulled up after he entered the gate and dismounted, then took a good look at the place. Moderately sized, well kept, a rather pretty place, if nondescript.

He made his way to the door and knocked. There was a great commotion from inside, with dogs barking and shouts from within, but at last the door opened and a rather beleaguered-looking older woman with a kerchief wrapped around her head stood there. The housekeeper, he thought, and smiled at her.

"Good afternoon, madam. I have come to call on Mrs. Montgomery. I have been told she is here visiting her parents."

The woman looked him up and down slowly with a faint sniff. "And who are you?"

He withdrew a card from the inside pocket of his jacket and held it out. The cards were meant to impress; he had designed them thus, with gold filigree and fine paper. "Mr. Owen Gregory, at your service."

"I don't think you are expected, sir. I wasn't told the family was receiving guests."

She moved to close the door, but Owen wedged his boot in at the last moment, stopping her from locking him out. "I understand," he said, forcing what he hoped was a friendly but firm expression to his face. "But what I have come to discuss cannot wait. I've news from London about Mr. Montgomery. *Urgent* news."

A bit of interest lit up in the housekeeper's expression, and she glanced him over a second time before she opened the door and motioned him into the foyer. "Wait here, if you will," she said. "I'll ascertain if they'll see you."

He nodded and took a seat on a bench along one wall of the foyer. He tugged his riding gloves off as he did so and stretched his fingers while he looked around the entryway. If the outside of the home had been nondescript, the foyer was trying for another impression: opulence. Every item, from the cushion on the benches to the wall hangings to the golden pitcher and other baubles on a table along the opposite wall, looked expensive. The entryway was clearly meant to impress whatever guests came. To tell them that the inhabitants of the home were important, even if Sir Timothy was only a baronet.

The housekeeper returned to the foyer, and he rose.

"The family will see you," she said, and motioned for him to follow her. He did so, taking a subtle peek into the rooms with open doors as he walked. Some were very plain, others all done up like the foyer. For show and for life. He supposed many families lived thus.

The parlor he entered was one of the plain ones. Perhaps the family had heard his name and not recognized it as one of import, so they hadn't felt a drive to move to a showier chamber. It didn't really matter. What he had to say would have to be said no matter the quality of the wallpaper.

His stomach hurt at the thought of it as he searched the inhabitants of the room for Mrs. Montgomery. Lady Hendricks and Sir Timothy stood at the sideboard together, a slim lady with dark hair and an older gentleman, all gray and angled, as he looked to his wife to address this situation.

Which left the woman standing next to the fireplace as his quarry. Owen had read up on her—as much as he could, of course. She was in her early thirties, and had been a spinster until the marriage had been arranged with Erasmus Montgomery after the briefest of courtships. Owen had made a picture of her in his head as he rode from London to perform this horrid duty: older than her years, made haggard by life.

The woman before him was not that picture. He caught his breath at how beautiful she was. She was tall and curvaceous, with dark auburn hair, like a fire that was smoldering and waiting to explode. Her eyes were a gray-blue. They held his with question and he thought a bit of hesitance, as if she had already determined that whatever news he came with, it wasn't good.

That dragged him from the inappropriate study of her beauty and back to reality. He was here to fulfill a duty, not to ogle the widow who didn't yet know she *was* a widow.

"Good afternoon—Mr. Gregory, is it?" Lady Hendricks said as she moved toward him. "I do not think we are acquainted, nor that we had an appointment."

"No on both accounts," he conceded with a slight bow of his head. "And I apologize for intruding upon your hospitality in such an uncouth way. But I have urgent news for Mrs. Montgomery and I could not stand on propriety, nor wait for an appointment to deliver it."

Mrs. Montgomery tilted her head and stepped forward. "The housekeeper, Mrs. Blythe, said that you had a message for me about my husband. I cannot imagine what it could be."

There was a hint of disdain to her tone as she said the word *husband* that Owen could not help but mark. She had no warm feelings for Erasmus Montgomery, it seemed. He would not ease that tension before this day was through.

"Yes, and why would our *dear* Mr. Montgomery not come here with the news himself?" Lady Hendricks said, stepping closer and all but cutting off Owen's view of Mrs. Montgomery. Lady Hendricks had clearly bestowed her daughter with those lovely gray-blue eyes, but the older woman's version was sharp, narrow, seeking. There was little warmth within.

Owen cleared his throat and side-stepped Lady Hendricks to focus, yet again, on Mrs. Montgomery rather than her mother. "There is no easy way to say this, and I am sorry for the pain it will no doubt cause you. I have come here to…"

He drew a long breath to steady himself for what was to follow.

"Mr. Montgomery is dead, Mrs. Montgomery. And I fear that is not the worst of the news I am bound to bring to you."

Celeste Montgomery felt the world stop turning in the moments this handsome stranger said those four words. *Mr. Montgomery is dead.* They hit her square in the chest like a shotgun blast, and she nearly went to her backside in front of the fire before she reached back and steadied herself on the mantel, toppling one of her mother's little figurines. She saw Lady Hendricks' eyes narrow at the sight of that unforgiveable indiscretion, even as she shrieked like it was her husband who was dead. Sir Timothy caught her as she slumped into an elegant heap.

Celeste had seen this kind of reaction so many times over the years, she refused to rise to the bait, but she was surprised when Mr. Gregory, the stranger who had just ripped her world out from under her, hardly reacted to it either. He continued watching her, not her mother as she heaved while she "came to" from her fit.

"Mrs. Montgomery, did you hear me?" he asked, stepping closer.

She realized she was still gripping the mantel with all her might, and released it as she stared at him. He was a very handsome man. An odd thing to think about in this moment, but facts were facts. He had brown hair that was a little too long, a well-defined jawline and a mouth that clearly smiled often, though he was certainly not doing so now. His eyes were also very fine, a pale brown that held hers steadily.

"Mrs. Montgomery?" he said again.

She shook herself. "I-I'm sorry," she said over her mother's hysterical weeping in the background. "I am shocked. You are telling me that Mr. Montgomery is...dead. Truly? And you are certain it is *Erasmus* Montgomery?"

He nodded. "I am very certain, I'm afraid."

"How...when...?" she whispered.

His gaze lit up a fraction, as if she had said something he approved of. "In London...quite suddenly, a few days ago."

She stepped toward him and her knees gave way unexpectedly. Mr. Gregory lunged forward and caught her elbow, drawing her against his chest as he guided her to the nearest chair. When she was situated, he released her and she felt a bit colder for the lack of his warmth. She gripped the armrests with both fists, clinging there for purchase.

As she did so, her parents each took a place on the settee, her mother wiping her tears with a perfectly monogrammed handkerchief. Lady Hendricks motioned to the chair beside Celeste for Mr. Gregory to sit.

"I cannot believe this terrible news! Oh, to lose one so young and *so* beloved!" her mother moaned. Then she leaned forward and speared Mr. Gregory with a pointed, bright stare. "Tell me *everything* about the circumstances."

Celeste caught her breath at the nosy cruelty of her mother's desire for gossip. "Mama!" she said, and earned a glare from her mother and a slight shake of the head from her very pale and normally silent father. She ignored them both and focused again on Mr. Gregory. "I don't understand, sir. My...husband seemed in good health when last I saw him."

"And when was that?" Mr. Gregory asked, his light brown gaze holding hers.

She shifted with discomfort, with humiliation as she dropped her eyes to her hands clenched in her lap. "Six—six months ago," she admitted.

She dared to lift her gaze and found Mr. Gregory had arched one of those brows and was watching her carefully. But before he could say anything to respond to that horrible admission, her mother leapt to her feet.

"Our Mr. Montgomery was such a busy man. If you knew him, you would be aware of how very important he was. The son of an earl, sir. How could he always be here when he had so much to do and influence? But when he returned to our daughter, it was always to the most wonderful reunion. Two so in love, I have never seen."

Celeste's stomach turned at that lie, the one that Mr. Gregory didn't seem all that moved by, though he looked her mother up and down carefully, as if he were taking the measure of her.

Why, Celeste couldn't say. If he were simply a messenger sent to tell her the news of Erasmus's death, why was he asking questions about her last meeting with the man? Why was he judging and seeking? And what had he meant when he told her there was worse news beyond Erasmus's death? She'd been so shocked by that fact, the rest hadn't sunk in, but now it did.

"—wasn't it, my dear?" her mother was still saying, though now she'd put the full force of her attention on Celeste's father.

Sir Timothy rose to his feet and gave a nervous glance first to Celeste and then to Mr. Gregory. "I-Indeed, the day our daughter married was m-most happy," he stammered, as he was wont to do when his wife made him lie.

Celeste tried not to be drawn back to that horrible day when her fate had been sealed. How she'd made an attempt to escape out a window, only to be dragged back in and marched, almost at bayonet point, to the altar. Erasmus Montgomery hadn't even looked at her when he said his vows. He'd yawned while she said hers. All his pretense was gone once he knew he'd have the little dowry that accompanied her entrance into their marriage.

As for the wedding night...well, that hadn't been much fun, either.

"Of course we will all go to London. Arrangements must be made for our *dearest* Erasmus," Lady Hendricks continued. "I'm sure the earl will be most pleased that we will make ourselves part of their deep grief. It is Erasmus's brother who holds the title, is it not?"

Celeste flinched, for her mother's ramblings were only making clearer the state of her marriage. She had been Mrs. Montgomery for almost a year and had never met her husband's family or friends. She had never been brought to London to see her home there. He had let her a...well, it was hardly more than a hovel here in Twiddleport, and she wasn't entirely certain he paid the rent on time on that.

But that didn't stop her mother from grasping, as usual. Seeing the death as an opportunity to insert herself into higher society if she could. Just as she had been Celeste's entire life.

Celeste cleared her throat, tired of the theatrics and the questions. "Mr. Gregory," she said above her mother's continued plots and plans. "You said a few moments ago that you had more to tell me than just that my husband was dead. Something worse than that news. I can be held in suspense no longer—what could be worse than that he is dead?"

Owen Gregory had been watching the room with interest, quiet but observant, for the last few moments. But when she asked that question, his posture changed. She could see discomfort take over and it...frightened her. This man didn't want to tell her the rest. Which meant it was very bad, indeed, for he had no affiliation with her, no reason to want to protect her.

"You might want to retake your seat," he said, and motioned to the chair she had abandoned. She did so and gripped the armrests with all her might. As if they might support her, for no one and nothing else in the room would.

"Please just say it," she whispered. "The suspense is horrible."

He nodded. "Of course. I am sorry, Mrs. Montgomery, your husband didn't just die. He was...he was murdered."

"Murder!" her mother screamed, and was about to launch into another round of hysterics when Mr. Gregory raised a hand.

"My lady, please! I am not finished." There was something about his tone that did the impossible: it silenced her mother.

Celeste leaned forward as the word *murder* echoed in her head. "What else is there?"

He swallowed. She watched the action move his Adam's apple, noted the subtle shift in his position. "It has been determined that... that Mr. Montgomery was a bigamist, madam. You are the third of three wives that the man held at his death. Your marriage, I'm afraid, was not legal."

CHAPTER 2

I f her mother had been screaming theatrically a few moments before, now the wails that echoed in the room around Celeste were more genuine. But she could scarcely hear them over the rush of blood in her ears. It was all just too much and she could scarcely fathom it.

Erasmus was dead. *Murdered.* And a bigamist. The last year of her life had been nothing more than a lie. And the future was now as cloudy and bleak as it could be.

She fought to suck in a breath but couldn't seem to do so as the truth of the situation settled over her, cold and heavy. Mr. Gregory seemed to see her distress, for his frown deepened and he crossed to her, taking the seat beside her. He caught her hand in his, his fingers warm against her own. He held her gaze steadily, almost intimately despite the fact that her mother carried on screeching across the room.

"Take a breath, Mrs. Montgomery," he said softly. "Through your nose and out through your mouth. Slowly now."

She blinked and did as he suggested. After a few focused breaths, she felt slightly less like she would sink into the floor and disappear forever. She forced a small smile. "Th-thank you." He nodded and released her hand.

"I say," Sir Timothy said, shaking his wife off his arm and crossing toward Celeste and Mr. Gregory. "You have come into my home and disrupted my wife and daughter. I think you need to explain yourself. We don't even know who you are—how are we to believe anything you say?"

Mr. Gregory looked at her rather than her father. "I am happy to explain if I can. Why don't we all sit? Mrs. Montgomery, do you need tea? Perhaps something stronger?"

Celeste blinked at the question and the earnest expression in his eyes when he asked it. He actually wanted to ease this for her. He had done so already by encouraging her to breathe, and he continued the pattern by offering her libation. When was the last time someone had done so for her? Thought of her, especially in times of stress?

She glanced at her mother, who had taken a seat on the settee but had her head in her hands and was still in minor hysterics. And her father, who was blustering now, but certainly at the behest of her mother, not because he felt some wild drive to protect Celeste.

She had been alone in the world for a very long time. It was an odd sensation to have someone thinking of her first.

"I'm fine," she lied. "Perhaps tea in a while. Right now I do think an explanation will go further in easing my mind. I cannot wrap my head around anything you are saying."

Mr. Gregory nodded. "Understandably. I have dropped a weight on your shoulders that I wish I could have avoided, but in these circumstances it is sometimes better to simply tear the bandage away all at once."

"Not exactly successful in wound management," she muttered.

To her surprise, the corner of his mouth tilted in a flash of a smile. He had a dimple, revealed and then concealed just as quickly. But she'd seen it.

"You have asked who I am, and I owe you that courtesy as I

start," he said, glancing at Sir Timothy. "I told you when I arrived that I'm Owen Gregory. I am an investigator."

Celeste shifted. "An investigator. You are looking into the murder?"

"Now, yes," he said. "But I was originally hired for another purpose. You see, at the time of his death, Mr. Montgomery was pursuing the marriage of a fourth young woman."

"Great God," Celeste breathed as she lifted her hand to cover her mouth. "A villain in every sense!"

"Yes." Mr. Gregory said, meeting her eyes. "The cruelty of his behavior was unconscionable. This young woman had a family, though, a very important family. A letter was received implying that Mr. Montgomery might already be in possession of more than one wife, and I was hired to investigate the claim and protect the lady in question…and her dowry."

"Of course!" Lady Hendricks said, her hysterics set aside now that there was a salacious story to be heard. "What family would not wish to protect the money at stake?" Celeste's cheeks heated as Owen glanced at her. Of course her mother would reveal her priorities in such an obvious way. "Who was the family?"

Celeste gasped at the inappropriate question. "Mama, that is hardly important now."

Mr. Gregory gave another of those fluttering smiles and said, "Indeed, my lady, I must protect the man's identity as much as I can, just as I will attempt to protect your daughter."

Celeste shook her head. There was surely no hope of that now. To keep an intended bride from the public eye was one thing. But she was married…or had thought to be married to Erasmus. The truth of his murder and his bigamy would become public fodder, there was no denying it. She was ruined. And while that terrified her, there were also other thoughts that moved through her at that fact.

Ones she pushed aside.

"So you investigated and discovered the truth of my—of Mr. Montgomery."

"Yes, and I was with the man who hired me, on our way to confront your husband, but when we arrived we found him dead in the parlor of his London home. Poisoned, it seems. And after some kind of altercation, for his eye was blackened, as well. There was some indication that arsenic was used."

Celeste squeezed her eyes shut as her stomach turned. She knew little about the poison, but she couldn't imagine that death in such a manner would be pleasant.

"The gentleman who hired me is acquainted with Montgomery's brother, the Earl of Leighton. Though the guard did come, the earl wanted the matter to be resolved more privately. So he asked me to continue with the investigation and try to determine who might have killed his brother. As well as help to resolve the mess with the multiple wives."

Celeste flinched. Multiple wives. That part still made her head spin. She pushed to her feet and paced the room. Already her mother had begun to talk, an endless stream of words that she blocked out. She'd had plenty of practice in doing so over her life, after all.

She stared out the window onto the drive, past it into the countryside. She still had so many questions, but with her parents in the room she would have no chance to ask them. At least not without interruption.

She pivoted back toward the rest of the room. "I need a moment to speak to Mr. Gregory," she declared loudly enough that she could be heard over the sound of her mother's voice.

That stopped the talking, and her parents and Mr. Gregory all looked at her at once. She shifted beneath their regard, their pity, their curiosity. If she found those things here in the parlor, it would only be worse out in the world.

"Then speak to him," her mother said, false consolation in every word.

"Alone," Celeste said softly.

"Certainly not!" Her mother leapt to her feet, and the understanding was gone from her voice and her body language. "I will not leave you. This is a family matter."

"It is not," Celeste said. "Mr. Gregory, am I to assume that you first came to look for me at my home in the village?" He nodded once. She arched a brow at her mother. "Then I would have been able to have this conversation in private had I not been calling here. I am an adult, this is my...my problem, and I would like a moment alone to discuss it further with this man. Please do not make me leave this house and force him to follow me."

Her mother huffed and was surely about to launch into a tirade when Mr. Gregory got to his feet. "My lady, your desire to support your daughter does you credit. But I can see how overwhelmed she is. Perhaps it would be better to allow her a moment with all this. I know you care enough to grant her that boon."

Lady Hendricks pursed her lips, and Celeste could see her struggling. To deny what he said would be to admit she didn't care about Celeste's feelings. And she desperately wanted to appear like that was her main concern. So he had effectively trapped her.

Celeste looked at him closely. Had he meant to do so? Or was it accidental?

His gaze slid to her and he gave a very small nod. The action warmed her. So he *had* meant to protect her. A kindness she appreciated, just as she appreciated the other kindnesses he had shown to her since his arrival. Certainly many a man would have made this much harder.

"I suppose I understand," her mother grumbled. She glared at Sir Timothy as if this were his fault. He hardly responded at all, probably because he was accustomed to such things. "Come, then."

She pivoted without another word and flounced from the room, Sir Timothy trailing behind her. Celeste shook her head in frustration at the fact neither had closed the door behind themselves. She moved to do so and then leaned on it. Mr. Gregory arched a brow.

"I would not do something so improper," she explained on a sigh. "But she is surely attempting to listen in."

He smiled, but it wasn't mocking or cruel, just something soft that made that dimple pop in his right cheek again. "Perhaps she means well."

Celeste laughed, though she found nothing amusing about this situation. "If that makes this more palatable to you, I will allow you to think that." She moved to the sideboard. "Now let me try to be a better hostess than I have been. I'm going to have the tea you suggested earlier. Would you like some of the same?"

He nodded. "Please. No milk or sugar."

She poured them each their cup and then motioned him to sit. They each did, she on the settee this time so she could look at him straight on. He did the same as he set his cup aside and leaned forward, draping his forearms over his thighs.

"I must ask you some questions," he said softly.

She blinked as she realized he meant about the murder. Questioning *her* about the murder. A strange thought. "Certainly," she choked out.

"Where were you four days ago?" he asked.

She sucked in her breath. "Was that when he—"

She couldn't finish the sentence and he didn't respond, just held her gaze evenly. His face revealed nothing to her about his thoughts, either negative or positive.

"I was here in Twiddleport," she said as she thought back to the day in question. "I will try to recreate my movements. Let me see, I was at my home during the morning. At one I took a meeting with —" She cut herself off with a blush. It seemed there would be humiliation after humiliation now.

"With whom?" he pressed, so softly the words barely carried.

"With the owner of the home I live in. My landlord, Mr. Greenley. He was insisting that Erasmus had not paid our rent and I was equally firm that he must have." She shook her head. "Though now I doubt it. The meeting lasted an hour."

"You are certain?" Mr. Gregory pressed.

She nodded. "I shall not soon forget that humiliation. Nor this one."

That caused a response. Mr. Gregory visibly flinched and inclined his head toward her. "My deepest apologies, Mrs. Montgomery."

Now it was her turn to recoil. "Mrs. Montgomery. Am I that? I'm not, not if there were two other wives. Nearly three." She bent her head. "God's teeth."

"Would you prefer I call you Miss Hendricks?" he asked.

She choked out a laugh. "That name comes with its own set of troubles, as you have seen."

He was silent a moment, watching her closely again. Reading her, she was certain, though she had no idea of the outcome of his observation. Finally, he said, "Then what about Celeste? I can call you by your given name, at least when we are discussing this matter in private."

"An improper suggestion," she said, examining him now. "But I suppose there is nothing proper about this anymore, is there? This entire situation is impropriety embodied. Yes, Celeste is fine."

"Then to be fair, I will ask that you call me Owen. In private."

Owen. She let the name roll in her head. It suited him, though it felt wicked to call him by it when they had only just met.

"Very well," she said. "I will give you Mr. Greenley's information if you'd like so you may speak to him. And after that meeting, I had other errands in the village and then joined my parents here for supper."

There was shouting at the door to punctuate that statement. Her mother, knocking hard and asking if they needed anything. "As you can tell, Lady Hendricks will be happy to discuss any and all details with you."

He raised both his eyebrows. "It seems so. Perhaps you would like to continue this conversation back at your home in the village later? I can give you time to collect what I imagine are some very tangled thoughts. And it will give me time to call on Mr. Greenley."

She blinked, shocked yet again by his calm and gentle support. Perhaps it had an ulterior motive; after all he was investigating the murder of her...husband, she would still call him even if it weren't true. Owen suspected she might have motive to have committed the crime, if his questions were any indication. Why not be kind? More flies were attracted with honey than vinegar, after all. If he were a spider, he was doing a fine job of luring her in.

"Yes, I would very much like a little time to collect myself. Once I escape the trap that my mother will surely spring the moment you depart."

He rose and she did the same. "I know Mr. Greenley's address, so I will not require you to share it. I'll go there and meet you, shall we say in two hours? Will that be enough time?"

"I hope so."

They walked together to the door and before he opened it, he smiled down at her. "I realize this must be shocking and over-whelming, Celeste. But I assure you that I will do all I can to relieve some of the pain of it if I can."

She didn't have a chance to respond, for he opened the door. Her mother immediately rushed to him, babbling that he should stay and trying to get more information out of him. He handled Lady Hendricks admirably, though, detangling himself from her attention, and then he bowed to the family before he departed with a promise to return to speak to them further.

He made no mention of his intention to come to her home and for that she was grateful. Her mother would certainly insist on joining their conversation if she knew. Once he was gone, Lady Hendricks all but shoved Celeste back into the parlor, shrieking for Sir Timothy to join them. Celeste sighed as she paced to the window while the two of them huddled together by the fire.

"This is *terrible*, Celeste!" her mother wailed. "Think of what it will do to your father and me!"

Celeste saw the glimmer of excitement in her eyes. Even when the world was about to fall, Lady Hendricks would bask at being in the center of it. Celeste could practically hear her sobbing to her friends, sucking in their pity and support.

While Celeste's world crumbled.

She pursed her lips. Normally she could be patient with this sort of display. She'd trained herself almost not to hear it over the years. But today when her life felt in tatters and her future was completely uncertain, she had less patience for the foolishness.

"Perhaps this is what you get when you grasp, then," she snapped.

Her mother's mouth dropped open. "Celeste Belinda Montgomery! How *dare* you speak to me in such a fashion? Timothy, speak to *your* daughter."

"Now, Celeste—" her father began, a sheepish expression on his face. As if he knew this was foolish but had no energy in him to fight it.

Celeste turned away before he could finish. "You wished me to marry Erasmus Montgomery and I did so. This is the result. In the end, what does fault matter? The cost is coming due and I will have to face it." She let out a long, shaky sigh. "Now I'm sure we have a great deal more to speak about, but I truly cannot even fathom it now. I must go and let all this horrible news sink in."

"But Celeste—" her mother gasped.

Celeste crossed to her and took her hands. "Please, Mama. I really cannot discuss it right now. I will return and we will work it out later. Good afternoon."

She pressed a brief kiss to her mother's cheek and the same for her father, and then left the room. Even as she called for her carriage to be brought, she could hear the histrionics of her mother in the parlor. She was meant to hear them. To feel guilty.

But at present all she felt was numb. And she had no idea when any other feeling would return to her body. Nor if she could bear the emotions when they hit her at last.

CHAPTER 3

O wen stood in Celeste's parlor two hours later, looking around him at the stark and worn-out room. The furniture was frayed and tired, a hodgepodge of threadbare fabrics and scratched wood that had clearly not been meant to match as a set. A cheap wallpaper had been hung, faded by time, curled at the water-damaged ceiling line, threatening to unfurl itself down to the floor. There was nothing of style to the chamber, nothing that reflected the woman who lived here. It was not quite a hovel, but only just barely.

He hadn't been allowed entry upon his first visit, just been told where the lady had gone. But the inside matched the out, much to Celeste's detriment, it seemed. He wrinkled his brow. Erasmus Montgomery was the younger son of the Earl of Leighton. He'd been raised with money and privilege. Certainly by outward appearances he could afford a nicer place than this one for his bride.

Even the third of three.

"Good afternoon, Mr. Gregory," Celeste said as she entered the parlor.

He pivoted to face her and had to fight not to catch his breath. She was truly beautiful. All curves and softness and bright blue eyes that met his even as her cheeks pinkened with embarrassment. She had been crying, that was evident. His stomach clenched at the sight.

"I believe we settled upon Owen in private, did we not, Celeste?" he asked. She tensed, and he frowned. "Unless you would prefer the formality. I would not ever cross a line against your will."

Suddenly she was looking at him very closely, indeed. "No, I don't think you would," she said softly. She shook her head and turned away to the sideboard. "Celeste is fine, of course, just as we agreed upon earlier today. I was only startled hearing it from your lips."

She seemed to put a little emphasis on the word *lips*, but Owen had to have imagined that. He had been instantly and powerfully attracted to her, because no man could look at her and not feel his heart lodge in his throat. But that didn't mean she returned the attraction. Why would she? He was the man come down to destroy her world. Her future. That she tolerated him was enough, especially since any other option was out of reach. He had a set of values, after all, unspoken rules of his profession.

"May I get you tea?" she asked, glancing back over her shoulder at him. "Or whisky. Is it late enough for whisky?"

He smiled. "It's late enough somewhere. I think we've both earned it."

She pushed the teapot aside and grabbed for a bottle along the back of the table. Her hands shook as she grabbed for two tumblers, and he moved forward.

"May I?" he asked.

She looked at him again. "I suppose it might be better or half the bottle will end up sloshed all over the room," she said before she backed away and walked to the fireplace, where he had been standing when she entered the room.

She smiled as he brought her the drink, but then sighed. "I assume you have more questions," she said at the very same moment he said something similar. They both laughed as she raised her glass to him and then took a sip.

She pulled a face, just as he did. "Oh, that is vile," she gasped. "My husband...Mr. Montgomery...he was never anything but stingy. I could count on that if nothing else." When Owen didn't say anything in response, she shrugged. "You'll have to write that down later. *Suspect found the victim miserly.*"

He tilted his head. "You think I believe you to be a suspect in the murder?"

"You'd be a fool not to. I'm the third of three wives, all of whom are living. I might be pretending my shock at that discovery. My husband's lies and the ramifications of them coming out would certainly give me a motive."

Owen nodded slowly. "An impressive analysis of the situation. But I needn't take down notes about you because I know you didn't do the crime."

"You *know*?" she asked. "How's that?"

"Your alibi," he said, motioning her toward the chairs before the fire. They sat, though he couldn't say the lumpy seat was comfortable. "I spoke to Mr. Greenley, and your landlord did verify that you were in a meeting with him on the day in question. You couldn't have reached London, a day-long journey on the best roads, in time."

She seemed to ponder that for a moment. "What if I had an accomplice?" she asked. "Or paid someone to poison Montgomery?"

He almost laughed at how hard she was working to convince him she was a murderer. "You really do think of everything."

"I try," she admitted. "I don't want there to be a question later, you see."

"Well, *I* think of everything too," he said. "I don't wish to offend, but I doubt you have the funds to pay an accomplice to kill in your stead."

Her lips thinned. "My current surroundings give me away, do they?"

"Unfortunately, yes. And I know this is not a recent development because Mr. Greenley complained incessantly about how your rent had been late over and over during the last nine months."

"Dastardly man," she grumbled, and the flush of her cheeks made Owen wonder if Greenley had offered her alternative methods to keep a roof over her head, much to her disgust. To his, as well.

"If you could not pay for the murder and you couldn't get to London yourself," he continued, slower this time. More gingerly, for what he was about to say might earn him a slap. "Then that would only leave one alternative. Someone you cared for would have had to commit the crime. I know your parents had supper with you that night."

"They don't care enough about me to kill for my honor," she muttered, her tone brittle and bitter.

"Then it would only leave a lover," he said. She jerked her gaze to his and the room seemed to get a little smaller as they stared at each other. "Are you the sort of woman who would take a lover, Celeste?"

Her shoulders straightened. "I did not have a lover, no. But I think, after a year of neglect and cruelty, that I would have been in my rights to take one." She arched a brow when he was quiet. "Have I shocked you, Owen? Have I reduced myself in your esteem?"

He narrowed his gaze. "Not at all. I happen to agree that based on all the circumstances, no one could fault you for finding...pleasure for yourself."

He shifted because this conversation was making his blood pump decidedly southward and he needed to get that under control before he shocked and horrified the woman. She'd suffered enough in the last few hours. Few months, if what was coming to light was accurate.

"No lover, no money, no way to get to London...it eliminates you from suspicion unless I uncover some other evidence to the contrary."

There was a flutter of a smile that passed her lips. "I'm glad of it." Her shoulders rolled forward. "I honestly have no idea what to think, Owen. Since I left my parents' home, I have been unable to consider anything but Erasmus's murder and this news of his other wives. But it is like it's being told to me in a language I don't fully understand. I can't…I can't fathom it."

He nodded. "I don't pretend to understand what your position is. The shock of all this isn't something I will ever diminish. But you asked me a moment ago if I had questions, and perhaps your answers will also allow me to give you more of the same." He leaned closer. "Can you tell me something of your marriage to Montgomery?"

She turned her head as if he had physically slapped her, and those blue eyes flashed. "Have you not mined the depths of my humiliation enough? Is there no bottom to this pit?"

He reached for her before he thought it through and caught her hand. For a moment they both stared at their intertwined fingers, and then he released her.

"Forgive me," he said, pushing to his feet and stepping away from her so he wouldn't be so foolish as to do something like that again. "I was too bold. I have no place to offer you comfort."

She shifted. "I appreciate the sentiment. I doubt I'll receive much support from anyone else."

He folded his arms. "I realize that confessing your past to me, a near stranger, one with an ulterior motive, is not pleasant. But I'm not asking out of some salacious desire to pry into your pain. It is merely to better understand the circumstances so that I might solve Montgomery's murder. And perhaps even help you detangle his deceptions of you."

She worried her lip a moment, which made him look at that same mouth. Even thinned with concern and displeasure, it was a kissable set of lips. And there went his mind again.

Clearly he needed a woman if he was panting over the widow of a murder victim. One of three widows. God's teeth, the woman was in trouble. She didn't need him to add to that burden.

"The marriage was arranged," she said, her tone low and rough, as if she had to force the words from her lips. "Erasmus showed up in Twiddleport a little over a year ago. He swept into a country dance and made himself known. My mother...well, you have met her. She knew he was the son of an earl and her eyes lit up like a thousand candles as she set her sights on him."

"She didn't know of his first marriage," Owen said. "Even though she had heard of his origins?"

"When pressed, I believe he told her some desperately sad story of losing his first wife quite tragically. He made it clear he didn't wish to speak of it, so my mother railed at me not to mention it. I had no interest in getting to know him any deeper, so I complied."

Owen wrinkled his brow. "You had no interest and she insisted."

"*She insisted* will be written on her tombstone." Celeste sighed heavily. "She hated that I was a bluestocking spinster and happy to remain such. She demanded I allow him to court me, and when that didn't work, she upped my dowry and made the arrangement behind my back. I was kept in the dark and sold off like so much chattel."

He could hear the pain of that statement. The anger that bubbled right at the surface of her. The helplessness she had felt then and continued to feel now thanks to desperate people who didn't think of her comfort or happiness in the least.

"And so you married," he said softly.

"I tried to jump out the window first, to escape," she said with a small smile. "But I was sadly caught and marched up the aisle, and became...well, I *thought* I became Mrs. Erasmus Montgomery."

"And how did he treat you?" he asked.

She clenched her hands on her thighs, rubbing them against the fabric of her gown as if that could comfort and soothe her. Make this more palatable.

"With...indifference, mostly. The moment he had his prize, the money, he no longer pretended charm. He took his husbandly rights, I suppose to give me no cause to annul the union. I asked him if I would go with him to London. After all, if I were to be chattel, at least in Town I could have some happiness. I have friends there."

"He refused," Owen supplied.

She nodded. "He laughed in my face, deposited me in this home and left. He never wrote. Occasionally he'd show up here, horse wet with exertion, face wild with emotions I didn't understand. But I think I saw him maybe three times in the year we were wed? We had no relationship, we had no connection. And now I suppose I understand the why of that much more."

"And he never spoke of his life in London when he came."

"No," she said. "He…oh God's teeth, this is all so humiliating."

"Any fact might help," Owen said softly.

She took a moment to gather herself. "He did talk in his sleep on the rare occasion he deposited himself in my bed. He often said the name Rosie. I thought it to be a lover of his, but perhaps it is one of the other wives?"

Owen straightened. "No. That isn't either of their names, nor the woman he was courting for his fourth marriage."

She covered her face with her hands. "There must have been legions of women he betrayed. What a club to be a part of. And news of this will spread, there will be no way to keep it from happening. The murder of a bigamist son of an earl? If no one else tells the tale, my mother will not be able to stop herself."

"Even though it will hurt you? Hurt herself?"

"Gossip is currency," she all but hissed. "She will revel in my pain as swiftly as she does in anyone else's if she gains some notoriety for the story."

She rested her head back in her hands for a moment, and that gave Owen the opportunity to observe her unhindered. He felt for her, of course. He felt for all the women Montgomery had betrayed, for he had seen their various reactions over the past few days. Their humiliation and their destruction did make them part of a small sorority.

But Celeste stood out from the others to him. She was so very clever and lovely.

And a plan began to form. One that might not be a very good idea, considering the instant attraction he'd felt toward her. But there were other considerations. She had already shown herself to be a mind that would work well within the job he was doing. She had provided him information he hadn't had before. And since he was certain she had not committed the crime, something he couldn't say about Montgomery's other wives, she might also be a useful tool in uncovering further information on that score.

Plus, in truth, he *wanted* to help her. He wanted to…save her in some odd way, even though he couldn't. But couldn't he make it easier?

"I am returning to London soon," he said slowly, as if hearing the words would help him decide if he wanted to continue saying them.

"Of course you must," she said, glancing at him briefly. "You have done your duty here. You must have a great deal to do in Town."

"Yes, and some of it might require additional answers from you," he said, feeling stronger about this with every word. "I will be examining timelines and looking into connections that you might have the only information about. The distance between there and Twiddleport will slow the exchange of that information and perhaps cause difficulty in my case. Would you…would you come to London with me?"

Her mouth dropped open and she stared at him in shock. "Go with you!"

He nodded. "Yes." He was convincing himself even as he tried to convince her. "It could be of great help to me."

She still looked stunned, but he could also see that the idea of escaping this horrible house and the parents that had forced her into this situation was intriguing to her. "Where would I stay?"

He hadn't thought of that. With him would be a very bad idea. "The…er, gentleman who hired me…if you are to go with me, you'll meet him. I might as well tell you."

"My mother would be hysterical to know I have the information she was so interested in. A secret pleasure amongst all this pain." She smiled briefly. "And who is he?"

"It is the Duke of Gilmore."

She leapt to her feet. "Great God!"

"Yes. I'm certain he will make arrangements when he realizes how vital you could be to the resolution of the case. As will Montgomery's brother. The two of them are friends and they both seemed determined to get to the bottom of this for their own reasons."

"I-I don't know," she whispered, but he could see she was poised on the edge of saying yes. How much she wanted to say yes.

"Please," he said softly.

Her eyebrows lifted and then she exhaled a ragged breath. "Very well. When would we depart?"

"Tomorrow, if you can be ready," he said.

Her eyes widened again. "You do not hesitate."

He caught that stare, holding it steadily, hoping she could see his honor. "No, I do not. And I do not lie. I promise you that you can depend on me and that I will make this as easy for you as I can."

Her breath hitched. It seemed that promise was not one she had been able to trust often in her life. Not from her family. Not from her false husband. He wanted to be able to earn that trust. An odd thing to feel toward a stranger, lovely or not.

"No one can do that, I fear. It will be a difficult path I'll just have to travel for a while." She set her shoulders back and he could see a steel enter her, a strength he might not have guessed just by looking at her. He respected it enormously, for he knew what it was like to have to step into the wide unknown and pretend that he was just fine.

"Good, I'll make some arrangements for us and whoever will accompany you, and send word ahead to the duke to see if he can provide accommodation." He dug into his pocket and handed her a card. "I'm staying at Twiddleport Inn just up the lane if you need

26

anything. Otherwise, I'll send you the information about a time for leaving in the morning."

She blinked as if she was slightly stunned by all this, but then she nodded. "Very well. I'll be ready."

She followed him to the foyer and they said their goodbyes before he walked away toward the inn. But he couldn't help but take a look back at her before he turned the corner. She remained on her doorstep, watching him, and lifted a hand to wave one last time. When he glanced away, he knew deep within himself that that something had shifted today. For his investigation. And perhaps for both of them. Now he just had to make sure that he didn't tumble them both into a worse mess than they were in right now.

"Mama, you are standing in Mabel's way," Celeste said softly, interrupting her mother's tirade.

There had been no way for Celeste not to send a quick note to her parents, telling them she would go with Owen in the hopes of helping him solve his case. And she had known Lady Hendricks would come crashing down on her house to whine and moan and talk ceaselessly.

She'd been right. For here they were, wedged into her chamber as she and her maid, Mabel, tried to pack her things. And Lady Hendricks was, as always, predictable in her theatrics.

"I cannot believe you are just going to flit off to London with some strange man you've never met before. *This* is how you got into this kind of trouble in the first place."

Celeste hadn't been fully listening to her mother's ramblings until that moment. She straightened up from the chemises she was folding and pivoted. "*That* is not how I got into this situation. You will not rewrite my history to make me a silly girl who chose poorly. I never wanted this marriage to Erasmus Montgomery. You nearly yanked my hair out hauling me back through a window to prove it."

Her mother grew red at the challenge of that statement and glanced at Mabel. "Not in front of the servants," she hissed, as if the maid couldn't hear that either.

Celeste rolled her eyes. "Mabel knows everything anyway."

Mabel stifled a small smile and went back to her folding and packing without comment. She'd learned long ago not to involve herself in the politics of the Hendricks family.

"You should take me with you," her mother huffed, and sat down hard in the chair before the fire. "I can help you."

Celeste nearly tore a chemise in her attempt to remain calm. "Help me with what? I'm certain it will be very boring, Mama. I'll be sitting around in home likely smaller than this one, waiting to find out if Ow—Mr. Gregory needs information I might be able to provide. I'm a widow, technically. I have Mabel as my companion, I do not need a chaperone."

"But Mabel will not be able to see what is to your advantage," Lady Hendricks insisted. "After all, how often do you have the prospect to go to London and partake in the opportunities it provides?"

"What opportunities?" Celeste asked with a side glance to Mabel, who shrugged lightly. "You've never been one to enjoy museums or parks."

Her mother's face twisted as if Celeste had said something vile. "Not parks, you ridiculous girl. I'm talking about gentlemen. It turns out you were never truly married. This trip to London could allow you to come to some other arrangement if it is played correctly. A *real* husband, perhaps this one with a little more influence."

Celeste froze and so did Mabel. She shot a look to her maid, and Mabel did the kind thing and slipped from the room without comment. Once she was gone, Celeste turned to her mother.

"Have you gone mad?" she asked, trying to meter her tone.

"What has happened with Erasmus is going to be *public*, Mama, if it isn't already circulating all through London. Everyone will know I am the third wife of a bigamist husband. It will not cause anyone to pile up at my door hoping to align themselves with this nightmare. I will be lucky if I am not booed out of Hyde Park if I'm recognized."

Her mother's face paled. "Well, I suppose...that is..."

Celeste shrugged. "In truth, it might be better for you and father to simply cut me off and forget you had a daughter."

That was a terrifying thing to say when Celeste had no idea of her future. Worse was that her mother pressed her lips together and was clearly considering the option. At last she said, "Perhaps staying here would be better."

"Yes," Celeste said, and went back to her worn portmanteau to begin to add things again. "And I will write you to let you know all the gossip."

That seemed to please her mother, for she brightened up considerably. With a sigh, she stepped up to Celeste and pressed the briefest of kisses to her cheek. "Do that. And I hope it won't be as terrible as you predict. Goodbye, dear."

That was all she had to say before she departed the room. Perhaps departed Celeste's life permanently, for she hadn't disagreed about the idea of cutting her off. It was a strange feeling, the concept that she might be free, at last, of her mother's meddling.

She jumped a little as Mabel re-entered the room and gave her a look of concern. "Are you well, Mrs. Montgomery?"

Celeste frowned. "I think we can't call me that anymore, can we? Back to Miss Celeste?" As Mabel nodded, Celeste managed a smile. "In truth, I'm not sad about that part. The role of Mrs. Montgomery never felt like it was mine. Turns out it wasn't. And yes...I'm as well as can be expected under the circumstances."

"What about this man who brought the news? Mr. Gregory," Mabel asked, sending her a quick side glance.

Heat rushed to Celeste's cheeks. An odd sensation considering they were talking about someone she had so little connection to.

But the circumstance was certainly fraught, so that must be why she felt so warm and odd when she thought of the man.

"No one can deny he is handsome," she said.

Mabel giggled. "I peeped from the window when he arrived earlier, and indeed, he's well favored. At least it won't be an unpleasant ride to London, there will be something to look at."

"Mabel!" Celeste gasped, but then laughed. She'd had Mabel as her maid for several years and they were often more like friends in private. She worried her lip a moment. "He is more than handsome, though. He could have been...horrible about all this. Many would have been. But he wasn't."

Mabel arched a brow. "Handsome *and* kind? Men like that don't fly by all that often."

"No." Celeste sighed. "But I'm certain after we arrive in London, he'll only call on me to answer questions if he needs information. We will hardly see him."

"Hmmm." They went back to packing as Mabel said, "And do you have a plan then, Miss Celeste?"

Celeste's hands trembled and she set the gown she'd been ready to pack down on the bed. "I don't know. But I will. I must." She fisted her hands and collected her resolve. "And I can tell you that none of those plans will likely involve ever coming back here again."

CHAPTER 4

T he trip started out most inauspiciously, with a clap of
    thunder and then a downpour that had continued for the
next two hours. Celeste and her maid Mabel were safe and warm
enough inside the carriage Owen had hired to ferry them to
London. But he was on his horse and it was a miserable ride,
indeed.

He glanced up at the sky, silently cursing whatever ancient,
vengeful god had brought this cold and unpleasant torrent down on
his head. Then again, perhaps whichever one had done so was only
trying to tell him that he shouldn't involve himself too closely with
Celeste Montgomery. Not bad advice, if cruelly given.

It was becoming painfully clear to him that he was already too
close to her. After all, he had dreamed of her the night before. Not
an innocent dream, either. No, he had unbound all those beautiful
red locks, let them cascade over them like a fiery curtain while he
stroked every inch of that luscious, curvy body with his tongue.
She'd rocked and keened beneath him until all there was left was
pleasure, pleasure, pleasure...

He'd woken hard enough that a cold bath had been in order
before he traveled to her home, where he'd had to pretend to be

proper so he wouldn't make her uncomfortable knowing he felt things she certainly couldn't want him to feel. The universe was now rewarding him with a second cold bath to keep his unexpected lust in check.

Why her? He'd never been the kind of man to pant over a woman in such a shameless way. He took a lover now and then. He wasn't a monk. But he didn't...pine. He didn't seduce. He didn't...he didn't dream of specific women the way he'd dreamt of her.

Only the why her was actually obvious. And it wasn't just that she was beautiful. She *was* beautiful, of course, that was just a fact. But all of the Mrs. Montgomerys were beautiful, and he didn't have naughty dreams about the other two.

Celeste was different...*interesting*. She was sharp as a pin, observant in a way he had spent years training himself to become. She didn't smile all that often, not that he expected her to do so under the circumstances, but when she did...well, she was even lovelier. He felt like he had to earn that expression, coaxed from that otherwise serious demeanor.

The window to the carriage opened in that moment, and the very lady he had been obsessively pondering appeared there. She had removed her hat and her red hair was in a sleek chignon, save for a few locks that curled around her chin. She smiled out at him. His heart, betrayer that it was, thudded hard in his chest.

"Mr. Gregory, won't you *please* join me in the carriage?" she asked, glancing up at the cloudy sky. "It is positively horrible out and I'm sure you could use the respite from the torrent."

He followed her look up at the dark skies and sighed. He *was* miserable. He signaled to the driver to stop, and he did so.

Celeste shot him another smile, this one brighter. "Good. I knew you were a man who could be reasoned with."

With that, she shut the window, and he took the time to tend to his horse and peel out of his soaked greatcoat so he wouldn't fill the warm interior of the carriage with steam and damp.

Finally he opened the door and stepped inside. He settled on the seat across from Celeste and her maid, who appeared to be asleep. As he did so, Celeste handed across a blanket.

"Much obliged," he said, drying his hair a bit with it before he laid it across his damp legs to warm himself. As they began to move again, he motioned toward Mabel, whose head was lolled back against the carriage seat with her mouth open a fraction. Every once in a while she let out a little snorting snore. "Is that normal?"

Celeste laughed as she tossed a side glance to the sleeping woman. "Incredibly, yes. She is like a rock once she's asleep. She'll probably be like that for hours."

He shifted slightly. If that were true then it was almost like they were alone. A dangerous proposition considering where his thoughts had been taking him not five minutes before. "So you called me in here for company."

She inclined her head at his gentle teasing. "Perhaps. I *did* lose interest in my book and you were the next best thing."

He snorted out a laugh at her directness. Yet another thing that appealed to him. She did not mince, this one. She was always direct, whether in jest or in seriousness. "Then I am at your disposal for entertainments of any kind."

The moment he said the words, she bent her head further and a little color entered her cheeks. He wished he could pull that sentence back, with all its innuendo that was so highly inappropriate.

"That sounds both fascinating and ominous," she said, her tone a bit breathier. "But I was thinking, as I was riding along with my maid snoring in my ear and my book boring me, that you know a great deal about me. At least about some of my circumstances. But I don't know very much about you."

"Ah, so you invited me into your carriage for an interrogation," he teased, hoping to put her at ease again. He found he didn't like the alternative. "Excellent choice. I cannot escape, you control the environment. You even softened me by offering me the kindness of the blanket."

She sat up a little straighter. "Oh no, that was never my intent!"

He shook his head at her shock and horror at the idea she might have been so devious. "I'm teasing you. Of course you're interested in some information about me. It's only natural, for I have certainly made your life more...complicated."

"Not on purpose, I don't think. But yes," she conceded.

He sighed. "Then what would you like to know?"

She worried her lip for a moment, a distracting action to say the least. Then she shrugged. "How did you become an investigator?"

Owen's brows lifted. He hadn't expected that question of all questions. But he had an answer. "I didn't start that way. I was actually the man of affairs for Lord Livingston. I helped manage his estate and finances, took care of odd jobs he felt were beneath a viscount. I was good at it, but not particularly engaged by the vocation. He wasn't particularly fond of a young lady his eldest son had taken an interest in, and one day he asked me to do a little looking into her background and her activities."

Her mouth twisted a little with displeasure. "You were to spy on her."

"I suppose that is one way to put it," he conceded. "I thought of it more as doing due diligence. The lady would become viscountess one day and a marriage to the son came with a great deal of money and power. It wasn't entirely cruel for Livingston to want to know more about her intentions. I did the work, dug into her past and her present. I found I truly enjoyed it."

"So you are nosy by nature?" she asked.

He smiled. "A little. But it was more that — I was assembling a puzzle. I'd get a piece of information—was it important? How would it fit into the overall picture? Sometimes I wouldn't know until days later when I had five more pieces of information, and suddenly it became clear what the first piece meant."

"You light up when you talk about it," she said with the flutter of a smile. "It's apparent you still have a great passion for the work."

He shrugged. "I do. It is my calling, I suppose, if you want to put it in somewhat religious and extremely dramatic terms."

"You are lucky to have one," she said, and glanced out the window at the streaking rain. "Gentlemen have that option more often than ladies. I'm supposed to see marriage and motherhood as my calling. But it can't be every lady's calling, can it? That you as a man can contain such multitudes and I can only have one future laid out before me?"

He frowned at the sadness in her expression as she asked the question. "I don't believe that. You clearly contain multitudes."

She snorted out a little bitter laugh. "I will have to now. This scandal will destroy all possibility of the life that has always been expected of me. Perhaps I should say a thank you to my...husband or whatever we'd like to call him."

"You're looking for the positive."

"What other choice do I have?" She sighed and then straightened up. "And now I have taken us off topic. You were telling me how spying on a potentially wayward lady turned into a career and I interrupted."

He hesitated, for his desire to push further on her was pulsing. Yet her face was a mask that told him she wanted space. Needed it, perhaps. And he didn't want to make this worse for her. She was vulnerable, and if his story evened the score a little then it was worth the telling.

"I suppose I couldn't hide my excitement from the viscount as I worked on the investigation, because when it was over he offered to sponsor me in starting my own business where I would do so permanently. I accepted. He helped introduce me to potential clients and spread the word that I was trustworthy and discreet when needed. And then he set me free."

"And here you are," she said. "Whatever happened to the lady?"

He laughed. "She was doing nothing untoward. In fact, she was very much in love with the gentleman. They married and Lord

Livingston adores her now. She teases me mercilessly about my grand investigation every time I come for supper."

"So Livingston is a man willing to admit he was wrong, too." Celeste shook her head. "As rare as a sprite. How wonderful to have such a benefactor."

"Indeed. He was a friend when I needed him and he hired me as his man of affairs. And he was my friend when he gave me the tools to my own freedom."

"You needed him?" she pressed.

He drew in a long breath. Here was where he would make himself vulnerable. He told himself it was only to balance the scales, but there was also a part of him that wanted her to know him a little more. To feel a little closer.

"My mother had died a few months before," he said, feeling out the pain that still accompanied that statement, even all these many years later. "I fear I was a bit rudderless. He was kind to offer me the job when I had no experience. And trained me patiently, kept me on for five years while I settled into the man I would be."

"I'm sorry about your mother," she said. "Were you close?"

"Very," he declared with a smile. She had been gone so long now and the grief never fully faded, but it had softened so that he could recall all the wonderful things about her, not just the heartbreak of her loss. "My father was a vagabond at heart. He'd just bought a commission into the army when my mother came up with child... with me. He was forced to marry her and then he went on with his life almost as if we didn't exist. I wasn't close to him—he died when I was sixteen. But she was...remarkable. She made the best of the worst situation."

"Then I suppose that gives me hope that I can do the same," Celeste said with another of those faint smiles. "I'm sorry I could not have met her."

He met her gaze and held there, drawn in by gray-blue seas. "So am I."

Those words seemed to draw all the air from the carriage and they stared at each other as time ticked by, perhaps a moment, perhaps a lifetime, it was hard to say. What wasn't hard to say was that he wanted to kiss her. It was a desire that rolled through him like a tidal wave, almost overpowering even if he knew it was so very wrong.

But there it was.

And from the way she held herself, held his gaze, he had to wonder if she wished for the same. If she would shudder if he touched her. If she would sigh if he claimed her lips.

But before he could do something so foolish, her maid started awake beside her and the spell was broken. "Oh, Mr. Gregory," Mabel said, rubbing her eyes as she stared at him. "I didn't realize you had joined us. I must have dozed."

Celeste met his eyes with a conspiratorial arch of a brow even as she said, "Yes, indeed. If dozed means fell into the sleep of the dead."

Mabel huffed out a little breath, but Owen could see that the two women were friends. Sometimes women of a certain station didn't lower themselves as such. His mother had been a seamstress when the money his father sporadically sent had been sorely lacking, and there were only handful of women she serviced who treated her as anything better than furniture in the room. Lady Livingston being among those who saw her as a human, not a means to an end. It looked as though Celeste was like that lady, one he respected a great deal.

"Well, you two must catch me up on everything I missed so that I might join in the fun," Mabel said.

Celeste cast him another glance, this one a little more furtive. As if she didn't want to share what they'd been discussing, even with a friend.

"We were talking about museums in London," Celeste said.

Mabel arched a brow as if she didn't fully believe that. "Were you now? Well, then let us continue the topic so that I might know what to look forward to when Miss Celeste and I make our rounds."

Owen stifled a chuckle. At least she had chosen a topic where he was well versed and might actually help her enjoy her time in the city. So as they began to discuss the much more benign topic, the tension between them faded a fraction, replaced by ease and laughter.

And for that he was both pleased...and disappointed. But he would have to put the latter reaction away because he could *not* involve himself with Celeste Montgomery. There was absolutely no way.

CHAPTER 5

The inn Owen had chosen for the night was exceptional, and as Celeste had come down for supper, she marveled as she took in the beautiful dining hall where travelers were gathered around tables, eating what smelled and looked like luscious food and talking softly among themselves.

She scanned the room and found Owen at a table set for three. He waved when she met his eye, and she crossed to him with a blush. "Good evening," he said. "I hope you found your accommodations to your liking."

She nodded. "Our room is lovely. Very comfortable." She shifted as he helped her to her seat and then retook his own. "I hope the duke and the earl will not be irritated that you chose such a fine inn. I wish I could say I could repay the expense but—"

He shook his head to interrupt her. "Celeste, on this count you must not worry yourself. You are coming to London to assist them in my investigation. This is a small expense and one I would have had to incur whether you came with me or not, as I would have had to stop on my way to London anyway."

She ignored the fact that he would not have let a carriage, nor had to pay for the extra rooms for their driver or for her and Mabel.

He was trying to reassure her and she attempted to be reassured as a response.

"Where is Mabel, then?" Owen asked when she didn't press the issue. "Coming in a moment?"

"She decided to take a smaller meal in our chamber," Celeste explained. "She wanted to do some mending of one of my gowns and said she had a book to read. It will only be the two of us tonight."

Something in Owen's stare shifted at those words. The same thing that had come into his gaze when they were talking in the carriage earlier, when the air had gotten heavy and a tingle had rushed through her like something was going to happen. He blinked it away swiftly, though, and smiled, popping that dimple in his cheek that was so very endearing.

"Then two it will be." He motioned for the serving maid to come over and she told them what the kitchen had as options for supper. Once they had chosen and were alone again, he leaned back in his chair, casual and comfortable. Strange how that made her even edgier when he was lounged in his chair like a king. "The circumstances are not the best, but are you pleased to be out of Twiddleport? When was the last time you traveled?"

She worried her lip. He had likely gone all around the country, perhaps even traveled in the wider world. She felt very much like a chawbacon when she stammered, "I-I have never traveled."

He stared at her a moment. "Never? You never went to London, even with your parents?"

She worried her lip. "I didn't. My mother had designs for me to wed one of the local gentry, so she focused all her attentions on him when I first came out rather than take me to London to exhibit."

"What happened to him?"

"He had designs on someone with a higher rank than himself, as is the way. My mother never had a chance. By that time, I had developed a reputation for being a bluestocking who would argue finer points of fact, and that scared off the rest."

"Was that by design?" he asked, and smiled up at the young woman as she brought their soup.

Once she had gone, Celeste drew in a deep breath of the delicious broth and took a spoonful. She couldn't help the rumble of pleasure that came deep from her chest. Owen quickly dropped his gaze to his own bowl and began to eat.

She shook herself back to the conversation and said, "It might have been a little by design, yes," she admitted. "I didn't want to marry any of those...those *boys* who didn't like the idea that I might have a mind of my own. Opinions that didn't entirely mirror their own. I was resigned to be a happy spinster when they foisted Montgomery upon me."

He shook his head. "I am very sorry about that."

"You needn't be," she said with a sigh. "It wasn't your doing."

"Perhaps not, but I can help make up for it a bit. If this is to be your first trip to London, then you will have to sample all its delights. I have lived in the city all my life and I will be your guide."

She caught her breath. "You would...you would do so? Won't you be very busy with your investigation?"

He shrugged. "Yes, but I do have private time, Celeste. A man can't work all day every day."

"I hate to intrude upon your relaxation."

He tilted his head. "If you do not wish to spend the extra time with me, I understand, especially given the circumstances of our...relationship."

Her lips parted. In her haste to keep him from troubling himself, she had made him think she didn't like him. And she realized in that moment that it wasn't true. She did like this man who had swirled into her life like a tornado and turned everything on its head.

"I fear I've offended you," she said softly. "And I didn't mean to. I would love a guide to London whenever you have the time or inclination. Though Mabel went on about museums with you today, I certainly pictured myself being tucked into some hidden home, only there to assist when I was needed, but if there can be more I will gladly take it."

He held her stare for a long beat, as the serving maid took their bowls and replaced them with the main meal. Celeste might have breathed in the scents again, noticed the bright beauty of perfectly roasted vegetables, but she couldn't drag her eyes away from her companion.

"Whatever more I can provide," he said before he was the one to break that intense stare.

She began to eat and for a little while they ate in silence. Not uncomfortable, but not exactly companionable either. She felt a drive to fill it as the food on their plates dwindled.

"Will I...will I meet the other wives?" she asked.

He lifted his gaze. "You would wish to do so?"

She nodded. "I admit I am curious. But perhaps they would hate me. Put the blame on each other rather than on Erasmus for what was done."

"I assure you neither of them are that kind of lady. You *will* meet them both, and I think you will get along just fine."

"Will you tell me about them?" she asked, pushing her food around her plate as she tried not to sound too eager or nervous.

"If you'd like."

"Oh yes. I hate being kept in the dark. I can imagine so many worse scenarios when left to my own devices."

"Let me see, the first wife is Abigail. She was married to Montgomery for almost five years. She is warm and very kind. And lovely, a very pretty woman."

Celeste felt a twinge of jealousy at that descriptor, but shoved it down because it certainly wasn't her place. "What was her reaction when she discovered what Erasmus had done?"

"Shocked, just as you were," he said, though his brow wrinkled slightly as if he had thoughts on that which he didn't share as he continued, "Angry, though she handled it well. She has been cooperative. And she was instantly welcoming to Phillipa, the second wife."

"Oh, so they have already met?" Celeste said, worrying her lip again. Perhaps she would be the odd woman out, then.

"They did, for Phillipa Montgomery was visiting London at the time of the murder."

Celeste searched his face a bit closer. "You count them both as suspects, don't you?"

He arched a brow. "What makes you say that?"

"I heard it in your voice."

"You know me so well after so short an acquaintance?" he asked. "Or are you simply that observant?"

Celeste ignored those loaded questions. "Why do you suspect them?"

"Both were in London. In fact, Phillipa Montgomery was in Town rather *unexpectedly*," he said. "And while both expressed surprise to hear the news about Montgomery's behavior, that could have easily been pretended."

"And we wives certainly have motive," Celeste mused.

"Yes."

"And what kind of woman is Phillipa?" she asked, mulling it all over in her mind.

"She was certainly the angriest of the three of you when she was told about Montgomery. She's a fiery spirit and seems to feel the injustice of what was done most keenly."

Celeste nodded. "I admit I'm very interested to meet them both. It seems we are markedly different people in temperament."

"And in appearance. Abigail has dark hair, Phillipa blonde curls and you have those..." He cleared his throat. "...beautiful auburn locks."

Her cheeks heated and she tried not to smile at the compliment. It was so rare that anyone told her she was pretty. It wasn't something she valued all that highly, after all. She liked to be recognized for her mind, for her values. She had always chased away men who waxed poetic about her face. It had never sat right with her when Erasmus did so during their halfhearted courtship.

But something about the way this man said it landed very differently. In the center of her chest. Which was wrong, wasn't it? She'd only just met him and she was supposed to be in mourning for a husband she had never loved and who had destroyed her world so carelessly.

"Why don't we take a walk?" Owen said, smiling up as their plates were removed. "The rain has passed and the moon came out. It might do us both some good to take in a little fresh air."

Celeste shifted. The idea of taking a walk in the moonlight with this man felt intimate and a little dangerous. But she also longed for it. "Very well."

She rose and took the arm he offered. It was impossible not to be very aware of how strong that same arm was. She hadn't touched him before, save for a few glances of his hand on hers. Under all those proper layers was a solid man, muscular. Why was her heart racing so fast?

She tried to draw a full breath as she allowed him to lead them from the inn. They walked down the lane together in the still, cool night, and she tried desperately not to tremble from being so near to him. She was no wanton—she didn't want to display as such.

"Th-thank you for thinking of a walk," she managed to croak out when the silence seemed to stretch out forever and become heavy.

"You looked troubled at the end of supper," he explained softly, then glanced down at her. "What can I do?"

She almost laughed. The man seemed created to solve problems. Put others at ease. It was very attractive, of course. Too attractive, just like everything else about him.

"I suppose I cannot lie and say I'm not troubled. I'm only trying to picture how this will all work...and I'm afraid I'm failing," she said with a sigh as she broke away from him so she could think more clearly. "It's such an untenable situation. I am a widow... except I'm not, because my marriage was never real. Am I expected to wear black and give a proper time of mourning? To gnash my teeth and display some emotional breakdown? Where do I stand anymore?"

"Do you feel sorry he is gone?" Owen asked.

She pivoted to face him and swallowed hard. Would he judge her for what she was about to say? "I'm sorry he was murdered. That is a terrible thing. But I will not miss him, if that is what you mean. We were practically strangers and I resented him every moment he was my husband." She threw up her hands. "I have no idea about my place in this world now."

She heard the wavering of her voice, felt the edge of tears sting her eyes. She moved to hide it, but it was too late. Owen had seen through her, and he caught her hand and drew her back toward him before she could escape. She staggered a little and he caught her elbows, drawing her tighter to his chest to steady her.

She found herself staring up at him, haloed in moonlight, that handsome face not lit with a smile at present, not warm with comfort, but dark with something else. Something that called to the same in her. Made her want things she shouldn't. Not with a stranger. Not in this horrible, twisted moment in time.

She ought to have pulled away. She didn't. She stood there as his lips parted and he let out a low, ragged exhale. He wanted her. She knew it in that moment in a way she'd never felt with any other man before. He wanted her even though they'd only just met and he'd come to blow her world to smithereens.

She wanted him too. Perhaps because he was so solid. Perhaps because he didn't really know her. Perhaps because she just wanted something nice or to steal a moment for herself. Why not? Everything was ruined anyway.

She lifted on her tiptoes, flattening her palms on his chest as she tilted her head and brushed her lips to his. She kissed him as he stood there, perfectly still, then less than perfectly still as his mouth moved just a fraction beneath hers. She felt the power of him. The strength that he held back as he captured her forearms in his hands.

And pushed her away gently.

"I'm sorry, Celeste," he murmured.

Her heart sank and blood rushed to heat her cheeks as she pulled from his grip. "I should say those words, not you. I ought not to have done that."

There was a long pause, as if he were contemplating that thought. Then he caught her hands in his, squeezing gently in what she supposed was meant to be a gesture of soothing or support. Instead it just made her want...well, she wanted a great deal more than a truncated kiss.

"Celeste, you are compromised by everything that has happened in the last day and a half." He sighed. "You aren't in any position to make decisions when it comes to kissing practical strangers in the moonlight. You might regret doing so soon enough and I wouldn't want that to be another disappointment you pile on all the others."

She blinked. Her world had always been filled with men who thought little about what was best for her. Her father had always danced to her mother's tune. And Erasmus clearly had never had her best interest at heart to put her in this untenable position.

And yet this man, this stranger...he stared down into her eyes and offered her protection. Even from herself.

"I might not have regretted it," she whispered.

He swallowed and she saw his throat work hard with the motion. His pupils were dilated, and for a moment she thought he might throw caution and reason to the wind and just kiss her all over again. But instead he stepped away, a very long step, indeed.

"We have a long day tomorrow," he said, his voice rough. "I think it might be best if I take you back inside."

She nodded even though that wasn't what felt best at present. Her mind was a cauldron of fear and anger, and his lips against hers had been the only thing to make it stop churning. Only he was making it very clear that this wasn't what he wished to do.

So she resigned herself to that fact and followed him back into the inn. But she wasn't going to stop thinking about what could have been. Not for a long time.

CHAPTER 6

Celeste didn't know what she had expected of London. She'd seen drawings and paintings of it all her life, she'd dreamed of coming here from the little village and pictured what her life as a city lady would be like. But now that the buildings rose up all on all sides of the wobbling carriage and the people and vehicles bustled around her, she was overwhelmed to say the least. Perhaps it would have been easier had she had a person to talk to about all she was seeing and feeling, but Mabel had never been to London either, and Owen...

Well, Owen had ridden outside all day, thanks to the sunnier weather. Or at least that's what he'd said that morning when he didn't join them. He hadn't talked to her about their kiss, he hadn't acted as though anything was different between them at all. Perhaps he meant that as a kindness. A way for her not to feel badly about her thwarted attempt.

It didn't work because now he was back to being a near stranger who had been sent to give her bad news. Her world felt a little... emptier for it.

They pulled through a high iron gate and up to a fine townhouse across from a park. She watched Owen swing down and speak to the footman who approached from the steps. The man nodded and then stepped away.

"Oh, gracious, Mabel," she whispered as she clung to her maid's hand. "Here he comes and I have no idea what to expect."

"Hope for the best," Mabel whispered. "So far he hasn't seemed the worst of men."

"No, he's certainly not that," Celeste murmured back, thinking of the faint taste of sherry on his lips when she kissed him.

The door to the carriage opened and Owen ducked his head in, giving them both a brief smile. "I wanted to be the one to escort you ladies from the carriage so that I could tell you more about where we are."

There was something…nervous about his demeanor as he spoke, and Celeste's hands began to shake as a response. "And where are we?"

"This is Montgomery's London home," he explained, and held her gaze steadily as if he could support her through this. "The one he shared with his first wife."

"Abigail," she whispered. Somehow she breathed when it felt like she was being dunked under water. "Are you telling me we're about to call on one of the other wives?"

Owen had already decided that Celeste had a strength like steel that made her steady, but now he was seeing it in action. Her fear, her anxiety, was clear all over her face, but her voice was calm. Her back was straight. She was ready to face a gauntlet if need be. He certainly hoped that would not be the case.

If it were, he intended to face it with her.

"Do I look well?" she asked, glancing first to him, then to Mabel, then back again.

"Beautiful," Mabel said.

He swallowed hard, for that was a loaded question if there ever was one. "I assure you, not a person could find fault with your appearance."

She let her breath come out softly. "That's the best I can hope for. I'm ready."

She held out a trembling hand and he caught it, squeezing it gently before he helped her from the rig, then did the same for Mabel. Celeste smoothed her skirts as she looked up at the house. She pressed her lips tight with displeasure.

"It's very pretty," she said softly. "Especially in comparison to my hovel."

Owen tucked her hand into the crook of his elbow. He tried not to think of the previous night when her body had leaned into his. At how her eyes had shone like diamonds when she stared into his face in the moonlight. How soft her lips were, even briefly.

"The man was an arse," he choked out. "Don't forget it."

A flutter of a smile was his reward. "I won't. I couldn't even if I wanted to."

The door opened as they crested the stairs and a stern-looking butler appeared from the house. "Mr. Gregory," he said. "They are waiting for you."

"Very good," Owen said. "Thank you, Paisley."

The butler inclined his head, even as he shot a glance at Celeste. She shifted against Owen's side and when he looked at her, her cheeks were bright pink. How he wished he could spare her this humiliation. But Montgomery had set this in motion for a long time. It had to play out if any of these women were to come to the other side of it.

Mabel was directed away to have a cup of tea in the servants' hall. Celeste sent her maid one forlorn look, but she didn't argue as they followed Paisley down the hall and he stopped at a parlor door, which he opened and stepped into, blocking the view of the interior of the room. "Mrs. Montgomery, Mr. Gregory is here with…with…"

"Mrs. Montgomery," came a soft, gentle voice from within. "We mustn't mince words, dear Paisley. Mr. Gregory is here with the third Mrs. Montgomery. Please show them in."

The butler stepped aside, and Owen allowed Celeste through the door first. She caught her breath and so did he. Abigail Montgomery stood before the sideboard, sleek dark hair pulled back from her face and equally dark eyes sweeping over Celeste as she made her entrance. She was not alone in the room. The second Mrs. Montgomery, Phillipa, stood at the fireplace, blonde curls straining to break free from her own chignon and green eyes flitting over Celeste.

Before the settee were two gentlemen, Owen's employers. Erasmus Montgomery's older brother, the Earl of Leighton, and the man who had set this entire nightmare off, the Duke of Gilmore.

Owen leaned in to Celeste, feeling her warmth, and God help him, he wished he could sweep her up and carry her away from all this. He didn't.

"You'll be fine," he breathed, and felt her press into him a little closer before she broke free. He hoped that would be true. He hoped it *could* be true because Celeste didn't deserve more heartache than she had already encountered.

But there was no way for him to protect her now.

"G-good afternoon," Celeste murmured, her gaze flitting from one face to the next because she wasn't certain where to look in this room full of strangers, whether they be potential enemies or friends.

But the dark-haired lady at the sideboard didn't hesitate. She rushed across the room, hands outstretched in greeting. "Mrs. Montgomery." Then she glanced at the other woman, who was already coming across the room. "This is going to get very confusing, isn't it? *I* am Abigail Montgomery. Missus the first."

"Phillipa," said the blonde as she reached Celeste's side and gave her a sad but kind smile. "The second. But call me Pippa, everyone does."

"Celeste, the third," Celeste sighed. Suddenly her exhaustion felt overwhelming, perhaps because she saw it mirrored on the expressions of the other two women. Only they would know how all this felt. Only they could have an inkling the fear, the humiliation and the regret of it all.

"What a club to be a part of," Abigail said with a gentle smile.

In that moment, Celeste stopped holding the breath it felt like she'd been keeping in for days. She'd been unable to picture how this meeting would go, if it ever happened. But instead of being horrible or filled with accusation, she found herself welcomed. Almost as if this were a sisterhood. One formed in pain, yes, but she felt no accusation between the women. She felt no cruelty.

She glanced back at Owen and found him smiling at her, encouraging with just that look. He was trying to tell her she could trust these women.

She wanted to do just that.

"Indeed, it is something," Celeste said.

Abigail glanced at the other gentlemen. "Let me introduce you to our other guests." She caught Celeste's arm and guided her further into the room. "This is the Earl of Leighton, our...brother-in-law." The earl flinched slightly and his gaze flitted from Celeste to Abigail and finally settled on Pippa before he darted it away. "And a rather decent fellow despite his attachment to the scoundrel who created this situation."

Celeste nearly choked at that description and at the fact that this handsome man who now extended a hand toward her shared Erasmus's pale blue eyes. Only on his face they looked kind, and it made her realize how distant and cruel Erasmus's expression had been in comparison. By the time she'd met him, he'd already been lost. She wondered if he'd always been that way. What had driven him to such a course of action that had altered all their lives?

"My lord," she said. "I am so very sorry that I have caused any—"

He held up a hand to stop her. "You have caused nothing, madam, I assure you of that. My brother was the villain who created this farce. It is I who should apologize to you for his role in this horror."

Her lips parted. That was not the response she had expected. But none of this was what was expected. This should have been a room full of sharks, bent on devouring her if they so much as scented blood.

Only it wasn't.

"And this is the architect of our destruction," Abigail continued as she motioned toward the other man standing before the settee. "The Duke of Gilmore."

The duke didn't look at Celeste, he simply kept his gaze on Abigail for one beat, two. His lips were thin, his eyes narrowed on her in severe scrutiny. But then he glanced away and looked at Celeste with far less intensity.

"Madam," he said. "I do regret that my investigation has caused any of you ladies grief. Though I do not regret, nor will I ever regret, seeking to protect my own sister."

"Of course you don't," Abigail muttered, and turned her back on him. "And now you gentlemen have seen the last of our number. We stand before you, the Three Mrs. Montgomerys." She linked arms with Celeste and did the same with Pippa on the other side. "So here we are. Take it in, and then I will ask you two and Mr. Gregory to leave us."

Owen had only been observing the interaction, but now he stepped forward, his lips parted. "I had thought to escort Mrs. Mont—Miss Hendr—*Celeste* to her intended home during her stay."

"I made arrangements," the Duke of Gilmore said softly. "I promise the accommodations will be of good quality and—"

Abigail shook her head. "That will not do. I will host Celeste here, just as I am hosting Phillipa."

Celeste gasped as she jerked her gaze toward Abigail, but the lady looked anything but uncertain of this decision. She met Celeste's stare with a quick nod.

"Mrs. Montgomery," the duke intoned, stepping closer to Abigail as she pulled from the linked arms of Celeste and Pippa. "Are you certain that is wise? The news of this terrible thing is already circulating through Town. If the ladies are staying with you—"

"Then the world will know we do not blame each other for our fate but place it firmly where it belongs, on Mr. Montgomery. Why should we be at each other's throats? *We* are the victims here, Your Grace. And we will stand together."

His mouth twitched. "As you wish."

"A fine sentiment," the earl said as the duke stalked away to the fire. "And I do not deny that it will be a powerful one. But I do think we all have much to discuss. There are many matters to resolve if any of us have any hope of escaping this scandal."

"And determining the murderer of Mr. Montgomery," Owen added softly.

Celeste glanced at him. He was watching the earl, and she realized with a start that Owen suspected him. But of course he would. Probably he suspected everyone in the room. One of them could very well be the killer and yet she felt no fear. If someone in this room had murdered Erasmus, well...they'd certainly had their good reasons.

"Yes, there is that," the earl murmured. Celeste couldn't help but mark the way his head bent. There was something guilty in his demeanor. Guilt over this terrible state of affairs? Or something deeper?

Abigail shrugged. "And we will resolve all of that. But not tonight. Celeste must be exhausted from her journey, and all of us need time to stare each other in the face and see what this sisterhood of the Mrs. Montgomerys will look like as we move forward. And none of you men are invited."

She gave a playful smile to the gentlemen before she settled into one of the seats before the fire. The Duke of Gilmore shot her a look. "I don't know how you can be so flippant about such a serious subject, Mrs. Montgomery."

"Which one of us are you speaking to, Your Grace?" Abigail asked.

Celeste's eyes went wide. The two of them were almost at each other's throats, even if they were oh-so-very polite about it. She would hate to see what would happen if the knives really came out.

She stepped forward to diffuse the situation before the vein that was pulsing in the duke's forehead popped. "I admit I am tired. It's been a very long few days. Perhaps a quiet night would be good for all of us. And then we will, of course, discuss all those important matters." Celeste shifted her focus to Owen. When he met her gaze, she found a fraction more calm on the violent seas. "Owen—Mr. Gregory, what do you think?"

"I think another night won't matter in the scheme of things," he said softly. "And that it makes sense that you ladies would wish to get to know each other."

"It seems it has been decided," the duke said with a shake of his head. "Then I will depart. We will meet again tomorrow then. Good afternoon."

He nodded to the group as a whole and then strode from the room. Once he was gone, Abigail pursed her lips and then spat, "I don't know why *he* must be involved in all this. He got his way, didn't he? He set in motion a destruction of us all and protected his family. Why can he not just leave us to the consequences?"

The Earl of Leighton let out a long sigh. "He truly isn't the beast you make him out to be, Abigail. And he's a powerful man, so don't completely disregard that his influence might make this easier. If you don't chase him off entirely by your obvious disdain." When Abigail shrugged, the earl smiled. "Good afternoon, ladies. Mr. Gregory." He once again gave a quick glance toward Pippa, but said nothing more as he left the room.

Owen was all that was left, and he met Celeste's gaze and held there as he said, "We will have much to discuss tomorrow, ladies.

But I hope your peace will do you all good. Celeste, I will make certain all your things are taken from the carriage."

"I'll join you," she said. "I left a book in the carriage and I think it might have slipped between the cushions. I'll find it easier."

He didn't argue, even though they both knew her book had been safely placed into her reticule. She smiled back at Abigail and Phillipa before she followed him from the parlor and out to where his carriage was still waiting. Footmen had unloaded it already, making her think that Abigail had always intended to take her in.

She and Owen stopped next to the open carriage door, and she stared up at him. "You'll be fine," he said softly.

She blinked. "Did I look worried?"

He nodded. "Since the first moment I saw you. But the other two wives seem like decent women. Your welcome was genuine, and I think you'll find them good allies for what is to come."

"Even if you're not certain if one of them is a murderer. Nor the earl. Nor the duke?"

His brows lifted and a hint of a smile tilted his lips. "You saw all that, did you?"

She shrugged. "It doesn't take too sharp a mind to deduce it, but yes. I saw you watching them all with more interest than just a casual observation. You still have a long road to walk to determine who snuffed out Erasmus's life."

"And I'll walk it," he assured her. "Carefully and prudently and hopefully with success."

She shifted because when they were standing like this, face to face, she couldn't help but think of when they'd kissed. That stolen moment played over in her mind whenever he looked at her like he was right now. Like he wished they could repeat it, even though he was the one who had turned away.

"Must you walk that road…alone?" she asked.

His eyes went wide. "Are you offering to walk it with me?"

"It might be foolish—I have not the experience you do in such things. But I want to help. Otherwise I'm just a victim of this and I don't want to be. Not only that."

He was quiet for what felt like a lifetime, searching her face with those bright brown eyes that seemed to see so much. Then he nodded. "If you want to help, then watch. Listen. You'll have access to far more honesty than I probably will. Make note of anything interesting and we can discuss it later."

"You'd do that?" she said in surprise.

He nodded. "Yes."

"And you won't...keep things from me? Try to protect me or think that I can't handle this?"

His brow wrinkled. "I believe you can handle anything, Celeste. And if I cannot tell you something, I promise to be honest about that. I won't keep you in the dark."

The relief that moved through her was far more powerful than it should have been. So many people had underestimated her, lied to her to manipulate her to their way. That he vowed not to do so meant a great deal. More, perhaps, than it should.

She reached out and touched his arm. "Thank you."

His pupils dilated and his gaze moved from her eyes to her lips. He wanted to kiss her, just as she wished to do the same.

Instead he cleared his throat and handed over her reticule from the carriage seat before he stepped away toward his horse, which the footmen had just brought around for him. "Good afternoon, Celeste."

"Good afternoon," she whispered, then turned away to the house where the ladies awaited her. Where an unexpected future was beginning to bloom.

CHAPTER 7

As Celeste returned to the parlor, she caught her breath. While she'd been outside with Owen, Abigail had apparently called for a full tea to be spread out on the table by the window. There were sandwiches and biscuits and tea. Celeste's stomach rumbled even as she forced a smile for the two women.

Pippa returned it immediately. "Abigail and I thought that it's going to be awkward, so we said we might as well eat like queens."

"My cook is divine," Abigail said with a light laugh as she motioned for Celeste to sit between them. "Everything she makes is heaven on a plate."

Celeste took her place and watched as Pippa and Abigail heaped her plate with all the delicacies that had been prepared for them. Once it was brimming and the tea had been poured, Abigail lifted her cup. "To us. The Three Mrs. Montgomerys."

Celeste clinked her cup to theirs. "I'm shocked you two can joke so easily about it. I'm still reeling."

"Well, you haven't known as long, I suppose," Pippa said. "I was in London and so was Abigail. But it took longer for word to reach you in Twiddleport."

"Aside from that, I think Pippa and I decided over the last few days that we can laugh or cry, and laughing makes my eyes swell less," Abigail added.

Celeste shook her head. "But you must have felt *some* pain over the realization about what Erasmus had done."

At that both women's expressions fell. "Of course," Pippa began. "I shall never forget when Lord Leighton and Mr. Gregory arrived at the room I was letting. I was so thrilled to meet my husband's family after two years of being kept from them. And then...the world crashed down."

"Did you not live in London?" Celeste asked.

"No," Pippa said. "I don't think Erasmus would have been capable of managing us all in the same place. He met me in Bath, where my father owned an assembly room, and he was happy to leave me there after the first six months of our marriage."

"The first six months?" Celeste repeated. "He stayed with you so long?"

"Yes, though he traveled, and now I realize he must have been coming home to Abigail all that time."

Abigail frowned. "Home or somewhere else, it seems. How long did he stay with you, Celeste?"

Celeste shifted. "We married a little over a year ago. He stayed with me just days and returned only three times."

Pippa reached out and caught her hand. "I can see you are blaming yourself for something or questioning why he might have stayed longer with me. Trust that it isn't you, it's him. He was a rambler and a scoundrel, and not in the romantic sense. He must have been getting more desperate as time went on and he *never* cared about anyone but himself."

"Why would he be desperate?" Celeste asked, marking the flash of bright rage in Pippa's expression. "I know so little of him. He was not my choice and he made it clear very quickly that only my money was his."

Abigail nodded. "Then we'll start at the beginning. I have been married to the late Mr. Montgomery for almost five years. And I have reason to believe that for the first three, I was the only one to carry that name."

"How did you meet?"

"As you do," Abigail said with a shake of her head. "My father is the second son of the Earl of Middleton, and he and Ras's father were cronies. They encouraged the match, but I desired it regardless of their machinations. I thought he did too."

There was a faraway sadness to Abigail's expression a moment before she blinked it away. "Courtship was followed by marriage, and for a while we were happy. He strayed, of course. He had more than one mistress, and it always came back to me. The first time it hurt me, but I convinced myself that was what men did. That I could be happy regardless, for he was affectionate enough when he was with me."

Celeste flinched. "I'm so sorry. To hear what happened with Pippa and with me must have caused you so much pain. To offer us such kindness speaks to highly of you."

Abigail smiled. "My dear, I might not have known he was strutting across the country, marrying young ladies, but by the time he began that foolishness, I was long out of love with him. He changed over time, you see. Became harder, sometimes even more cruel. He despised me for not providing him with a child, especially a son whose existence might allow him to demand his father give him more money. And when his brother inherited the title, it only got worse."

"How so?"

It was Pippa who answered rather than Abigail. "They're half-blood, you see. Erasmus grumbled ceaselessly about his brother and how he was so big for his britches after inheriting. But having met Lord Leighton now, I see that the real trouble was that they are such different men. Leighton is genuine and serious. Erasmus was...well, he made a bed his brother wouldn't abide by. He cut him off a year before he married me."

Celeste's lips parted. "Is that why he started marrying all of us?"

Abigail nodded. "That is what Pippa and I theorize. He'd already run through my dowry, but Pippa's was generous. I assume yours was the same?"

"My parents threw money at their problem, and their problem was me," Celeste admitted, because at this point they were all so vulnerable she felt no reason not to carry that through. "And one can only assume that the Duke of Gilmore's younger sister would be the biggest prize of all."

"But that was where he made his mistake," Abigail said. "He had chosen you two because your families lived in the country and neither of your fathers had powerful connections to London or the Upper Ten Thousand. But Gilmore was too big a fish for Ras to land."

"Why do you think he did it?" Celeste asked.

"Desperation?" Pippa suggested. "Hubris? Who knows? I long ago gave up on trying to read his mind. Though I did chase him to London, so that tells you something about me, doesn't it?"

"I think it completely rational that you would seek him out when he'd been unresponsive to your letters for months," Abigail reassured her. "It says you are a decent person, nothing more or less."

Celeste leaned back in her chair and observed the two women. It was impossible not to like them, but she couldn't help but think of Owen's suspicions when it came to them. He'd said for her to watch and listen. This was an opening for both options.

"Who do you think...killed him?" she asked, then took a sip of her tea so she could watch the pair surreptitiously over the edge of her cup.

Pippa flinched, but Abigail didn't move at all. For a moment the room was silent and then Abigail sighed. "There is no shortage of suspects, I suppose. His brother, all of us, probably untold others... all had a motive for the killing."

"And the Duke of Gilmore," Pippa added.

At that Abigail did react, her gaze darting to Pippa swiftly. "I suppose him, too. Mr. Gregory seems driven to uncover the truth.

And he comes off clever enough to do it." She leaned in and met Celeste's eyes evenly. "You spent a few days with the man, much longer than either of us. What do *you* think of him?"

Celeste sucked in a breath at the direct question she should have expected but somehow hadn't. She'd been trying to obtain information, but here she was being asked for it. "He is…he was kind about his revelations," she began slowly.

"Yes, he was," both Abigail and Pippa said together.

Ignoring the flare of jealousy that worked through her at that statement, Celeste continued, "He has done nothing but try to set me at ease. He is very intelligent and observant, and I think driven to do his duty."

"And he's very handsome," Abigail said with a tiny smile. "You didn't add it, but it's clear you think it."

Celeste's eyes went wide. "I—he—" She gathered herself as best she could. "The gentleman is attractive. There is no denying it, for it is fact. I noted it, of course. But it isn't a factor in this situation, is it? Erasmus was handsome, after all, and it didn't make him decent or good or true. Mr. Gregory's looks will not change his ultimate actions."

Pippa stifled a smile into her cup as she finished her tea before she said, "No need to get ruffled, my dear. As you say, Mr. Gregory will determine the answers in the end." Her smile fell. "There will likely be no stopping him."

Abigail sighed. "Yes. Now I'm certain poor Celeste must be exhausted after the last two days on the road. May I show you to your room? We will have plenty of time to get to know each other over supper. And I'd like to discuss *anything* but the wicked Erasmus Montgomery. We are more than our wayward husband, ladies. We always have been, and by God we will be again."

There was something about the way Abigail declared it that made Celeste believe it could be true. So as she followed her hostess and Pippa from the room to find her chamber, she chose to go with that feeling. Because it was hope. And hope was what she needed to carry on with whatever would happen next.

~

O wen hadn't been surprised to arrive home to a missive from the Duke of Gilmore demanding he join him at his home for supper. He hadn't even been surprised that the Earl of Leighton was also in attendance when he arrived. The two men, after all, were splitting the bill for his services. Gilmore because Owen had uncovered the truth about Montgomery's marriages. Leighton because he claimed to wish to discover who had struck his half-brother down.

What he was surprised about was how untroubled the men seemed to be when he joined them in Gilmore's parlor.

"Mr. Gregory," Gilmore said as he gestured him into the room with a nod for his butler. "Good to see you again. Would you like a drink?"

"Is that whisky?" Owen asked, as he stared at the drink in the duke's hand.

"It is. I have property in Scotland and there may or may not be a still on the land. I suppose as a man of the law, you disapprove the smuggling of such contraband?"

"Not at all," Owen said with a smile. "I've always enjoyed a good whisky when I can get it. I'll have the same."

As Gilmore poured, Leighton shook his head. "And so what do you think of the threesome of ladies my brother treated so callously?"

Owen took the drink offered to him and sipped it slowly, both to savor the flavor and also to consider what to say next. Leighton's disgust with Montgomery had been clear from the start. Owen knew the two had not been close—they had different mothers and very different attitudes, and that had clearly put a wedge between them.

But was Erasmus Montgomery's behavior troublesome enough to the earl that he might snuff out his own kin?

"I'd be more curious about your thoughts, my lord, Your Grace," Owen said at last.

Gilmore snorted out a laugh. "I'm sure you would, since you obviously still suspect both of us in the bastard's murder."

Owen inclined his head apologetically. "This is the duty I have been hired to fulfill. I would be remiss if I didn't consider all angles. At any rate, you two have likely spent more time with at least the first and second Mrs. Montgomerys."

"We're using Christian names, aren't we? I don't want to spend every moment we're talking trying to determine which woman we're discussing," Gilmore asked.

"That seems the wisest," Owen agreed, and tried not to think of the way the name Celeste tasted on his tongue. "What about Abigail?"

Leighton opened his mouth to speak, but Gilmore slammed his glass down on the sideboard before he could speak. "*That* woman," he grunted. "All accusation and glares and trying to make me feel guilty about protecting my own flesh and blood. Beautiful as she is, she is mightily unpleasant, and I will be very glad when this is all over and I never have to see that troublesome sprite again."

The earl stared at his friend a moment. "Are you finished?"

Gilmore grunted and downed the remainder of his drink before he poured another. "Quite."

Leighton shrugged at Owen as if to apologize for the outburst. "Abigail is the only wife I met before this unpleasantness. Ras married her nearly five years ago, and though my brother and I were strained even then, I found no fault in her."

"No fault," Gilmore snorted.

Owen glanced at him from the corner of his eye. As much as he groused and as much as he and Abigail butted heads, there was something in the man's eyes when he talked about her that indicated he felt something more for the lady than just frustration and disdain. Which was an interesting development, indeed. One he would have to keep an eye on as it could ultimately affect his case.

"If you think so low of the woman, do you suspect her of having a part in the murder?" Owen pressed.

Gilmore's eyes widened. "No, of course not. The woman may be a fly in the ointment, but she could not be a killer. She wouldn't do such a thing."

Owen held his stare for a moment. Gilmore was as passionate about defending Abigail as he seemed to be about his complaints regarding her.

"And what about Phillipa?" Owen pressed, so they wouldn't become mired down in whatever was in Gilmore's head. He marked it, of course. He would watch them more carefully together.

"She seems a decent enough lady," Gilmore said, all his ire gone with the change of subject.

Leighton shifted. "I-I did not know her, of course, before this all began. But in the short time we've been acquainted, I have found her to be very...very pleasant."

"What do you think of her traveling to London from Bath, more than a day's travel, just before your brother's death?" Owen pressed.

Leighton's brow furrowed and his fingers gripped a little tighter on his glass. "She has explained it, has she not? She said that she had been trying to reach my brother for months and he had not replied. Her coming was a way to determine his health and well-being."

Another interesting defense of one of the wives. It seemed each lady had her champion.

"And what about Celeste?" Leighton asked.

"Yes," Gilmore added. "You spent time with her on the road, you are likely the best source of information regarding her.

Owen shifted, not wanting to reveal his attraction to the men as they had done to him. "I do not suspect her," he said. "She has a strong alibi for her location during the murder. As for her character, like all the wives she is a strong woman." He didn't add he thought her the strongest of them all. That would *certainly* reveal too much.

"Then it seems there has been little advancement to the case," Gilmore said with a heavy sigh. "I would surely like for this whole mess to be over."

"You and me both," Leighton said. "The scandal is already brewing, there is no way to keep this kind of nightmare from the ears of the ton."

"Yes, I realize it is not easy," Owen said.

"What can we do to help?" Leighton asked. "I want a part in this. For my family's sake, as well as for the sake of my honor."

"Yes," Gilmore added. "I would like to contribute more than simply my money."

Owen set his jaw. Normally he wouldn't allow anyone to come near his case, let alone two of its prime suspects. But the more he allowed them near, the more closely he could observe them together, with the women and individually.

"Well, I say we all call on the ladies again tomorrow," he suggested. "And we can continue trying to parse out exactly what to do next."

"Excellent," Gilmore said, and both he and Leighton looked relieved by the idea. "And now I see my servant motioning, so that must mean our supper is ready. Gentlemen?"

Owen followed the men into the dining room, and he should have been thinking about his next move. About whatever subtle thing he could do to read these men and their intentions and motives more clearly.

But instead he found himself thinking of Celeste. And wondering what would happen to her when the smoke had cleared and everyone's lives had moved on.

CHAPTER 8

Celeste smoothed her skirt for what felt like the tenth time since she'd stopped before the parlor door. Owen was behind it. Mabel had told her that a moment ago, and also that the gentleman was as of yet alone. Her heart throbbed, her hands shook, both against her will, as she opened the door and stepped inside.

He was standing at the fireplace and turned as the door opened. She caught her breath as he smiled, that broad, welcoming expression that popped the dimple in his cheek and made her want to move toward him.

Made her want to repeat that kiss that should never have happened in the first place. She wanted to cling to those solid shoulders and pretend like it wasn't wanton or foolish or desperate to do so.

"Good morning, Celeste," he said as he crossed to the room. His hand flexed at his side as if he might want to reach for her, but he had more self-control than she did.

"Good morning." Oh, how she wished she didn't sound so breathless. "It is just you, then?"

"The earl and the duke will arrive shortly," he said with another quick smile. "They can afford to be fashionably late, while I am forever early, I'm afraid. On time is behind schedule for me."

"I am the same," she said. "And so I was up with the sun, ready before nine and pacing the halls like a fool while the other ladies slept."

He tilted his head. "The other ladies. And how did you find them?"

She moved a little closer and clasped her hands together. "Oh, Owen, they were wonderful. Both of them are so lovely. We talked about the situation we find ourselves in, of course. But then at supper we talked about books and music and the state of the world. We have so much in common, and that which is different is interesting, rather than something that pushes us apart."

Now he did reach for her, and squeezed her hand gently. "I am very glad for it. I admit I was nervous when I left you last night."

"Why?" she asked, trying not to focus on the weight of his fingers as they tangled through hers.

He tilted his head. "I blew up your life and I brought you here. I feel a keen sense of responsibility for you. From what I knew of the ladies, I believed you might connect and develop a friendship with them both, but there was always the possibility that it could go wrong."

"And so you laid awake all night, worrying yourself over me like a mother hen?" she asked.

His pupils dilated. "If I lay awake at night, Celeste, it isn't motherly thoughts that plague my mind."

She caught her breath, but before anything could escalate in that charged moment, he released her hand and paced away, his smile replaced with a frown as he ran a hand through his hair.

"I...er...I did make some observations that could be useful to you," she said, trying to bring him back to her in some way.

It worked, for he turned back, but instead of pressing her to share what she'd learned, he glanced at the door. "I think it might be better to share those thoughts later, when we're alone."

Just as he finished the sentence, Paisley announced the arrival of the Duke of Gilmore and the Earl of Leighton. By the time they entered and everyone said their good mornings, Abigail and Pippa had also joined the fray. Owen stepped away, but even when he did, it didn't change the fact that he'd said they would be alone together later.

Celeste thrilled at the thought, even if she didn't understand how that would work in the slightest. Not that she had time to ponder it. Abigail directed everyone to sit and casual small talk faded away to something more purposeful when the Duke of Gilmore said, "We cannot avoid discussing the murder of Mr. Montgomery, can we?"

Abigail rolled her eyes. "Trust in you to make things unpleasant."

"What is unpleasant, madam, is ignoring a difficulty just because it's not easy," he snapped in return.

For a moment the two of them glared at each other, then Abigail folded her arms. "I don't think anyone believes we can ignore anything, Your Grace," she said. "Though in truth, I don't know what part you have to play here. Pippa, Celeste and I are affected by Ras's lies because we are the victims of them. Lord Leighton, as well, will be directly damaged by the scandal that will come."

"Has already come," the earl said.

Abigail ignored him. "But why, exactly, do *you* insist on remaining part of this tale of woe and ruin? Is it only the enjoyment you receive from watching us all fall?"

Celeste nearly choked at the pointed accusation and the fact that the duke's cheeks were flaring a dark red. But Abigail seemed unafraid, despite the fact that the man had power and could likely squash her like a bug if he desired. Celeste couldn't help feeling envious of how certain Abigail was in that moment. How unaffected.

"I involve myself because the man was trying to make a victim out of my sister," he said through what sounded like clenched teeth. "And because I know I set in motion a series of events that will cause pain and ruin both to my friend, the Earl of Leighton, and to you ladies. So I feel a responsibility to help resolve the issue in whatever way I can."

Abigail drew back at that statement. "Oh," she said.

Leighton raised a hand. "You two can argue about how little you think of each other later. We have a limited amount of time to spend as a group, and I think we'd better use it by discussing the very scandal you are debating."

Celeste glanced at him. "How bad is it?" she asked softly.

Leighton exchanged a look with Gilmore and then sighed. "I brought this morning's paper." He pulled it from his inner pocket and smoothed it on the table between them. "The story is on the second page. Not on a gossip sheet, not a blind item...it is listed as fact and details are given."

Celeste leaned in and read aloud where he indicated. "*The Honorable Erasmus Montgomery, brother to the Earl of Leighton, was recently murdered. Speculation is that the nature of his untimely death could be due to his questionable actions. Montgomery was discovered to be a bigamist.*"

She lifted her gaze and stared at Owen. "It lists our names. It lists the names of our families and where they live."

"Names? Let me see," Pippa gasped, and edged in a little. The way she snatched the paper to read the horrible black-and-white truth herself made Celeste look a little closer.

But her own emotions overwhelmed her before she could glean much about Pippa's thoughts. Celeste got up and paced away to the window. She stared outside as the group behind her began to talk all at once. The words faded into a mindless noise behind her, and that left her with only her thoughts buzzing in her mind.

Erasmus's death had given her...hope, as morbid as that was. Coming to London, she had pictured that she might be able to make a life here. A small life, perhaps, but a life of her own at last.

But the whispers that had likely been filtering through higher society since Erasmus's murder would now become screams in all corners of London thanks to the news going public. Her name was now associated, maiden or married. And she might never be accepted in any way, not in high company nor low.

She realized someone was saying her name. It pierced through her desperate fog. She turned and found the group staring at her. Owen had stood and moved a step in her direction, but it was Abigail who was saying her name.

"Celeste?" she repeated, and this time it didn't sound like it was coming from under water.

"I-I need a moment—" she stammered, and stumbled for the door. Abigail said her name again, but she ignored it. After all, there was nothing anyone could say now that could change the truth...or the future.

Owen watched Celeste stagger from the room, and his heart ached in his chest to see her in such pain. To not be able to soothe it, even though he so desperately, foolishly wanted to do just that.

Abigail scrambled to follow, but he held up a hand. "Let me."

The room at large stared at him and he shifted beneath their now-focused regard. He was showing his hand. Revealing himself in a way he didn't do. He'd trained himself not to do it over the years when he worked on a case.

But something in Celeste broke all that. In that moment, at least, he didn't care what they saw or what they thought. She was more important.

He scowled at the questioning faces and stalked from the room, twisting and turning through the halls, looking for her in each open room. At last he came to the back of the house and a large drawing room there. She wasn't inside, but he saw the door that connected to the terrace was open within. He slipped through it and there she was, standing with her fists gripped on the stone wall of the balcony, face turned toward the sunlight, eyes closed.

When he got closer, he realized a tear slid down her cheek, and he caught his breath as he reached for her. "Celeste."

She opened her eyes but kept her face upturned and away from his. "You don't owe me tenderness, you know," she whispered in a broken tone. "You don't owe me anything."

"I'm not counting debt," he said as he turned her gently. She looked up into his face for a moment and then rested her forehead against his chest. He folded his arms around her and held her.

They stood there for a lifetime, with her breath coming short, her hands clenching and unclenching against his chest, him smoothing her hair. At last she seemed to calm herself and she lifted her face to his again.

The last time she'd done this, she'd kissed him. He'd been able to rein in control over himself then. Now he wasn't certain he could do the same. He wanted so desperately to offer her nothing more than comfort. He didn't want to let the deeper, darker desires he felt for her overtake his moment. But when he moved to pull away, to distance himself from her, she tugged him closer.

"Owen," she whispered, and her breath stirred his lips because he was already leaning down into her, too close, too powerful, too out of control.

He captured her mouth, telling himself it would be a brief kiss, nothing more. He wouldn't let it be more. But he wasn't the one in charge, it seemed, just like the last time. Her arms came around his neck, her mouth opened, she demanded and he was too weak to her not to give exactly what she wanted.

He took her mouth as he hadn't allowed himself to before, tasting her, teasing her, driving into her the same way he so wanted to do without clothes, without hesitations.

She didn't mince or pull away. Instead, she melted into him. Dueled with his tongue, let out a low, hungry moan that seemed to burn through his bloodstream and settle heavily in his cock. He burned for her and he realized in that instant that if he kept dancing

71

around her, eventually that fire would rage out of control. It would lead to the inevitable. It would lead to his bed.

He broke away from her with great difficulty and they stared at each other, panting. Her pupils were dilated and she rested a hand against her flushed throat.

"I'm sorry," he gasped even though it was a lie. "I shouldn't have—"

She shook her head. "Oh, please don't. I wanted this. I wanted you to touch me. To kiss me. I don't regret it. If you do, then…" She blushed. "Well, then I suppose I owe *you* the apology because I keep doing this like a little fool."

"You're not a fool." He shook his head. "And I don't regret it. I just don't want it to…to cause more pain than you've already endured."

She worried her lip and he barely contained the groan that rushed to his lips. Did she not know what that little motion did to a man? More specifically, did to him?

"If this is pain, then let me feel it," she whispered.

He cupped her chin, exploring that lovely face, memorizing every facet of the blue in her eyes. He bent his head and kissed her again, savoring the sweetness of her flavor, the softness of her lips and the gentle sweep of her tongue against his.

This time when they broke apart, it wasn't desperate or driven. He smiled down at her and she returned the expression even as her cheeks became pink.

"I came out here to determine if you were well, you know," he said, stepping away so that she wouldn't feel too much pressure.

She laughed. "I'm certainly better now. But I do appreciate it. I must have looked like quite the fool to the rest by rushing out as if I'm the only one to be affected by this news."

He wrinkled his brow. "You are not responsible for anyone else's feelings. And I doubt anyone begrudges you yours. This is a very difficult situation."

"But Abigail and Pippa don't want to see me fall apart, not when they have their own feelings and reactions to manage," she insisted.

He cocked his head. "Then tell me. Pour it out on me and I promise you it won't break me."

Her lips parted. "That's asking too much of a stranger."

He swallowed, trying not to feel the sting of the truth. "What about a friend?"

"You would be my friend?" she asked after a hesitation that seemed to fill a lifetime.

"I would."

She bent her head, and it was as if he could see every bit of the weight that bore down on her slender shoulders. See that she had carried it all for almost her entire life. That she couldn't let even a small portion of it go, for fear it would misbalance everything.

"I had...hopes," she said at last. "That I could stay here. That I could build a life. I was foolish to think that the facts of Erasmus's actions wouldn't circulate through Society, through everything. I was foolish to think I wouldn't burn on the pyre of that scandal."

He pressed his lips together. "We don't know the future, Celeste. You do not yet burn, so let's not plan for your social funeral just yet."

"But—"

He shook his head. "Let us take the time to try to work it out. There are a dozen paths before us now. We'll narrow them down."

She sighed. "When you say it, I can almost believe it."

"Good."

She held his gaze a moment and then blushed again. "I told you before that I had information for you. Is now a good time to share it?"

"You are singular," he teased, and loved how her lips fluttered in that smile. "But I still don't think now is a good time. Why don't we get out? Air will do you good. We can see a bit of London and you can tell me everything you know after your night with Phillipa and Abigail."

Her eyes went wide. "Truly?"

He blinked at her utter disbelief, and ached for the life that must have caused so much of it. "Yes. Celeste, I promised you I'd show you the sights of the city. I don't lie. Now come, we'll tell the others."

She caught his arm and followed him back into the house. And he tried not to think too hard about why it meant so much to make her happy. Why he wanted to keep doing it, over and over, until she smiled more than frowned.

CHAPTER 9

C eleste had felt the curious stares of her new friends when Owen announced that they were going to escape for a turn about Town. She had seen the slight exchange of a look between the duke and the earl, as well. A knowing stare that she might have been offended by if she hadn't been kissing Owen passionately just a short time before.

But now she stood on the drive alone with Owen, waiting for his rig to be brought around, and she pushed all that from her mind. What did it matter what anyone thought? She was going to see London at last.

The phaeton that was brought to the step made her eyes go wide. It was a fine model of the rig, probably very expensive. The top was pushed back so the riders could enjoy the summer sunshine that almost seemed a gift from the gods. The two matching chestnut horses seemed to vibrate with as much excitement that they would be allowed to draw such a thing as she felt in being able to ride in it.

"You brought a phaeton?" she gasped as Owen took her hand and helped her up into the high vehicle.

He came around to the driver's side and clambered up himself.

Once he had taken his seat, he turned to look at her. "Yes. I promised we would do this. Even before we...*talked* on the terrace, I thought today might be a good day to start. The phaeton is open air and the best way to see the city is from the road."

She clapped her hands, knowing she was acting a country fool but somehow not caring. "Oh, it's wonderful, Owen. My father had this horrible dogcart for hunting and he tried to pretend it was a fine open carriage. He even called it a barouche sometimes—it was dreadful."

"Why didn't he buy a barouche if he desired one so greatly?" Owen asked with a shake of his head.

"You've met my mother." She rolled her eyes. "Do you really think he had any say in it? She liked a fine carriage, not a racing rig. At any rate, I always wanted to ride in a phaeton like this. Is it very fast?"

She might have been a little embarrassed by the enthusiasm she seemed not able to control, but he laughed as he signaled for the horses to drive on and they eased onto the bustling street. "Not in the city, of course. But if we went out onto a less populated road, we could frighten the devil out of any poor passerby."

She bounced in her seat with uncontrollable glee at that thought. "May we?"

"If you wish. I'll plan it for another day." He winked at her. "You can even drive."

"I would love that!"

She settled back against the seat in pure bliss. For the first time in days—no, months—she felt...*content*. And it was due in no small part to the remarkable man at her side who could both coax desire from her that she feared and present her with hope and happiness even in the worst of situations.

They rode for a while with Owen pointing out the landmarks she had read about so many times. They bounced past Covent Garden and its famous theatre, peered into Hyde Park with his seemingly sincere promises to return, and oohed and aahed over the fine houses in Twickenham.

Every turn seemed to reveal some new pleasure more wonderful than she had ever imagined when she dreamed of escaping her rustic village and coming here. She leaned so far out of the vehicle to sneak her peeks that several times Owen had to place a hand on her lower back to steady her so she wouldn't tumble from the rig and crack her head open.

Not that she minded when he touched her. There was something wonderful about the warmth and weight of his hand. It both enflamed feelings she hardly recognized in herself and also soothed her. An odd dichotomy she was beginning to crave.

Finally, he turned the rig into a glorious green haven and slowed the horses as they meandered down the tree-lined lanes of a park.

"This is lovely," she breathed.

He smiled. "It is Pettyfort Park. It's not as showy as Hyde or St. James, but it's my favorite in the city. I come here as often as I can to walk and take in the air. My home is just on the other side there."

He motioned past the entrance, and she craned her neck. Through the trees she saw a pretty neighborhood, quiet and peaceful. She wondered which of the colorful little row of houses was his. Not that she would ever see it.

"It's also not so crowded. Those are places where those who wish to be seen go to exhibit and someone is always watching. But here you and I can have that conversation you've been so desperate to start."

He winked, and her stomach flipped. "Conversation?" she repeated.

What could he mean by that? Had he read all her wicked thoughts that afternoon as he toured her around the city? Had he felt her desire for him to kiss her again? And again? And then maybe more than kiss her, even though that sort of thing had never appealed to her all that much in the past? Sex with Erasmus had been...well, she'd spent a lot of time staring at the ceiling and thinking of anything but him grunting over her.

Now she found herself wondering what it would be like if *Owen* touched her. Stripped her bare. Claimed her.

"About what you learned," he explained with a chuckle that yanked her from her wicked thoughts. "You look so nervous right now, Celeste, almost like you've seen a ghost. I only meant that back at the house you tried to talk to me twice about your observations regarding Abigail and Phillipa."

"Oh, of course," she gasped, gripping her hands together in her lap. "I wasn't thinking. Yes, yes."

He turned his attention back to the road ahead and tipped his hat to a couple walking the path. He remained so at ease while it felt like a weight had been pressed to her chest now.

"They are both good women," she said, and heard how defensive she sounded.

He glanced toward her and arched a brow. "I don't think anyone ever said differently."

"And yet you still suspect them of murder," she said.

He tugged on the reins, and the meandering horses came to a stop by the side of the road. He pivoted in his seat, resting his arm along the back of the bench, tantalizingly close to her own shoulder, though he never touched her.

"The two things do not have to be so separate," he said. "Celeste, I have seen murder before. It's always ugly. But the motives behind it range from horrific to understandable. If either Abigail or Phillipa had uncovered Montgomery's trickery, if they had been pushed to the brink by his behavior, or even threatened by him when they confronted him...those would be understandable motives. They wouldn't indicate that either woman was evil or bad or indecent."

Celeste swallowed. "I suppose that is true. But what would you do if one of them *did* kill Erasmus? What if it had been done out of self-preservation? If one was threatened, as you described?"

He arched a brow. "Is that what happened?"

She drew back. "I don't know. I have observations, not answers."

He nodded slowly and she felt him reading her. He always read her, but this time he was looking for a lie. She didn't like that. It sat heavily on her skin.

"Then tell me those," he said, and she noted he didn't answer her question.

"Pippa is angry," she said softly. "She pretends she isn't, but I sense it there under the surface. She said she was looking for Erasmus before his death. Trying to get him to respond to her. When he wouldn't, she came to London looking for him." She worried her lip because what she had said now painted her new friend in a poor light. "I don't know if she is capable of harming anyone, though."

"Nor do I," he said. "I knew she'd come to the city before the death. Well done sensing the anger, though. She hides it well, but I've felt the same from her. Did you notice how she jumped to look at the paper this afternoon, too?"

Celeste nodded. "I did, though barely through my own fog. It was when I said our names were listed. It could be she just felt the same sting I did, knowing our secret would be out."

"But you think it was more."

She shrugged. "I don't know. Perhaps."

"What about Abigail? Anything to say there?"

Celeste shifted. Abigail had welcomed her into her home. She hadn't yet made Celeste feel anything but accepted into their odd sisterhood.

"She is clever," she whispered. "And observant. She knows you suspect her of the death. She seems...oddly resigned to that. I don't know if she remains so calm about it because she is certain of her innocence...or because she is equally sure you will eventually catch her and that will end her freedom. It could be either thing."

"Anything else?" he asked.

"She doesn't hate the Duke of Gilmore as much as she acts like she does," Celeste said.

"Why do you say that?" Owen asked.

"She stood up for him when we discussed Erasmus's death, if only for a flash of a moment," she explained. "She doesn't *want* him to be the guilty party. It matters to her that he isn't." Owen was silent for a beat, and she examined him more closely. "How did I do?"

"Very well," he said. "I'm impressed, Celeste, and I don't say that lightly."

She saw the truth of that on his face, and her chest swelled with pride. Impressing him was a pastime she could surrender herself to. The outcome felt so good, it was addicting.

"So what do you think of my fair city?" he asked with a wider grin. The dimple popped and her entire body clenched with a desire that was so strong it was unseemly.

"It is everything I could have dreamed of and more," she said. "I'm sure I sound like a bumpkin when I go on and on about what I'm seeing."

"You sound excited, you sound like you're open to new experiences and sights and sounds. There is nothing wrong with that. It has made me see my own city through new eyes. I ride around the streets we rode today all the time. I see the things we saw regularly, but today I truly looked at them."

Her cheeks heated. "Well, I appreciate the effort," she said. "I had a wonderful time and I will never forget it."

He tilted his head. "Do you think it's over?"

"What do you mean? You promised a tour and I certainly got one. I wouldn't dare trespass on your time more than I already have."

"I'm not sure where you got this idea that you are some terrible burden to me that I am anxious to rid myself of. You were *never* trespassing," he assured her. "And this tour today was only the overview. If you would like, I'm happy to take you to a few of these places for further exploration. Some of the museums, for example.

And we already said we'd go to Hyde Park again. Is there anyplace else especially you'd like to see?"

She stared at him. Owen was practically a stranger to her, and yet he was offering her the world. His world. Without hesitation and thus far, without price.

"Celeste?"

She blinked. "I...have you heard of Lady Lena's Salon?"

His eyebrows lifted. "I have. Everyone has. Lena Bright is one of the most scandalous and popular women in London. The bastard daughter of a duke who calls herself Lady Lena to draw people to her salon? One who is...very open with her *progressive* thoughts and ways? But I am not sure I could garner you an invitation. It is the most sought-after literary and political salon at present. We could drive by the location if you'd like."

"I would very much like that." She shifted slightly. "Although *I* might be able to get us an invitation if that is something you would be interested in."

He leaned back. "And just how would you do that, fair lady who was calling herself a bumpkin not three minutes ago?"

She laughed. "It has nothing at all to do with my sophistication or lack thereof. You see, Harriet Smith was my governess."

"Lady Lena's...companion?" he asked, and she could see he was being delicate.

"I thought you said she was open with how progressive her life is. I've heard it's common knowledge that they are not just friendly companions."

"It is," he said.

Celeste met his eyes as if challenging him to say something about that fact. He did not. "Harriet and I have kept in touch for years. I would dearly love to see her and finally meet Lena, if it can be arranged."

"You write the letter telling them of your arrival in London and let me know the day and time. I will be your escort," he promised.

She stared at him, both wanting to believe this was simply the kind of man he was and also hesitant to do so. "Why are you so kind to me?"

He returned her stare with a blank one of his own. "What do you mean?"

She narrowed her gaze. "Are you just observing me like you do with all the others? Is it that you want something from me? Why?"

His lips parted, and then his hand inched forward on the back of the bench. His fingers brushed her shoulder and even through the layers of silk of her gown she felt the pressure. The warmth of him that made her hot and cold all at once.

"I won't lie and tell you I don't want *something*."

Her eyes went wide. "You do? I wasn't certain when you pulled away from my kiss, not once but twice."

He shook his head. "I pulled away because you are vulnerable and I didn't want to take advantage. But I can't sport with your intelligence by pretending there isn't something that burns in me whenever I'm near you."

She caught her breath at those words and the passion in his expression when he said them. "O-oh."

"But I am kind to you because you deserve kindness. It doesn't come with a cost."

Could she truly believe this man? In her life she'd never known anyone who didn't trade on their love or affection or kindness. She almost couldn't picture that someone like that truly existed.

But Owen made her *want* to believe.

"Now we've been out a long time," he said. "And I would not wish to make you late for your supper plans with the ladies. Shall we go back?"

For a wild moment she wanted to say no. To tell him to ride around the city with her forever, because the afternoon had been so perfect that she didn't want it to end. But that was a dream, just as everything about this man was a dream.

"Yes," she said instead, and tried to temper her disappointment when he shot her one more of those world-brightening smiles and then urged the horses back into motion.

Back to the real world, which had its fears and frustrations that she didn't want to face, even if Owen made them seem a little more bearable. Which was a dangerous thing, indeed.

CHAPTER 10

Owen stared at the list before him on his desk, but as it had been all afternoon, it blurred before him. It had been two days since he'd spent the afternoon with Celeste and thoughts of her had plagued him ever since. More than thoughts. Dreams. Wicked dreams.

"Pardon me, Mr. Gregory."

He lifted his head and found his butler was standing in the doorway to his study. "Yes, Cookson?"

"The Earl of Leighton is here to see you. Are you in residence?"

Owen arched a brow, his attention now fully back where it belonged. He hadn't been expecting Leighton. That the man had arrived here without sending word that he would call was…well, it might mean nothing and it might mean something.

"I'm in," Owen said. "Show him here."

Cookson inclined his head, and after he left, Owen got to his feet. The past two days he had been focusing his efforts on the Duke of Gilmore's guilt or innocence in the murder. Gilmore was a difficult read, and his rage when he'd discovered Montgomery's duplicitous behavior had been violent and hot.

But now Owen had the opportunity to explore Leighton. He would take that, expected or not.

Cookson reappeared. "The Earl of Leighton, Mr. Gregory."

Owen rose as Leighton entered. He could see the man was troubled, perhaps hadn't been sleeping if the circles under his eyes were any indication. Was that from guilt or grief or something else? Certainly the man had a great deal of trouble to wade through, no matter what his involvement in his brother's death.

"My lord," Owen said, coming around the desk and offering a hand.

Leighton shook it. "I'm sorry to call without a prior appointment."

"You needn't be. You are one of my employers, after all. You are welcome any time. Would you like a drink?"

"I would," Leighton said with a harsh, humorless laugh. "But I think it's a bit too early for me. I hope you have time to talk."

Owen motioned him to the seat across from his desk and then took his place again behind it. "I do. I'm joining the wives at Mrs. Montgomery's residence, but I have an hour before I must depart. What can I do for you?"

"I was calling to check on your progress. I haven't heard much from you in the last few days."

That the man was concerned about the progress of his investigation was a mark in his favor, but perhaps not as strong a one as a layperson might believe. Owen had known many a villain who had pretended interest in the outcome of an investigation to push suspicion away from themselves.

"I'm working through the suspect list," he said, and it wasn't a lie.

Leighton leaned back in his chair and folded his arms. "Is there a point where you will stop pretending I'm not on that list?"

Owen lifted his brows. *That* was unexpected. "Why do you think you're a suspect?"

"Because Ras was my estranged half-brother. We had several public altercations, including one just before his death. I cut him off three years ago. And this discovery of his bigamy could and *has* created a scandal that…" Leighton trailed off with a shake of his head. "It will be years before I am welcomed without whispers and shakes of the head, if I'm ever truly welcomed again. A murder, had it gone off without too much fanfare, might have solved the problem."

Owen watched the man closely. There were a dozen ways to play out this moment, a dozen ways to react that might bring him the information he required. But honesty was the one that jumped out at him, both because he thought it might have the desired effect and also because he liked the earl.

"Very good points, all. I must consider you, of course. I have. You are lower on my suspect list because the murder *didn't* go off without fanfare. Whoever did it left things so that the worst might come out. It would not have served you to do it, though in the heat of passion you could have not been thinking." He didn't add that poisoners weren't usually heat of passion killers. He wanted to see Leighton's reaction first.

The earl didn't appear to be offended. He let out his breath in a long sigh before he said, "What can I do to remove myself from that list in your head, Mr. Gregory? To get you closer to the real killer?"

"You are anxious for this to be closed," Owen said.

"Obviously." Leighton pushed to his feet. "My brother was many things. Many more terrible things than I even knew. But he did not deserve to be poisoned. He didn't deserve to be murdered. I want justice, Mr. Gregory. I want to be able to mourn my brother without questioning. And yes, I want to be able to rebuild every-thing he so foolishly destroyed without the specter of this resur-facing down the road."

"Can you tell me where you were the night he was killed? Nine nights ago?"

"Has it been nine days?" Leighton breathed. "It seems longer. And it seems like it was yesterday. The message that I received that day that told me my brother had been murdered shines greatest in my mind, but let me see if I can recreate my day otherwise. I met with my man of affairs around two. We spoke for two hours."

"A long meeting. About anything specific?"

"No. We always meet on the first Wednesday of each month to go over the state of things. It was a regular meeting. I'll give you his particulars so you may speak to him." Leighton rubbed his thighs as if he were uncomfortable. "Afterward I bathed and dressed for my evening. At seven I took supper with a...a lady friend at her apartments. I was there until ten. I returned home by ten-thirty, and the message about Ras arrived a few moments later."

"So a mistress," Owen said gently.

Leighton ran a hand through his hair. "Not exactly. Not officially, at any rate. Just a woman I sometimes meet with to pass the time. It isn't serious on either of our parts. She is an actress."

"And what is her name, my lord?" Owen asked.

Leighton tilted his head. "It is necessary?"

"While I appreciate you wishing to keep her out of this situation, the fact is that you were with the lady during the very time I believe Mr. Montgomery was killed." He leaned forward. "So I *must* speak to her. I will be discreet, of course."

"Bollocks," Leighton muttered under his breath. "Very well. Her stage name is Violet Vickery. She lives on Glenhill Lane."

Owen wrote it down. He would, of course, speak to the lady, but he had a sense that Leighton was telling the truth. There had been nothing artful or practiced about Leighton's recalling of the day or evening. And his hesitance about his alibi seemed to genuinely come from a desire not to reveal something delicate, both for himself and the sake of the lady.

"I will speak to her tomorrow," he said. "Until then, I hope you won't see her, just so I may have her uncoached and unpracticed response."

Leighton laughed, but it was bitter. "There is no need to worry about that. When my brother's death became public, she wrote to me to break things off. She didn't want to be associated with such goings on, even before she knew there was a murder."

"I am sorry if you are pained, but it will make my duty a bit easier," Owen said. "I wanted to ask you another question, though."

"Anything to help," Leighton said, but he looked very tired. Not that Owen could blame him.

"Who do you think killed your brother? Who do you see as the list of suspects?"

Leighton shook his head slowly and then met Owen's eyes. "That, my friend, will take longer than a moment to detail. And I think it will also require that drink I declined earlier."

Owen smiled as he got up and poured them each a sherry. When he handed one over to Leighton, the earl took a long sip before he said, "I've not been able to stop thinking about potential suspects, though I'd not shared my thoughts because I wasn't certain if you wanted to feel these things out yourself."

"It does help to do so," Owen admitted. "But I also like to get the insider view of a situation."

"Then I am not your man." Leighton sighed. "Our estrangement put me firmly on the other side of the glass. But I suppose one would be a fool not to think that the wives are all suspects in his killing. Especially Abigail and...and Phillipa."

Owen marked Leighton's hesitance to say Phillipa's name. The way his fingers flexed on his glass when he did manage to choke it out. Interesting.

"Yes. They were both in London. And while both deny knowing anything about Montgomery's bigamy, they could easily be lying about that. It would give either of them a solid motive." He watched for Leighton's response and the earl's jaw tightened.

"Indeed, I cannot imagine how any of those women felt when they heard the news."

"And what about Gilmore?" Owen pressed.

Leighton's gaze darted to him. "The Duke of Gilmore?" he gasped.

Owen nodded. "Surely you must see why."

"I do. He is very protective of his younger sister Ophelia, and he must have been enraged that Ras chose her. Especially since he and I have been friends for...years. Since we were boys at school. He knew Ras, played games with him when we were children. He hasn't spoken to me about the betrayal, but he must feel it with some variation of the keenness that I do."

Owen marked that fact in his mind, knowing he'd later have a great deal to add to the notes he had on the case. Gilmore was so serious a person, it was hard to picture him as a child, playing games with a man who would later try to snare his beloved sister.

But it certainly made the man's motives sharper.

"God's teeth, I hope that isn't true," Leighton murmured. "His investigation into my brother was understandable, though I wished he'd come to me first. But to kill him..."

"It may not have been Gilmore," Owen said. "Are there any other possibilities?"

"Have you spoken to the other woman?"

Owen sat up straighter. "Other woman?"

"Yes. Perhaps it means nothing, but more than five years ago, before Ras married Abigail, he was involved with another woman. She was the daughter of a pub owner. She'd worked as a serving girl for her father, and that was how Ras met her. He believed himself in love with her. He wanted to marry her, but our father nipped that in the bud. Ras was very angry—they nearly came to blows." Leighton flinched. "Funny how our father was trying so desperately to avoid a scandal, and yet here we are." He slugged back the remaining alcohol in his glass. "Here we bloody are."

"What was her name?" Owen asked gently.

Leighton shook his head. "God, I can hardly recall. What was her name? Rebecca? Regina? Something with an R."

That didn't do much to narrow the potential persons of interest. There were dozens of pubs around London, with dozens of servers and patronesses whose name began with R. But it was, yet again, a new piece of information to add to the pile.

"In truth, I hope it isn't one of the wives," Leighton continued with a sigh. "I knew Abigail all along, of course. She was the proper wife. And though my brother and I were estranged, I never had a cross interaction with her. Phillipa and Celeste are newer to me. But I would hate it if my brother pushed either so far." He flexed his hands against his thighs. "You know. I'm certain you are as loath to suspect Celeste as I am to suspect Phillipa."

Owen blinked, thoughts of his investigation fading at those pointed words. "I—what do you mean?"

Leighton leaned back in his chair. "Come, man, I'm not blind. There is clearly a connection between you. I see it whenever your eyes meet. And why not? She's a lovely woman and seems a good sort. This mess created by my brother will make things difficult, but..." His gaze darted away. "You don't have the hindrances another might have for such a thing."

Owen pursed his lips at the implication. It was more evident than ever that Leighton had some attachment to Phillipa. And he could, indeed, see how difficult that would be for him. Leighton was knee deep in this awful situation. Developing a relationship with one of his late brother's wives wouldn't ease the talk, only multiply it.

"It is still complicated," Owen said softly.

"Why?"

Owen choked on a laugh. "*You* ask me that?"

Leighton threw up his hands. "Come now. She isn't married— she never was, thanks to Ras's selfishness. So there is no limit on her for a mourning period. I also get the impression that Celeste never had any feelings for my brother."

"No. I think it was an arrangement and not one she was very pleased with."

"Then there is no guilt for her or for you." Leighton shrugged. "If you have the inclination, why not follow it? You might be good for her."

Owen couldn't help but think of Celeste's soft sigh when he took her lips. Of the sweetness of making her smile or teasing some clever observation from her mind. He shook his head.

"I would like to be good for her," he muttered, and then immediately wished he could take it back. Whether his suspicions about the man had been alleviated or not, Leighton wasn't his friend. He was his employer, at best. It wasn't right for Owen to hand over personal information, personal connection to a stranger. "I beg your pardon."

Leighton shrugged. "My brother created chaos, Mr. Gregory. It was his forte for all the years of his far-too-short life. If any kind of happiness or pleasure, permanent or temporary, could come out of what he's done, I would be glad of it. Certainly there is little I can do to create it."

Owen wrinkled his brow. "Is there anyone in particular you're thinking of?"

Leighton's lips thinned. "No. There cannot be. I know that. I accept it, however reluctantly." He pushed to his feet. "And now I have intruded upon your privacy for far too long. Please let me know if I can be of any assistance."

"I will," Owen said as he followed his guest to the door of the study. "And my lord?"

Leighton turned back. "Yes?"

"Perhaps it isn't my place, but I do feel that sometimes when the relationship wasn't...easy, then the rest is harder when it comes to loss. To grief. But you *are* trying to do right by Mr. Montgomery. That makes you a good brother."

Leighton's expression softened slightly, a trickle of relief cutting through the stone of his countenance. "Thank you," he said softly. "Good afternoon."

The earl tipped his head and then he departed toward the foyer. Owen shut the study door and leaned back against it. He had a great deal to think about when it came to his case. But it wasn't all the new information that ricocheted through his mind like an errant bullet.

No, it was thoughts of Celeste, and the idea that pursuing the desire, the connection he felt toward her might not be a losing proposition.

CHAPTER 11

"Is there any letter, Paisley?" Celeste asked as the butler brought a tray of tea into the parlor and set it on the sideboard, arranging it to perfection.

He smiled at her. "No, madam. However, you did only send out your missive this morning. So it might be too early to expect a reply."

Celeste's cheeks heated. She had taken almost two days to write her message to Harriet after Owen's encouragement. Partly because she didn't know exactly what to say to explain her arrival in London. Partly because she feared the response. And now she was anxious and worried and silly as a schoolgirl.

"Of course," she murmured.

"May I get you anything else?" Paisley asked.

"Nothing, thank you," she said.

"And what about you, Mrs. Montgomery?"

Celeste turned and realized that Abigail was standing in the doorway, observing the room with that quiet, intelligent elegance she always portrayed. Unreadable, as always, but never unkind. "No, thank you Paisley. That will be all."

The butler left the room and Abigail closed the door behind him. When she turned back, Celeste's heart leapt a bit. In the handful of days since her arrival in London, she had begun to know her fellow wives better. She liked them both immensely. Where she had feared censure, she had only found kindness. Where she had expected judgment, only understanding.

Pippa was softer about it. More direct in her offers of a shoulder to cry upon if it were needed. Celeste had taken her up on it a few times, though Abigail always seemed capable of controlling her reactions to the situation they found themselves in.

She also showed her affection through action. She had determined Celeste's favorite tea and biscuits and always had them on hand. She offered books that might be to her liking. She slid the paper away from her side of the breakfast table, since the sight of the gossip splashed across its pages was so upsetting to Pippa especially. She protected, but did so without fanfare or requirement for thanks or recognition. She fixed things.

Celeste only hoped she hadn't attempted to fix the situation with Erasmus and that it had gone all wrong, that he had ended up dead in the parlor. She didn't want to believe Abigail could do that. She didn't want to think of the consequences for her friend if she had.

"You look very pretty this morning," Abigail said with a smile as she moved to the sideboard Paisley had abandoned and poured them each tea. "That blue suits you very well."

Celeste smoothed the skirts of her gown with a smile. "Oh, thank you so much. I've always liked this dress."

Abigail motioned to the seats before the fire and they each took one. "How are you settling in?"

Celeste sipped her tea, giving herself time to ponder the answer before she spoke it. "I'm...well. As well as can be expected. I feel a little restless. Like I should be *doing* something, rather than sitting around waiting."

"Waiting for Mr. Gregory," Abigail said softly. "I hear he is coming to collect you today."

Celeste couldn't help but shift because Abigail had speared her with one of those all-seeing stares she possessed. She never missed a thing. "Yes. He has promised to continue his tour of London for me."

"And I suppose you two will also be talking about the case," Abigail said. "I know you are assisting him."

Celeste nearly choked on her tea and jerked her gaze to Abigail in surprise. "Why do you think that?"

"Because I'm not a fool. You weren't in London, unlike Pippa or myself or a half dozen other suspects he must be considering. Don't worry, I don't disapprove. The sooner he ends this, the better."

There was something bitter in her tone, but her expression remained serene. Still, Celeste wished she could...comfort her somehow.

"Certainly, he suspects *me*," Abigail said with an arch of her brow that all but dared Celeste to deny it.

Celeste shifted. Owen hadn't given her directions on what to do if one of his suspects addressed this sort of thing directly. Did she deny it? Did she say yes?

Abigail was clearly still waiting for a response and Celeste's cheeks burned as she stammered, "I-I—"

Abigail held up her hand. "Gracious, don't hurt yourself. It's all right. I wouldn't respect him much if he *didn't* suspect me. After all, I had every reason to kill Ras, didn't I? I am the humiliated first wife. Ras spent any fortune we might have once had, so I will be penniless." She sighed. "The scandal is already dragging me to hell. Friends have begun to cut me off because of him."

"I'm so sorry, Abigail," Celeste whispered. And she was. Abigail was, by nature of being the first and legal wife, the public face of this situation. The one with the most to lose, the most to confront.

"Why? It isn't your fault," Abigail said on a heavy sigh. "It was Ras's and Ras's alone. And Mr. Gregory knows that as well as anyone—he's a clever sort. I'm sure he looks at all my motives and adds them to the fact that I was here in London, I have knowledge of herbs and I have no alibi."

Celeste's heart sank with every admission of possible guilt. She liked Abigail so much. She didn't want her to suffer even more because she was accused of murder.

"No alibi at all?" Celeste pressed. "You weren't out with friends or with a servant?"

"No." Abigail looked around, a suddenly faraway sound to her tone. "I was right here in this house, the very place where Ras died. It was late, so my maid had gone to bed. There would have been nothing to stop me from coming down and confronting him about what he'd done…" She trailed off with an almost wistful expression.

Celeste's hands shook as she leaned closer. "And…did you? Did you go into that parlor where he was found, the one that's all locked up on the other side of the house, and confront him? Did you?"

"Did I kill him?" Abigail whispered. "No. By the end, my love for him had disintegrated to cinders. Hardened to a shell that I wore to protect myself from him. And yes, I did want to be free of him. But not like this. Never like this."

Her voice cracked, and Celeste couldn't stop herself from grasping for her hand. Abigail smiled at her, the vulnerability gone from her face as if it had never been there.

"I *am* sorry."

Abigail squeezed her hand gently. "And as I said before, you needn't be. It wasn't your fault, nor is it your place to fix it. I don't think your Mr. Gregory has a vendetta toward me, nor does he seem to be a careless person. I'm sure he'll determine the truth soon enough and that will be the end of it."

"He is not *my* Mr. Gregory," Celeste gasped.

Abigail arched a brow. "Is he not? Because it is very clear how much you like him."

Once again Celeste found herself speechless. "I—"

Abigail waved her hand. "It's obvious, so you needn't deny it."

"How is it obvious?" Celeste asked, barely able to make her voice carry.

"It's written all over your face, my dear, the moment he enters a room."

"Oh dear," Celeste whispered as she clenched her fists against her thighs. She wanted to find words to deny this, but she couldn't. "What you must think of me."

Abigail tilted her head back and laughed. "I think you are a woman, with as many desires and needs and interests as any man, even if they lie and tell us we are supposed to be behave differently than they do. Honestly, you could have chosen a worse object of affection. Mr. Gregory is *very* handsome."

"I cannot deny that—it is a fact anyone can see," Celeste breathed.

Abigail chuckled. "But he also seems kind and intelligent, even-handed. Attentive and that will always translate well into a more... intimate situation."

"Abigail!" Celeste burst out as she leapt to her feet and paced away, as if distance could silence this untoward conversation. "I wasn't even *thinking* about...about...intimate situations."

That was a lie, of course. She *had* thought of such things, dreamed of his hands on her. She shivered even now at the memory.

"Why not?" Abigail said with a laugh as she got to her own feet. "I think each of us deserves a bit of fun after what Ras did." She moved closer. "But have a care, my dear, if you do decide to pursue such an arrangement. A broken heart stings like nothing else."

Abigail's gaze went faraway, as if she were thinking of something personal. Something painful.

"Abigail—"

Abigail ignored her and continued, "I would hate to see you make a mistake by clinging to anything that seems solid when you're in a vulnerable state. Protect your heart. No one else can be depended upon to do so."

Celeste swallowed. She hadn't dared to seek permission for the feelings, the desires Owen stoked in her. But having that permission was heady and her mind leapt to wild, wanton scenarios where she might get what she wanted for once in her life.

"I don't know," she whispered. "It seems like a dream to even consider it."

"We all deserve dreams," Abigail said, and moved to the window. She glanced down at the street and then turned back toward Celeste with a smile. "And now he's here."

Celeste caught her breath and rushed to stand beside Abigail. Down below, one of the footmen was standing by as Owen came down from his phaeton. Owen straightened his jacket, smoothing his hands along the lines of it as he spoke to the servant for a moment.

"He does cut a fine figure," Abigail murmured. "There is no denying that. At least you'll have fun."

"Fun," Celeste responded softly. "There's a thought."

Owen turned his head toward the window, and Abigail caught Celeste's arm, drawing her back as the two of them began to giggle. It felt so good to be foolish and girlish with a friend. Back in Twiddleport Celeste had always felt the odd one out. She was too bookish for some of the girls and too unaffiliated for others. But now the bond between her and Pippa and Abigail was growing. She didn't want to lose it.

She didn't want to lose any of it.

"Mr. Gregory," Paisley said as he stepped into the doorway, then moved aside so Owen could enter the room.

Celeste's face grew hot as she and Abigail both acknowledged him with a bend of their heads. He had certainly seen her in the window watching him. But he made no mention of it and merely smiled at them both.

"Ladies, good afternoon."

"Good afternoon," Abigail said with a very real and welcoming smile of her own. "I would offer you tea, but I hear you and Celeste are pleasure bound today."

Celeste caught her breath and shot Abigail a look. "Abigail, you...we..."

"What sights will you see?" Abigail continued with a little look for Celeste.

Now her heart began to pound. She'd been so caught up in thinking of wicked things, she'd thought Abigail dared to speak of them right in the parlor. But of course she meant their tour of London.

"I wasn't certain what Celeste would be in the mood for," Owen said with a brief smile for her.

Abigail nodded. "Had you considered the British Museum? I've always liked their herbarium."

"I had thought of it, madam, as I am as much a fan. Tuesday next was my plan for that."

"Excellent. I shall be excited to hear Celeste's report on it." Abigail smiled again at Celeste and then moved toward the door. "I will not keep you. Good day."

She left them then, shutting the door behind herself most inappropriately. And now that they were alone Celeste couldn't help but feel...awkward. All this talk of fun and pleasure and naughty desires made her look at Owen in a most inappropriate way.

"Are you well?" Owen asked.

She jolted at the question, as well as the concerned expression on his face. "Yes. Yes, of course. How are...how are you?"

He chuckled. "I'm very well."

She nodded and paced away, wishing her hands didn't shake so much.

He was watching her. She felt his stare boring into her back. "Celeste, have a few days apart changed that we are friends?"

She pivoted back and found he had a truly concerned expression. "No, of course not. I am sorry, I know I'm behaving out of sorts."

"And why is that?" he pressed gently.

"Because being around you makes me...nervous."

He stared at her for what felt like forever, though it couldn't have been more than a second or two. Then he moved toward her. "That doesn't bode very well," he said softly as he reached for her hand. She wasn't wearing gloves and he had removed his before he entered the room. His palm was rough against hers, his fingers tracing a pattern on her palm that made her shiver.

"You needn't be nervous about me, Celeste," he said, watching her face for every reaction to his touch. "Because I'll never do anything you don't want me to do. I promise."

Her lips parted as she stared up into his face. His pupils were dilated, the pressure of his fingers increased and for a brief, powerful moment she thought he might kiss her again. She *wanted* him to kiss her again.

But he stepped away instead, releasing her from his grip and his spell. "Now let us talk about today. I didn't make solid plans because I wasn't certain if you had reached out to your friends in Town. Are we going to Lady Lena's Salon?"

She swallowed. "Er, no. I only just sent my letter to Harriet this morning."

His brows lifted in surprise, but he said nothing about it, just smiled as he motioned toward the door. "Then we can carry on. Are you ready?"

"I am," she said, but as she followed him from the room, she knew that was a lie. She wasn't ready, not at all. Not for him, not for London and not for the things she wanted that were beginning to squeeze all other thought and desire from her mind.

Unlike the first time he'd toured her in his phaeton when she'd all but tumbled from the carriage in delight, today Celeste had been quiet on the ride across London. She was restless, listless, and he wanted desperately to fix it, foolish as that inclination might be.

But he still wondered what had caused this particular hesitation in her.

"Do you want to tell me why you didn't write to your friend earlier than today?"

She blinked and her gaze slid to him furtively, like he had uncovered some horrible secret she had hoped to take to her grave. "I didn't mean to put you out."

He wrinkled his brow. "You didn't. But we spoke about your former governess days ago. I assumed you would be thrilling at the idea of meeting with her again, especially without your parents involving themselves or limiting you."

Celeste let out a long sigh. "I suppose I must be honest with you after all your kindness. I came home just as excited to reach out as you describe but I sat in my chamber and stared at a blank piece of vellum, just...not knowing what to say."

"You might try 'Greetings, old friend, I'm in London and wish to see you,'" he suggested gently.

She folded her arms. "But the real message is 'Greetings, sophisticated friend, I am in London because my husband turned out to be a murdered bigamist and I am the laughing stock of the city. Do you want to lower yourself to see what I've become?'"

He frowned. Celeste was so good at showing her strength. At lifting her chin and making the best of the worst in the world, it was easy to forget that she had to be flailing at the deepest part of an ocean. That she couldn't picture her future because her past and present were so clouded by lies and gossip and pain.

"I just don't know my place in this world," Celeste continued. "In any world." She was quiet a moment, then smiled at him apologetically. "I swear you will regret taking me out today when I am in such a maudlin mood."

"I certainly don't," he said, and meant it. Truth be told, he'd missed seeing her during their time apart. Missed that soft floral scent of her hair and skin, missed the way her hands fluttered when she was excited, missed the sound of her laugh.

That was incredibly dangerous and also totally undeniable. This woman had begun to bewitch him and he didn't want free of her spell.

He slowed the rig and moved it to the side of the path, then turned toward her. "You must be exhausted because the future is filled with such question. You want to see things resolved?"

She nodded. "Perhaps I could better see the path then, yes."

He smiled. She was so very clever—of course she liked to set herself a path to follow. Of course she would be troubled by how rocky and twisted the one before her seemed. "Then why don't we go to my home instead of a museum or a park today?" he suggested.

Her eyes went a little wider and her pupils dilated, and for a moment every muscle in his body contracted with wild, unfiltered desire. She had no idea what that look did to him. No idea what her presence in general did.

"Go to your home...alone?" she whispered.

He nodded slowly, hoping to mask some of his eagerness for just that. "Yes. I could use your help with some elements of the case. Your eyes and observations might help me move along a little faster."

She bent her head. "Oh, yes, of course. Your case. Yes, I'd be very happy to join you there and assist in any way I can."

He nickered at the horses to jog on and for a little while they rode in silence. Then he grinned at her. "Also, I think it wouldn't help your situation if I kissed you in the open rig in the middle of the road. But alone in my study, I can do so with far less worry."

Her mouth dropped open, and he reveled in her surprise at that forward suggestion. "Unless you don't want that."

She barked out a little laugh that she smothered with her hand. When she lowered her fingers, he could see the corners of her mouth twitching like she was trying to suppress a smile.

"I think, Mr. Gregory, that I would very much like that. Is there no way to make the horses go faster?"

He threw his head back to laugh before he flicked the reins and they rushed even more quickly toward his home, toward his case... toward whatever would happen when they were alone and he could do all the wicked things that had been haunting him since the first moment he met her.

CHAPTER 12

Celeste was focused mainly on controlling her breath as Owen pulled the phaeton onto a small circular drive before a brightly painted blue house in the little neighborhood they had observed a few days before. She clasped her hands as she stared up at the narrow home snuggling along the row of others.

"What do you think?" he asked as he climbed down and came around to assist her.

"I was hoping it would be the blue one," she breathed. "I love how happy the color is."

"I was drawn to the color too," he admitted. "Let us hope you don't find the inside a disappointment."

She took his hand, climbed down from the rig and shook her head up at him. "Owen, you saw my awful little home in Twiddleport. I don't think anything could be disappointing after that."

"Thank you, Jenkins," he called to the young man who had swept up into the rig to take it away. He offered Celeste an arm and guided her to his door, where a smiling lady with graying hair had stepped outside.

"Good afternoon, Mr. Gregory. Welcome home."

"Mrs. Cookson," he said with an equally wide smile. The one that made his dimple pop. They followed her into the foyer. "Good afternoon. This is Mrs. Montgomery, a client."

"Ah, well, welcome, welcome," the woman said. "I assume you'll be going to the study. Should I have tea sent in?"

"That would be wonderful, but wait a few moments."

Mrs. Cookson nodded and smiled at Celeste again before she slipped off to start those preparations.

"She seems very kind," Celeste said.

"She is. She and her husband, my butler, are the best of us. And discreet, which is imperative in the business I perform."

Celeste smothered her relief at that statement. The last thing she needed was a gossipy servant talking about how she'd come unattended to Owen's home. There were enough ugly things being said about her at present. And yet she hadn't refused the man when he asked her to come.

Did that make her a hypocrite?

"You look troubled," he said, and his hand flexed at his side as if he wanted to reach for her but restrained himself. "Is it so terrible?"

She blinked and looked around. "On the contrary," she breathed. "It's lovely so far. I love that painting over the table there."

"Ah yes, it's one of my favorites. I bought it from a vendor on New Bond Street. We ought to go there. There are shops and confectionaries enough to excite any imagination or desire."

"Oh, that would be lovely. I can just look, can't I?" she asked, and blushed because it revealed so much about her financial state that she couldn't even afford to buy a sweet.

But he said nothing, only nodded. "Of course. Now would you like a small tour?"

Celeste followed him into a parlor just off the entrance. It had the usual accouterment, but along the wall across from the window, there was also a small desk on wheels.

"Why a desk in the sitting room, if you don't mind my asking?"

"Not at all. Although I do my real work in my study, I occasionally see clients in this room. New clients, usually, and almost always when I am conducting multiple investigations at once so that I may protect the privacy of those I serve."

"It's a comfortable room," Celeste said. "The bay window gives so much light. I could read forever here."

"It is where I do much of my reading," he said, and she realized he was just watching her as she moved around the room, taking in the details around her.

She blushed as she glanced at him. "Well, it is lovely."

"I'm glad you approve. Would you like to see more?"

She nodded and followed him to a small dining room, as well as another parlor that looked out over the garden behind the house. Down a side hall he led her into the study, and she caught her breath as she entered the room.

It was the biggest of the chambers she had seen, and beautiful, with tall bookshelves lined with tomes on the law, the city and history; a fine fireplace; a cherry sideboard where tea was already waiting for them; and a large matching desk that faced the door. It looked like a professional place to take a meeting, and yet it was still comfortable and warm.

"This is where I spend a good deal of my time," he said softly. "Too much, some of my friends would say. But I like to work."

"I can see why. You've created a space that tells a person that they can be comfortable and share their secrets."

"I hope so. My business is secrets. Often it is the worst moment of a person's life. Something they regret or fear. If I want to understand their circumstances enough to help, I must see into them a little."

"You're very good at that," Celeste whispered. "I always feel as though you can see right through me."

He moved toward her a step and the air in the room got heavier. What she wanted, those wicked things she wanted, those things Abigail had all but given her permission to take, hung between them. And Celeste was terrified. If she reached for him, everything would change, and so much had already changed. Could she bear even more chaos?

Could she bear it if he pulled away like he had that first night she kissed him?

So she did so first, turning her back to him and moving toward the desk. Behind it papers had been affixed to the wall, and she realized they were sheets on each of the suspects in Erasmus's murder. A list of the names was on the far left, and she saw that her name and Leighton's had been crossed off.

"You've been busy," she said.

He chuckled, a low, rough sound behind her that seemed to work up her entire spine. "But not productive, in reality."

"How can you say that?" she asked, pivoting toward him.

"In more than a week since the murder, I have crossed two suspects from my list. I'm not closer to narrowing the rest." She could see his discomfort in that fact by the way he shifted his weight.

"You are too hard on yourself," she insisted. "For four of those days you were riding to and from Twiddleport and handling me. If you throw out that time, you've only been on the case half a week."

"You will soothe me even if I don't deserve it," he said.

"I would argue that you do deserve it," she said.

He was silent a moment, simply staring at her in the quiet room. Drawing her in with those light brown eyes, making her feel tingles in her body that could only lead to trouble and confusion and...and... oh God, pleasure. She could only hope they would bring pleasure.

He cleared his throat and fiddled with some papers on his desk. "The problem with working for those in power is that it's difficult to get information. They want an answer, but not to reveal anything embarrassing to get it. So it's a constant tightrope act."

She nodded. She could see how that would be true. Those of a certain sphere liked to remain high above regular people by pretending to be perfect. Men like Owen were a reminder that they weren't. The amount of pushing back against that had to be powerful.

"Well, you have me," she said. "I can ask questions that perhaps you couldn't. And if I am not a good tool for you, you are a resourceful, seductive man. I'm certain you'll figure it out."

He came around the desk, and now there was nothing between them. He held her stare. "Seductive?"

She gasped. Had she said seductive? Blast and damn, she hadn't meant to—it was just the word that had popped into her head in that moment.

"Er, I..." She bent her head and fought to contain herself. But when she looked up at him again, his pupils were dilated to nearly black, and he at last reached out a finger to trace it across the top of her hand. She shivered with the contact, so delicate, almost chaste, and yet her body reacted so powerfully.

Her mind equally so. The desire for this man becoming so loud in her head that it drowned out reason, resistance, prudence.

"You know you are seductive," she whispered. "You must know I can't...I can't stop thinking about you. I want to be better than my desires, more than those impulses. But I feel what I feel."

He swallowed, and for a moment she could see the struggle plainly on his face. A mirror of her own, it seemed. An argument with himself about whether he should let propriety take the reins, or surrender the way she was.

She couldn't breathe as she awaited his response, though she had no idea if she wanted him to give in or push away. Either outcome had its benefits, although being rejected in the midst of this trial didn't sound fun.

"Celeste," he whispered, his voice rough and low. "Celeste, Celeste, Celeste." Each time he said her name, he lowered his head and she lifted to him until their mouths touched.

Relief flashed through her, but it was quickly erased by other feelings. Powerful feelings that lit like flint on dry tinder when he cupped the back of her neck and his tongue slid past her lips.

She shivered against him, sensation rolling through her like powerful waves, settling in the most sensitive places. Only this time he was kissing her in a private room where they wouldn't be interrupted. And that meant she didn't have to pull away.

She didn't want to.

But he had more control and he moved to step away. She tightened her hands across his back and looked up at him as he parted his lips from hers. "I don't want to do something you'll regret later," he whispered.

She caught his hands and drew him toward the settee where she stopped. "The only thing I'll regret is walking away. Everything has been terrible, Owen...everything but you. If you want me, if I'm not mistaken that you feel the same powerful draw as I do, then give me something good. I just want to feel something good."

He shut his eyes and let out a low, rough curse. She smiled at the idea that she could tempt him. Torment him. He was so strong that it felt odd to have such power. He caught her in his arms again, kissing her as he lowered her back on the settee and partially covered her with his body.

"I feel the same thing you do," he promised her, his voice reverberating against her throat as he pressed his lips there. "I dream of you, Celeste. I dream of this."

"Then let's make it a reality," she gasped, rising beneath him as pleasure shot from the place on her neck where he scraped his teeth and settled between her legs. She throbbed there already.

He grunted an answer and then pushed off of her. She sat up and watched him walk to the door. He locked it and smiled at her. "No interruptions."

She nodded. "No interruptions."

As he returned to her, he shrugged out of his jacket and unwrapped his cravat, tossing each aside as if they didn't matter. When he dropped back down to cover her, she wedged her hands between them and partially unbuttoned his shirt. As she pushed the edges wide, she sucked in a breath. She hadn't seen a man like this in a very long time. And Erasmus didn't hold a candle to him.

Not only had she had no interest in her late "husband," but he hadn't felt so warm, so solid, when he covered her. He hadn't held her stare with such intensity, making her feel like she was the only woman in the world. The only woman who mattered.

She felt that way in Owen's arms and she never wanted it to end. He sat up a little and tugged the shirt off, and she stared.

He was lean and lanky, with defined muscles along his arms, his chest, his stomach. She bit her lip as she stared, mesmerized by the lines and curves and angles of him.

"You look like a statue," she whispered.

"I may be hard as marble at present," he agreed with a chuckle. "But I assure you I am alive and here to please. May I?"

She tilted her head at the request. She'd already given consent, and yet here he was, asking for more. Checking in to ensure nothing had changed. As if he actually gave a damn for her pleasure and her well-being. What a concept. "Yes. Oh yes."

"May I undress you?" he asked.

She gripped at the cushions of the settee with both hands. "I... I'm not sure I would please you."

His brow wrinkled. "What would make you think that?"

"Erasmus...he..." She turned her face. "He made it clear I didn't please him."

"Well, Erasmus was a fool," Owen whispered as he tugged her to a seated position and stripped the line of buttons along her spine open. "In more ways than one. There is no way you couldn't please me, Celeste. I am already vastly pleased."

As he said the words, he peeled her dress and chemise forward as one, and she was bared from the waist up to him. She fought the urge to cover herself, to look away, but he wouldn't allow it. He cupped her chin with one hand, holding her steady while he dragged his fingers across her breast with the other.

She hissed out a breath, pleasure so powerful it bordered on pain. Need so loud she feared it could be heard as surely as a brass band screaming through town.

He bent his head and swirled his tongue around her nipple, lowering her back against the settee as he did so. She let out a low moan, one that echoed in the quiet room. He smiled against her skin as she did so and sucked her. She jolted at the tug, the heat of his mouth, the wild sensation that ripped through her entire being.

She couldn't help but compare this moment to all the ones she'd been forced to endure before. This one made the rest pale in comparison.

"Don't roll away in your thoughts," he murmured as he moved his mouth from one breast to the other. "Stay here with me."

"I only want to be here with you," she promised, and meant it on more levels than just this one. But those were foolish thoughts, ones that could hurt them both, so she shoved them aside and put all her focus on sensation instead.

He rocked against her as he sucked her, licked her, teased her. She felt the hard length of him bumping her belly, and lifted to meet him. She pressed her fingers into his bare back, memorizing the muscles there, the lines of the body that was so pleasing her own.

She wanted to remember every part of this moment for later. Forever.

He lifted his head from her breasts and smiled at her. "I want to make you come, Celeste. I want to taste you come."

She blinked. *Come.* She'd heard of the word before. Felt it at her own hand. But she wasn't certain she was capable of having that kind of release from another person and she didn't want to let him down.

She didn't want him to think less of her.

"Owen," she whispered.

His brow wrinkled, an expression of concern and care. "He never made you come?"

She shook her head. "He…he didn't care about my feelings. He always reminded me that our sharing a bed was a duty, one created by the vows we took. We only did it a few times and I...no, he never made me come."

His lips thinned. "Well, that is his loss, my dear. But I don't consider touching you a duty, I don't consider..." He let his hand drag down her body, over where her gown was bunched at her waist, around to cup her hip and pull her more flush to him. "...I don't consider this anything but a gift. And I want to make you shake, Celeste. I want to make you cry out my name. I want to make you come."

She nodded. Right now she would have given him anything he asked, anything at all. But he didn't take advantage. He didn't do anything but tug her dress down her waist. She lifted her hips and he freed the wrinkled mass of fabric and set it aside. Then he removed her slippers and her stockings and she was entirely naked, spread out on his settee like a wanton.

"My God, you are everything," he whispered, it seemed more to himself than to her. She blinked at the tears that entered her eyes, turning her face so he wouldn't see. But of course he did. "Celeste, please don't cry. We don't have to do this if you're not ready or changed your mind or just don't want to."

She caught her breath. "It isn't that. It isn't any of that, Owen, I promise you. It's that...you said I was everything. I've been nothing to anyone for so long, I can hardly believe anyone could think otherwise."

CHAPTER 13

Owen stared down at the beautiful woman naked on his settee. He had never met any other person like Celeste, and yet she thought so little of herself. He understood why, of course. He'd met her horrible parents. He'd researched her awful husband. And given his own past, he knew exactly why she might feel less thanks to their actions and words. His father, or lack of a father, had certainly worn him down, made him question himself. He'd been lucky enough to have a life filled with people who helped him find the light inside himself.

All he wanted was to do the same for her.

"If you have been surrounded by fools," he said, caging her in with his hands, "who were so blind that they couldn't see your worth…" He bent to nuzzle her neck. She shivered and he smiled against her skin. "Then that is on them, not you, Celeste."

He drew his mouth lower, across her collarbone, lower to her breast. "Because you are the most remarkable person I've ever met." He kissed lower, over the curve of her stomach. "And I'm lucky to get even a moment with you."

His lips trailed across her hip and he pushed her legs open a little wider, allowing himself a space there. He scented her desire, saw it glisten on the folds of her sex, and his cock twitched.

But this wasn't about what he wanted. He'd get his pleasure and it wouldn't even take effort. Celeste, on the other hand, deserved to be worshipped. And that was what he was going to do.

She leaned up on her elbows and looked down at him, watching through a hooded gaze as he peeled her open, as he smoothed his thumb across her wet entrance. She gripped at the cushions of the settee when he did, a little groan escaping her throat.

He stroked her again with his thumb, pressing against the hooded nub of her clitoris. He flicked it gently, revealing the shining pearl beneath. Now when he touched her, she arched, her eyes widening. He stroked his thumb around her in a slow circle, increasing the pressure with each turn, watching her reaction to find just the right rhythm, just the right touch.

She was so responsive, it was almost effortless to make her moan. The fact that her bastard of a husband hadn't even tried to give her release was a crime in itself. And yet that meant Owen had a unique opportunity to give her that pleasure himself.

He bent his head, closer and closer to her sex, and at last he let his tongue join his thumb in torment. And then just his tongue, around and around her clitoris. Never stopping, never ceasing. He wanted her to come, hard and fast. He wanted her to see immediately and without question, that she deserved pleasure. That any man who touched her should give her this without hesitation.

She lifted against him, her head lolling back and forth on the pillows, her feet flexing against the settee, her hips surging to meet the strokes of his tongue. She began to shake, his breath coming shorter and faster, and then, with a guttural gasp of relief, she shattered.

C eleste had come before, at her own hand, both before and after her marriage. But this...this was something entirely different. The wall of pleasure that Owen built with his magical tongue was so high she almost feared it bursting, and when it did?

She couldn't control herself. Her entire body quaked as she covered her mouth with her hand to smother her moans and cries. On and on he went, tormenting her through the crisis, drawing out every drop of release from her until she was weak against the settee, residual trembles rocking her even as he lifted his head and smiled at her.

"Do I live?" she asked breathlessly.

He laughed, and in this moment of pure vulnerability it felt so good. Erasmus had always been so dire about sex, had always treated it like this solemn duty neither of them could ever truly enjoy.

But as Owen moved to cover her, he seemed just as pleased as she was. Just as light as she was, and he hadn't even had his own release.

"Let me check," he said, and bent his head to take her lips. She tasted herself on him, and her laughter faded as he deepened the kiss. She sank into the wicked flavor of pleasure, letting her hands travel to his hips, pressing there as she lifted into him.

He pulled away from her mouth. "Little minx, I definitely want the very thing you are seeking. But if all you want today is to come beneath my tongue, I can wait."

Her eyes went wide as she stared up at him. "What if I can't wait?"

"Then I'm happy to serve. Very happy. Incredibly happy and very relieved."

He kissed her again, then sat up and unfastened his trousers. She sat up with him, holding her breath as he let the fall front drop away, and there he was.

"Oh my," she whispered, unable to stop herself from reaching out to touch him. He bent his head back with a garbled moan as she took him in hand and stroked.

He was hard as steel, the skin soft as velvet, and she had never wanted a man so much in her life. She shook with it as she smoothed her fingers across his length, loving the surge of him against her palm, loving the tension in his face when she looked up at him and marked every reaction to her touch.

He stood, pulling away from her as he did so, and shed the trousers entirely. She had the wildest, most wicked urge to lick him like he'd licked her, but before she could, he dropped onto the settee on his knees, pressing her back with his weight as he kissed her.

She opened her legs wider and he settled there, but to her surprise he didn't just thrust into her and take. Instead he focused on her mouth and on smoothing his fingers through her hair. She felt liquid, languid in his arms, all her troubles melted away, all her tension forgotten because he was there and he would make it right. Make her forget. Make her whole.

"Ready?" he whispered, his hand trailing between them, positioning himself at her entrance.

"Yes, yes, yes," she murmured, the same word over and over because her mind had no other words, no other thoughts, no other needs but having this man.

He smiled, but the smile quickly faded as he slid his cock into her body. Inch by inch, he took, filling her completely as he let out a low, heavy moan of pleasure.

It had been months since she'd done this. It had always been uncomfortable, and she'd been bracing herself for the same, ready to revel in the pleasure that had come before and endure the rest. But there was no enduring what he was doing.

He filled her completely and she felt...alive. Every nerve ending in her body was stimulated, firing at once until there was nothing but sensation. She rose up against him, her fingers digging into his back, and he ground his hips in a circle to meet her, stimulating her still-sensitive clitoris and making her jolt with renewed pleasure.

"Slow," he murmured as he traced her ear with his tongue, but she wasn't sure if he was telling her or himself. It didn't matter. It was all the same now. One body, one pleasure, and she wanted it all.

He thrust, arching his hips against her over and over. She ground up to meet him, her mouth finding his while she drowned in pleasure, drowned in touch, drowned in him.

He increased his pace, grinding harder against her with each thrust, and she realized with a jolt of surprise that he was trying to make her come again. This way. Was that possible?

The question was answered when he took her hand and drew it down, wedging it between their bodies so she could touch herself while he took her. She did so, finding the pace she liked, matching it to his, surrendering to whatever he would give, whatever she could take.

The waves built higher, her fingers moved faster, and then it was happening. For the second time in less than half an hour, she was cresting over the peak of release, rocking against him, her cries caught by his lips as she came and came and came forever.

He gasped into her lips as her body gripped him, his pace increasing again, this time with purpose. She felt the change in him, the loss of control. She saw it by the way the veins in his neck pulsed, by the way his arms shook. When he growled out her name and withdrew, she welcomed the splash of his heat across her stomach and the renewed weight of him as he covered her a second time, panting as he kissed her neck, her shoulders.

She held him close, letting their breath slow together. She had never felt anything like this before. Never been so connected to a person. And even though she had to believe it couldn't last, she would never be sorry for what she'd done or who she'd done it with.

Owen wasn't certain how long they lounged on his settee, legs entangled, his fingers threading through her red hair, hers clenching against his chest. He knew it wasn't long enough. But at some point, they had to move. To address the surrender, because there would be consequences to it.

He shifted and held her steady as he got to his feet, searching around on the ground for his discarded clothing, handing over hers.

She dressed, and when she turned her back so he could fasten her gown, she said, "So what does this...mean?"

He leaned down, pressing a kiss to the side of her neck, loving how she shivered in pleasure at the touch. "We are two consenting adults, are we not?"

She faced him with a nod. "Yes."

He stared into that lovely face, so lined with uncertainty. He wanted to soothe all that away. For a few moments while he touched her, he had. "I would very much like to give you pleasure. You deserve so much pleasure, Celeste. So if you want more, I'm here."

"And if I...don't?" she asked, worrying her lip.

He tilted his head. The idea that she would walk away was troubling. But he wasn't certain she actually wanted to do so. This was, he thought, a test. What kind of man would he be when rejected? And he intended to pass.

He took her hands gently. "Nothing would change. If you don't want me to ever repeat what just happened, I will admit I'll be disappointed because it was...spectacular."

She blushed, but a little smile tilted her lips at the compliment.

"But *you* get to decide what you do and what you don't want to do. I'll respect your decision. And I hope I can continue as your friend."

She examined his face carefully. "Is that what we are? Friends?"

He nodded even though his heart screamed something different. "I hope so."

She paced away from him to the mirror mounted above the sideboard and went about fixing herself. He thought that was to keep from having to look at him when she felt vulnerable. Uncertain.

"And if we continue this...affair," she said, her gaze darting to his in the reflection. "Would our being friends change then?"

"Why would it?"

"Well, perhaps this is all you'd want to do," she said. "Once you didn't have to seduce me, you wouldn't want to take me around London or let me help you with your case."

He crossed to her, turning her to face him. "I didn't offer to take you around London or ask you to help me on this case as a seduction, Celeste. The two things are entirely separate. If you decide to come to my bed for a while, I will be very happy. But our friendship doesn't hinge on it one way or another."

She seemed to consider that for a moment, and he couldn't read her expression or if she liked that answer one way or another. But at last she nodded and stuck out her hand as if to shake. "I think it's a good bargain. I'd like to be...lovers."

He glanced down at the extended hand with a laugh. "Very formal." He took her hand and shook it, and she smiled. "Now, may I help you with your hair?"

Her brow wrinkled as her hand fell away from his. "You think you could do my hair?"

"I know I could," he said. "There were times growing up when my mother could not afford a maid, so she taught me a few simple styles."

Her eyes went wide and he swallowed hard. He'd never told another lady that in his life. Yet he didn't regret the vulnerability. On the contrary, it felt...right to connect with her this way.

She nodded and he motioned her to the chair across from his desk. He gathered up the pins that had fallen from her hair earlier and gently tugged free the ones still stuck in the tangles. Once he had placed them on the desk top, he went around to his drawer and pulled out the brush he used on his own hair the many mornings he had a client call and he'd forgotten to go to bed the night before.

With tools in hand, he began to brush out her knots. Stroke by stroke, enjoying the little sounds of pleasure she made that were so close to the ones she'd made when she came. Giving her that was powerful no matter how he got there.

He began to shape and twist the locks, binding them in a loose chignon at the base of her neck with a pretty twist along the sides of her hair.

"How can I help you?" she asked.

He continued to pin and work. "Help me? I suppose you could hold this strand right here a moment."

She lifted her fingers and pressed them against the lock he needed pushed aside. "I meant with your case," she clarified.

"Oh, *that*," he said with a smile. "You can let go of that strand now. The case, yes." He thought about it a moment. "Well, I'm working on some clarification when it comes to the Duke of Gilmore," he said. "As well as...another lead that I'll talk to you about later if it pans out. And there's a great deal that is public record when it comes to Abigail, as she was the first and legal wife. But Phillipa is more of a mystery to me."

Celeste worried her lip. "She's a bit more of a mystery to me, as well. Abigail is so welcoming, but her personality is to sweep in and take over. Not in a bad way, but she fills a room. Pippa is quieter. Harder to read. What would you like to know specifically?"

He marked those observations with interest. She really did pick up on human foibles and individual quirks with a natural flair. "Well, first why did she come to London seeking Montgomery?" he said. "I've never had a satisfactory response to that, always something that diverts attention to another issue."

Celeste nodded. "That's true, actually. I realize it now that you say it."

"Also, you and I both noted her strong reaction when the article in the paper about the scandal mentioned names."

"I remember. You want me to try to find out why she had such a powerful response?"

"Yes," he said. "And if there is some kind of alibi that can be established for the time and date Montgomery was killed, it would help. She's been vague about it all."

Celeste was quiet a moment. At first it felt like she was just thinking, but then it shifted. Her discomfort became far clearer. It permeated through him as he slid the last pin in place and her hair was finished.

"Do you not like my questions?" he asked gently.

She glanced up at him. "It's not your questions. I like them both so much. I just worry I'm doing something...wrong. Betraying them somehow."

He nodded. "I understand. But realize I'm not trying to prove a hypothesis that Phillipa is guilty. I don't think that. I don't think any one of those involved is the culprit at this point. By collecting information, I may very well clear her name, as I have yours and the Earl of Leighton's."

She worried her lip. The same lip he wanted to nip with his own teeth. "That would be worth it," she said softly.

He dropped down closer to her and cupped her cheeks. "If you don't feel right about it, don't do it. I won't be upset."

She held his gaze, as if trying to parse out the truth of that. Then she straightened her shoulders and he saw the steel come back into her. "No. I said I would help and this is helping. I'll speak to her."

He leaned in and kissed her, because how could he resist such temptation? When he pulled away, he tugged her to her feet. "And now I am finished with your hair. I hope you think you are presentable."

She moved to the mirror and her eyes went wide as she stared at herself. "That is perfect, Owen, I can scarcely believe it."

He shrugged, that flash of vulnerability back and just as uncomfortable as a moment ago. "She taught me well."

"You told me on our journey to London that she passed."

He cocked his head. "Yes, she died twelve years ago." He flinched because it certainly didn't feel like that many years had gone by. "I'm surprised you recall that fact given all you were going through during our trip."

"I remember every moment of that carriage ride," she said softly, and for a moment the air between them grew charged again, just as it always did when they connected in this way or in a more physical manner.

"I am still very surprised to hear you fixed her hair." Now she ducked her head, breaking the connection that crackled in the air around them.

He nodded. "Well, I think I told you it was just us."

"Yes, that your father died, too." She shifted slightly. "That he was not...available."

He held her gaze a moment. He had met her parents, so he knew that she understood the complexities of having a poor one. And though this wasn't a subject he often broached with anyone, he felt drawn to do so. After all...she wasn't exactly a stranger, not after the settee.

"No, he wasn't. He made it clear through both deed and word that he didn't want us. When I was younger, it troubled me. I was always trying to prove my worth, as if he could...as if he could love me if I was just good enough."

"Oh, Owen. I am so sorry."

He shrugged even though he felt far more than that dismissive action implied. He'd litigated and relitigated all his complex emotions toward the man who'd given him his name. Nothing ever changed, and it never would.

"You needn't be sorry," he said. "I'm not the first person to have a lousy father and I won't be the last. I wasn't very old when I realized I couldn't earn what he didn't feel. And I was more lucky in my mother. She was a seamstress—she actually made gowns for the wife of my mentor, Lord Livingstone."

"The viscount," Celeste said.

He smiled because she remembered that fact, too. "Yes. It was impossible not to like my mother. She had the most beautiful laugh. I used to collect jokes and funny stories just to make her smile. I was very lucky to have her, even if I didn't have her nearly long enough."

Celeste caught his hand and squeezed gently. "Thank you for telling me more about her. And for allowing me the benefit of your skills."

"Of course," he said. "I'm happy to have them if they are of service to you."

She smoothed her skirts and shook her head, breaking the moment. "And now I should probably go back. They'll wonder where I am if I don't send word or return."

He glanced at the clock. "Yes. I'll have the rig brought around." He moved to the door, and there he turned. "Celeste?"

"Yes?"

"Thank you for today," he said softly. Then he left her there, staring after him. He was completely unaware of whatever thoughts were going through her mind. And far too aware of his own thoughts and how swiftly they were taking him to dangerous places. Places where he could be more to this woman than a lover or a friend.

CHAPTER 14

As Owen pulled the phaeton back up in front of Abigail Montgomery's house, he smiled at Celeste. She'd been quiet during the short ride, but it wasn't an uncomfortable silence.

"I know we didn't do exactly what you hoped—" he began.

She turned a little to face him. "That was exactly what I wanted to do, Owen."

She covered his hand with hers and they both watched as their fingers interlaced. She let out a sigh. "If I'm quiet, it is because I'm thinking of how to best approach Pippa."

He wrinkled his brow. "If you can speak to her, wonderful, but please don't trouble yourself. This is my investigation and I will find another way if there is no route through your connection."

Her lips parted and she leaned a little closer. Too close, perhaps, for propriety, but it didn't matter in that moment. "I promised you I'd try," she said softly. "That I'd help. And I keep my promises, Owen Gregory."

He swallowed hard at the spark in her eyes. The determination that was so attractive to him because it was so much like his own. Then she blushed and turned her face and the moment passed.

"I should go in," she said, motioning for the waiting footman who came to help her down. "Thank you again for the day."

"I'll see you soon," he promised, and watched as she trailed up the stairs and into the house.

At the door, she paused and looked back at him, but then she was gone, and he drew the first full breath he'd been able to take since the moment when he'd come here to collect her. That's what she did, after all. Took his breath away.

He settled back and was about to pull his phaeton from the drive when he saw a flash of movement from the park directly across the street. The figure of a man, who ducked behind a tree as if trying not to be seen.

Owen clambered down from the rig and crossed the quiet street, searching for the person as he scanned the bushes and trees in the park. Seeking out people that weren't on the trails and walkways.

The movement flashed again, from behind a bush this time.

"You there!" Owen called out. "I see you, so there's no purpose in hiding. Come out."

A brief silence followed and then a rustle from the bush. To Owen's shock, the Duke of Gilmore stepped from behind the shrubbery, brushing small leaves from his fine greatcoat as he did so.

"Your Grace?" Owen said. "What are you doing here?"

He had a thousand guesses as to the answer to that question. After all, he hadn't yet cleared Gilmore from his suspicions, but he wanted to hear the excuse the man would come up with for this very odd behavior.

The duke pursed his lips and then sighed. "I apologize, Mr. Gregory. I ought not to have been so childish as to hide from you like that. I was embarrassed about being caught staring at Montgomery's home and I did not act my best. Perhaps you'd like to walk with me a moment and we can talk."

Owen recognized the man had not yet answered his question about why he'd been in the park hiding behind trees, but for the moment he set that aside. "Of course, Your Grace. I could use the exercise."

They walked into the park as the lamplighters began their early evening work. For a moment, the duke was quiet and Owen didn't push him to speak. He would when he desired to do so, it seemed. At the moment, he was getting enough from observing the other man's demeanor. His tight shoulders, his pursed lips.

Gilmore was troubled.

"I...I hate myself for not protecting Ophelia," Gilmore said at last. "My sister."

Owen lifted his brows. "Though I don't have siblings of my own, I can see how troublesome all this could have been for you. But you *did* protect her. She didn't marry Montgomery, after all."

The duke let out a long sigh. "I suppose not, but she came close enough to make it uncomfortable. I should have been more involved. She's always been...wild...and I should have been paying closer attention. Then all this mess could have been avoided, all this pain for people I know and care for."

"I'm not sure that's true."

Gilmore glanced at him, his eyes wide, as if he were shocked someone would dare disagree with him. Owen had the impression it was rarely done. "What do you mean?"

"Perhaps it would have been delayed a bit," Owen said. "But the truth of Montgomery's duplicity would have come out eventually. It is too big a secret for a man like that to manage forever. The pain would have still come."

"I suppose that's true. But I don't like being the architect of it regardless." Gilmore huffed out a breath of frustration. "Dastardly wicked business, this."

"I agree." He was careful about his tone as he asked, "Where is your sister at present?"

Gilmore jerked his gaze to Owen. "Why do you ask?"

Owen stopped in the path. "My duty now is to investigate what happened to Montgomery. I have curiosity about all the players in his final days and weeks on this earth."

Gilmore shook his head. "My sister *isn't* a killer. Even if she wished to be, she wasn't in Town to do such a thing. As soon as I realized what was afoot, I had her spirited away to my estate in Cornwall. She is far, far away, Mr. Gregory, and will remain there."

"She must have been grieved to know the man she thought she loved enough to marry was untrue," Owen said.

"She's young," Gilmore muttered. "So very young. And she feels deeply. So yes, she is heartbroken, indeed."

"I'm sorry for it."

Gilmore cleared his throat. "You must think me a great fool for not knowing what was happening in my own house. Especially since the man involved was brother to one of my closest friends. A man I grew up with off and on."

Owen nodded. "I admit the question has crossed my mind."

There was a long pause before Gilmore spoke again. "What you must understand is that though I had a passing acquaintance to Montgomery when we were children, we were never close. He and Leighton were always at odds and were often kept from each other. When Leighton inherited the title, he cut his brother off and I hadn't seen the man since an ugly encounter more than three years ago. When I thought of him, which wasn't often, I always assumed he was simply living his life in London."

"But when you discovered your sister was secretly involving herself with someone, didn't the name tip you off?" Owen pressed.

"The secret was the problem," Gilmore said with a heavy sigh. "I knew there was an interested party and that he could not be a man of honor because he was sneaking around, violating the bounds of propriety in order to see Ophelia alone."

The way Gilmore's jaw clenched did not alleviate any of Owen's suspicions about him. In that moment, the duke looked like he could kill.

"And that was when you hired me," Owen said.

"Yes." Gilmore shook his head. "God's teeth, this is nothing but horrific. When you told me it was Erasmus Montgomery and that there were other brides...it became clear that the man was a bigamist. It's too much. I despise Montgomery with every fiber of my being."

"Enough to kill?" Owen asked softly.

Gilmore turned on him and their eyes locked. "I wanted him dead, yes. But I never would have killed him. There were ways to deal with this problem without it being public but murder certainly wasn't one of them." He shook his head. "To cause harm to my sister, to my friends...to Abigail and the other wives? I despise it to my very core."

Owen examined his companion more closely. He'd learned over the years that there were pieces of evidence that proved and disproved, unadulterated facts that could be measured and shown to others. And then there were the kinds of feelings that he had learned to trust in himself. He'd trained himself to see lies, to see pretended emotions.

When he looked at Gilmore, he saw nothing disingenuous. He *believed* the duke. And the fact that the man had brought him along to confront Montgomery the night they found his body also was a point in his favor.

So although he couldn't dismiss Gilmore completely, Owen wiped his name from the top of his list of suspects and felt comfortable with doing so. Which meant he could focus on other topics that the man might assist with.

"Leighton mentioned an earlier love of Montgomery's. A barmaid? Since you were acquainted with the family, do you recall anything about her?"

Gilmore nodded. "I think I remember something of the scandal, yes. Our fathers were friends, you know. I'm certain they must have spoken about it. Would you like me to seek out the late duke's diaries and correspondence and see if I can uncover any facts of that situation?"

"That would be very helpful, yes," Owen said.

"Very good." They had almost completed a full circle around the small park, and Gilmore stopped just at the gate where Owen had first seen him. "Then I will say my farewells, Mr. Gregory. Unless you have further inquiries."

Owen stepped closer. "I realize you never answered my initial question, Your Grace. Why were you here tonight?"

Gilmore glanced up at the house across the street again, and Owen followed his gaze. The duke was looking at the front window of the Montgomery home. With the gathering dusk, the lamps had been lit within, and Owen could see Abigail standing at the window, turned in profile, laughing at something another unseen person in the room had said.

"No reason," Gilmore said, his voice rougher. "Just idly passing by. Good evening, sir."

Owen didn't believe him, but he tipped his head regardless. If Gilmore had his secrets, they didn't seem directly linked to the murder. Owen had too many of his own entanglements with one of the three Mrs. Montgomerys to question anyone else's, unless that connection led to information that might help solve his case.

So he said nothing else as Gilmore strode from the park and down the street away from the Montgomery residence and the alluring ladies inside.

❧

Celeste stared at her plate, filled to the brim with delicious venison and perfectly roasted potatoes and carrots. Even though she'd eaten very little that day, she didn't find herself hungry. Probably because her mind and body were distracted by other things. Like the memory of Owen's hands and mouth on her, doing such wicked things that—

"And so what did you and Mr. Gregory do this afternoon?" Pippa's voice pierced through Celeste's wicked thoughts, and she blinked as she was brought back to the room and her two friends within it.

She swallowed. "Just...drove around a while," she said, and it wasn't exactly a lie.

From the head of the table, Abigail arched a brow, and Celeste felt speared in place by the pointed look. "Very interesting. Where did you drive to?"

Celeste cleared her throat and set her fork down. "To the... parks..." she muttered.

Abigail smiled and it softened her expression. "Oh yes, the parks. Any one in particular?"

There was no answer. The name of every park in London fled from Celeste's mind in that moment, leaving only a blank space. "Er, I...we...it was..."

"Oh dear, you are turning the color of a plum," Abigail said. "Please don't feel like you have to hurt yourself coming up with some falsehood. You owe us no explanations and I fear my teasing has gone too far."

"It's not a falsehood—"

Abigail arched a brow. "My dear, your hair is different."

Pippa stared at her. "It is. Oh, it's very pretty."

"Thank you," Celeste muttered, and then covered her face with her hands. "Oh, trust you to be so observant, Abigail."

"It is what I do," Abigail said, not at all apologetically. "Under normal circumstances I wouldn't say a word. But we are friends, I think."

Celeste lifted her gaze and looked at the two women. "Yes," she said softly. "We are friends. A strange thought considering what we all went through. Society must assume we would be at each other's throats."

Pippa shrugged. "Perhaps, but who cares what they believe? There is no reason in the world for me to be angry at you or Abigail for Ras's actions. He is the guilty party, not any of us."

Abigail nodded. "Well put, my dear. We are a sisterhood created by his duplicity. And if my sister were to...say...go out with a gentleman in the afternoon with her hair in one sort of twist and come back in the evening with it in another, I would lean on the table with my elbows and ask her to tell me all about what she was up to today."

"Oh, dear," Celeste whispered.

"Not to judge you," Pippa said swiftly. "I don't think either of us want to do that."

"Lord no!" Abigail agreed. "I want to know because this entire situation is untenable and I would like to know that one of us, at least, is getting some kind of amusement out of it. Especially considering our conversation before you left with Mr. Gregory this morning."

Celeste sighed. There was not going to be any getting around this, it seemed. And even if there was, she found she didn't want to. What she had experienced was so different than what she'd ever felt before. She needed to talk about it.

"Very well. Owen and I intended to go to a museum, but instead we went back to his home and we..." Her cheeks felt so hot she feared she might melt right into the floor without another word. "We did exactly what you think we did. I'm a widow...sort of. I'm allowed to do this kind of thing, aren't I?"

"I think you are allowed, widow or not," Pippa said. "The constraints around a woman's modesty and pleasure are ways we are kept in line by the worst of men." She leaned a little closer. "How was it?"

Abigail was leaning nearer too, and Celeste laughed at their excited, pensive faces. They were truly engrossed. "It was...lovely. Wonderful. I've never felt anything like it, truthfully. You know how Erasmus was. When he took me to bed, it was like a chore that had to be fulfilled."

Abigail and Pippa exchanged a look, brief but meaningful, and Celeste's brow wrinkled. "Was it...was it not like that for you with him?"

There was a long and very uncomfortable silence, and Celeste could see neither of them wanted to be the one to answer first. She folded her arms. "Am I to be the only fool who reveals herself?"

"Erasmus and I married a long time ago, five years past now," Abigail began slowly. "And at first he was very attentive. I learned about pleasure and I enjoyed what we shared. It was only after his brother cut him off that things changed. I suppose around the time he began his attempts to find other brides, other fortunes to raid with his lies."

Celeste blinked. "But he...wanted you." Abigail nodded, and Celeste's gaze slipped to Pippa. "And you?"

Pippa worried her lip, and Celeste knew the answer before she even spoke. "He was trying to seduce me even before we wed," she whispered. "And for the first year was extremely...passionate."

Celeste's throat felt like it was closing at this news. "Oh."

Abigail pushed her chair closer and caught Celeste's hand. "It was never real, though. I think that's very clear, isn't it? If he made more of an effort to pretend affection or connection to me or to Pippa, it only indicates his level of desperation, not anything about you."

Celeste bent her head. "I didn't want to marry him. I should not care that he wasn't driven to touch me. I shouldn't care."

"But you do," Pippa whispered. "And that's fine."

"You shouldn't judge yourself for it, though," Abigail added. "After all, you're saying you and Mr. Gregory were...together today. He is twice the man Ras was and he clearly wants you to distraction."

"It's written all over his face when he looks at you," Pippa agreed. "I would much rather have that kind of regard from a decent man like him than interest from a lying charlatan like Erasmus Montgomery."

The heat to her voice made Celeste look at her a little closer. Owen suspected Pippa still. It was hard not to mark her words as a piece of evidence against her, even if Celeste only wished to be comforted by them.

"I suppose you're right," she said, shoving those difficult thoughts away. "Owen is a far superior man. And he…"

When she trailed off, Abigail squeezed her hand gently. "Don't leave us in suspense—Pippa and I need a good romantic tale."

"A steamy tale," Pippa corrected.

Celeste laughed. "I will only say that he pleased me more than I could have ever expected. Ever hoped for. He made me feel things…" Her cheeks grew hot again. "I never knew a man's touch could be like that. Or that I could want it more and more."

"So are you two…what is your relationship? Is he a protector? A fiancé?" Pippa asked.

Celeste worried her lip. "I think we're just lovers. I cannot imagine trusting my heart to a man. I never did with Erasmus, of course, but I know the fact that you both…did…has hurt you even more."

Abigail flinched slightly, and Pippa let out a sigh. "We all have our pasts to grapple with. And futures to try to see clear. And guarding your heart does seem wise."

"Very wise," Abigail agreed. "We must think like men. We can trifle and have our fun, but perhaps not open ourselves to something deeper. And now, perhaps we should speak on something less shocking. Poor Celeste's cheeks will burn off if she blushes any hotter."

"Very well," Pippa said with a laugh as she raised a wineglass to Celeste.

Celeste was relieved when they changed the subject. Yet her mind still turned on what had been said. Guarding her heart did seem wise. But was she doing so?

Or were these constant thoughts of Owen only bound to cause her grief in the end?

CHAPTER 15

Celeste sat before the fire in the sitting room, her needlepoint in hand, halfway through a stitch, and yet her thoughts were anywhere but in the room. Instead her mind was a jumble, both of good and negative thoughts, memories and fears. She had never trusted the future, after all, but now it just felt so foggy.

"There you are!"

She glanced up as Pippa entered the chamber, a wide smile on her pretty face. Her curly blond hair was just barely tamed today and ringlets swung around her cheeks.

"Good morning," Celeste said.

"Will it trouble you if I play the pianoforte?" Pippa asked, motioning toward the instrument tucked into the corner of the room.

"Not at all!" Celeste said. "I'm rubbish at it, I fear, but I love to hear others play."

Pippa smiled and took her place, resting her fingers on the keys with a contented sigh before she began to play. It was a rather melancholy song, but Celeste set her needlepoint aside and shut her eyes, allowing the music to permeate through her. It was such a relief.

After a little while, she opened one eye and peeked at Pippa. She had not yet approached her to find out more about her involvement in Erasmus's death. If she could do nothing else, at least she had to try to keep her promise to Owen.

The fact that it would give her an excuse to see him was certainly not the reason. Not at all.

"I was thinking about our conversation last night," she began carefully.

Pippa continued to play. "About?"

"Erasmus."

There was a slightly mangled sound to the next few notes Pippa played, but she righted herself swiftly. "Erasmus, Erasmus, Erasmus. We three are certainly more interesting than just our ill-fated unions to one liar of a man. I do look forward to the day we don't *ever* have to speak of him again."

"As do I. But so much is left unanswered yet." Celeste shook her head. "Like his murder. And also if there were other women, perhaps even other wives." A thought crossed her mind and her stomach turned. "What if there are children?"

Pippa stopped playing abruptly. "None of us had children," she snapped.

Celeste's brows went up at the harsh reaction. She treaded carefully as she continued, choosing her words wisely. "No, none of us three did. But in his desperation, it seems the man was not careful in *any* way. Why assume he would be with lovers he didn't marry? There *might* be children."

Pippa began to play again, but her posture had changed. Her notes were more staccato and some were slightly off key. Celeste couldn't help but mark all these things and pursue their reason if she could.

"I was also thinking back to when the news of this first broke in the paper," Celeste continued. "When our names were listed. That seemed to trouble you."

Pippa glanced at her over the instrument. "It troubled us all. A death knell to our individual futures, was it not? How could one not react?"

"You wanted to see the names, if I recall," Celeste said softly. "Pippa, were you looking for one in particular?"

"Mine, of course," she said, but there was no strength to her tone now and her gaze went faraway.

Celeste shook her head. "Not your own. We already knew our names were there. Were you looking for the name of someone else?"

Pippa stood up with a clanging crash of keys and then paced to the window. She stood there, shoulders shaking, for what felt like a lifetime. Finally, she pivoted back. "Why are you so curious, Celeste? Why press this?"

"Because, as Abigail said, we are a sisterhood of sorts. And I hope I can help you."

That was true to a point, of course. Celeste did want to help. She wanted to find that one piece of information that could remove Pippa from Owen's list of suspects. She wanted to free her friend for a life and a future once this was over.

But Pippa stared at her like she couldn't trust her now. She pursed her lips. "Ras didn't only hurt us, Celeste. There are many others who will suffer for his foolishness. And I will fight to protect them. That is all I will say on the matter."

"Fight?" Celeste whispered. "Pippa, what are you—"

Pippa came forward a long step. "Your lover wants to know if I'm the killer, does he? And he's using you to determine that answer?"

Celeste flinched at that assessment, true but not exactly one to paint her in a good light. "If he can eliminate you as a suspect, it will move him closer to whoever did this, won't it? And you can go on with your life."

Tears suddenly filled Pippa's green eyes and she ducked her head. "My life doesn't really matter. Ras destroyed every single thing I dreamt of, everything I hoped for. I know that, I'm working hard to accept it. But there won't be any *going on* with my life. Only creating something new, if I'm lucky."

Celeste stepped toward her. Pippa was being evasive about the entire situation, of course, but Celeste could feel her deep pain. It was right there on the surface, and all she wanted to do was take it away. She wrapped an arm around Pippa's shoulder and was happy when she sagged against her. For a moment they stood that way, Pippa drawing deep breaths while Celeste squeezed her shoulder and tried to pour every bit of strength she had into her friend.

"He isn't a bad man, is he?" Pippa said at last.

"Who?" Celeste whispered.

"Owen Gregory."

Celeste sucked in a breath. "He isn't. He is decent, Pippa, so very decent. He genuinely cares about the truth and I think he would do everything in his power to protect us if he could. We can trust him and his motives. I may not know anything else, but I know that."

"You are truly under his spell," Pippa breathed, leaning back to look at her. She shook her head when Celeste took a breath to respond. "Oh, don't argue, it will only be a tiresome exercise for us both. You trust him and I trust you."

She squeezed Celeste's waist and then pulled away to cross to the fireplace. She stared into the flames for a moment, drawing a few long breaths. Celeste allowed her that moment to compose herself before she said, "One easy way to take yourself from the list of suspects is to tell me where you were the night Erasmus was killed."

"Murdered," Pippa corrected as she faced her. "Let us not sugar-coat what happened. I try not to think about what Erasmus must have suffered. I don't know much about arsenic, but I've been told most poisons are not pleasant deaths. He must have been..." She caught her breath. "Afraid. No matter what I think of him, no matter how much I have grown to hate him, I cannot think he deserved that kind of end."

Pippa's eyes had filled with tears again, and Celeste turned her face. She had not allowed herself to picture what his final moments had been like. Now she did, and it felt like someone had reached into her chest and squeezed her heart.

"No, no one could deserve that," she whispered.

"But you asked me where I was that night," Pippa continued. "And hope that it will absolve me of being the monster who would let another person die in such a fashion. I have no good answers. I came to London seeking him, angry at him for...for betrayals he committed that aren't even related to his multiple marriages. That certainly gives me motive. As for alibi..."

Celeste held her breath, waiting for the answer. She found herself leaning closer, hands clenched.

"I have none," Pippa whispered. "I was alone that night in a room at an inn that I let before the truth came out and Abigail so kindly invited me here. It was busy there, I doubt anyone saw me go up to my room. And it could just as easily be said that no one might have noticed if I slipped out to poison a man who shattered all our lives. I can tell you the truth, that I didn't do it. But Mr. Gregory will need more than my word. The word of a woman who had every conceivable reason to take revenge."

Celeste's heart sank. Here she had hoped to free Pippa from the suspicion that had to be heaped upon her. But she hadn't. Her inability to explain why she'd come to London, her lack of alibi, all of those things were very good reasons to keep her on the list.

And yet Celeste believed her when she said she was innocent. Pippa's strong reaction to the mode of Erasmus's death, her passion about his not deserving such an end, felt like a suggestion of innocence.

Just not the kind one could prove. It was a feeling, nothing more. And Owen might not accept that. Certainly no other man in her life had ever taken her feelings, her intuitions, seriously.

She crossed to Pippa and caught her hand. "If you say you didn't do it, I believe you."

"Thank you," Pippa whispered. "But in the end, it won't matter what you believe, but what Mr. Gregory believes. What...what the Earl of Leighton believes."

"There are other suspects," Celeste said. "I'll talk to Owen. And perhaps you're wrong. Perhaps someone saw you go up to your room or heard you inside that night."

"Someone peeping on me, then?" Pippa asked.

Celeste pulled a face. "An admirer, yes. That could be. You are very pretty, Pippa. I suppose someone might have been watching you with interest and will tell Owen so."

"So my hopes lie on the ears of some man who watched me for likely a nefarious purpose," Pippa said with a laughing shake of her head. "How fitting."

Celeste couldn't help but join in on the laughter. This was such a horrible situation, but to be able to joke, even in a dark way, helped.

"Pardon me, ladies." Both of them turned to find Paisley standing in the doorway. "I have a letter for Mrs. *Celeste* Montgomery."

Celeste's heart began to throb and she dug her fingers harder into Pippa's arm as she fought to steady herself. "Thank you, Paisley," she managed to croak out as she released Pippa and came to fetch the folded sheets he held out.

Once he had departed, she glanced at the letter. The hand was so familiar she would have known it with only a glance.

"Who is it from," Pippa asked, "to inspire such a reaction from you of first terror and now the smile of the deepest comfort?"

Celeste looked up at her with a light chuckle. "I'm a fool, I know. I only have one acquaintance in London, my old governess, Harriet. After much hemming and hawing, I wrote to her yesterday to tell her of my being here, and she has written back."

"And yet you stare at the letter and don't open it," Pippa said. "Why? Your old governess must only be happy to hear from you."

"Perhaps," Celeste said slowly. "I adored her when I was a girl. She was not that much older than I was. Perhaps fifteen years my senior? She told me to want more than what the world expected from a girl like me. She taught me to think more and read more. That was why she was let go, I'm sure. My parents didn't support the bluestocking I became."

Pippa nodded. "Oof. Well, in that we are similar."

"When Harriet left, she eventually settled here in London, found a partner and together they opened Lady Lena's Salon."

Pippa's mouth dropped open. "Lady Lena's! *The* Lady Lena's? That place is legend. Only the best thinkers are invited. They discuss everything from abolition to the conditions of workhouses, as well as discussing literature and theatre. It is everything a salon should be!"

Celeste smiled at the passion of her friend. "I'm sure Harriet and Lena would love to hear your opinion. I know they are proud of what they've built. But I'm so...I fear they will see me as a bumpkin, especially since the news of my marital...er...problems is so public."

"I cannot imagine that is true," Pippa said. "Why don't you open it and see?"

Celeste drew a deep breath. "Very well."

She broke the wax seal that bound the papers together and unfolded them. She felt Pippa watching her as she scanned the words, then lifted her head with a smile.

"They wish to see me this afternoon!" she said.

Pippa clasped her hands together with a gasp of delight. "Of course they do. They would be fools not to want to see you! When?"

"For tea," Celeste said, and glanced at the clock on the mantel. "Oh, I must send Owen a message, then get ready."

Pippa tilted her head. "Why involve Mr. Gregory?"

Heat filled Celeste's cheeks and she folded the letter to have something to do with her hands. "Owen encouraged me to reach out to them and said he would escort me if I was called to visit."

After clearing her throat, Pippa said, "I see."

"What does that mean?" Celeste asked. "What do you see?"

Pippa arched a brow and held Celeste's stare evenly a moment. "Bedding a man is one thing, my dear. But please be careful."

"You sound like Abigail," Celeste said. "You two are so concerned with me guarding my heart."

Pippa crossed to her and caught her hands. "You didn't love Erasmus, and for that you are lucky. But it also means perhaps you don't understand the grief of a broken heart. Neither of us would wish to see you experience it." She leaned in and bussed Celeste's cheek. "Now go up and pick your prettiest dress and do your readying. We can further discuss your heart later."

Celeste smiled at her, but it fell as she left the room. She had told herself that her heart didn't have to be involved with Owen. But when she'd read the letter from Harriet and Lena, the only person she'd wanted to tell about it was him.

Which meant that same heart was in danger and she would have to protect it.

~

Owen had let a carriage for the ride today and he shifted inside it, peering past the curtain every few seconds to see if they had yet arrived at the Montgomery house. He reached into his pocket and his fingers brushed the message he'd received from Celeste just a few hours ago. He withdrew it and read it for what had to be the twentieth time:

Harriet wants to see me! Would you please accompany me to Lady Lena's Salon today at three? I would dearly love you to be at my side. Celeste

Her hand was very elegant, with swirls and slants and beautiful little embellishments. It fit her, and he smiled as he replaced the message in his pocket. He had no idea why he'd brought it today.

The carriage turned into the drive and he straightened up, smoothing his jacket as they came to a stop and the footman rushed to open the door for him. He came down and looked up at the door that Paisley was opening in greeting. Behind him, Celeste and Phillipa stepped into view and then past the butler. Celeste said something to the man and he smiled briefly before falling back into more proper butlerly expression.

No one was immune to her charms, it seemed.

"Good afternoon, ladies," Owen said as he met them at the bottom of the stair.

"Good afternoon," Phillipa said, meeting his eyes evenly.

She knew he suspected her, that was clear. Celeste must have spoken to her—Phillipa was too smart not to know exactly why even if Celeste attempted subterfuge. That was fine. He wasn't trying to be secretive about it.

"Oh, Owen, you brought a carriage?" Celeste said.

"I thought it would be better for the longer journey across town to the salon. Plus, it looks to rain and I would not wish you to get sick from it."

She smiled up at the cloudy sky. "You think of everything."

He almost puffed out his chest at her compliment, but managed to rein himself in. "Are you ready to go, then?" he asked, motioning to the vehicle.

"Yes." Celeste turned back to Phillipa, and for a moment they whispered together. Then Celeste nodded with a furtive glance for him. "Goodbye, I'll see you later tonight," she said.

"Phillipa," Owen said.

"Mr. Gregory." She gave a hint of a smile and then turned back into the house.

Owen helped Celeste up into the carriage, then followed her up, taking a seat across from her, even though he very much wanted to slip in beside her and give her a much more proper welcome. It felt like forever since he'd touched her, even though it had only been a day.

They began to move and she smiled at him, though the expression was nervous. Everything about her was nervous, like a fluttering little bird. Was it only because of her meeting, or did her discussion with Phillipa come into play with her emotions?

Her knee was bouncing and he reached out to cover it gently. She stared at his hand there and then up at his face. He smiled to ease her mind. "You are going to have a wonderful visit with an old friend," he said. "You have nothing to fear."

She blushed and it was so very pretty. He couldn't help but recall the same blush when she shattered with pleasure. She didn't erase that image from his mind when she tugged her glove off and let her fingers smooth over his own. Suddenly the carriage felt very close and warm.

"I just wanted to touch you," Celeste said, and he realized he had tilted his head toward her. She must have read that as a question. "I feels like forever since I touched you."

The sound that escaped his throat was more animal than any other noise he'd ever made in his life. He moved to her side of the carriage and let his arms come around her. She sighed as she tilted her face up and he took her mouth.

They kissed and it felt like forever. It felt like nothing but the briefest of moments. When her tongue traced his lips, he wanted to flip up her skirts and do the same between her legs. He wanted to make her shake and shatter and moan his name. He wanted to make her forget all her fears and uncertainties and pains that plagued her at present.

Only making her come undone would only cause temporary relief. Once it was over, she would have to fret over her hair and whether she should have or shouldn't have. He might want her, but not if it caused her more worry in the long run.

So he pulled away, difficult...impossible...but he managed it somehow. She rested her head on his shoulder and he held her there, smoothing a hand over her back in comfort.

"You're nervous about seeing Harriet and meeting Lady Lena," he said. She nodded against his neck without speaking. He felt her draw in a shaky breath. "Would talking about it help?"

"I fear I would only make myself more nervous," she admitted. "I fear I would say out loud everything that could go wrong and then I won't be able to breathe."

"Then we'll talk about something else," he said. "Phillipa had an odd look when I arrived this morning. It makes me think you spoke to her."

Celeste lifted her face toward him. "I-I did."

"Then perhaps that would be a good distraction on the ride."

She worried her lip a moment, brightening the color and making him want to nip it himself. Make her gasp against his mouth.

"I suppose we will have to have it out eventually," she murmured.

"That doesn't bode well," he said.

She sighed and slipped from his arms, moving to the opposite side of the carriage, where she met his gaze. There was strength in that, but also nervousness in how she clenched and unclenched her hands in her lap. In how she fidgeted and tried to find someplace where she would be comfortable in how she faced off against him.

He tried to reserve judgment about what it all meant until she had said her piece.

"Pippa and I had a long conversation about Erasmus just before you arrived," Celeste admitted. "I wish I could give you more information, more real evidence, but she doesn't want to tell me why she was nervous about names being in the paper. She's trying to protect someone, that is very clear, but who? She holds her tongue on that score."

Owen pursed his lips. "I'll look more into it. Erasmus Montgomery wasn't a careful man. If there is evidence to be found, I'll just have to find it."

She nodded. "Pippa knows she's a suspect, just as Abigail does. They're both too clever not to believe it to be true. But she cannot give me hope that her whereabouts would be accounted for on that night. She was staying at an inn when she arrived in London."

"The Nightingale House," Owen said. "Yes, I know."

"And she says that she was there all night when Owen was

murdered. But she was alone. So unless someone noticed her of their own accord and would recall the time or date without confusion, I'm afraid I found nothing of interest for you. Nothing that absolves her of the crime."

Owen could see she was disappointed in that fact. No, it was more than that.

"Are you angry with yourself?" he asked.

She huffed a breath. "Of course I am! You asked me to do one thing and I failed at it spectacularly. I added nothing of value to the investigation, and after you brought me all this way so I could help."

"First off, that is not the only reason I brought you here, and I think you know that after what we've shared," he said. "And secondly, you must understand that there isn't winning or losing when it comes to gathering evidence, Celeste. You've given me two further pathways to pursue. Which will move my investigation forward, no matter what the outcome. So I thank you."

He expected her to smile at that. To find relief in what she'd accomplished. Instead, she turned her face and stared out the carriage window pensively. The tension came off of her in waves, and it was evident that wasn't just because of the visit to her friends or because of guilt regarding Phillipa.

"Talk to me."

She jerked her gaze to him. "You can read me so easily, Owen?"

He stared at her a moment, taking in every curve and angle of her face, memorizing the bow of her lips, remembering how she tasted and felt in his arms. He skimmed through the images and sounds and feelings of every moment they had spent together since they met. And he nodded.

"It isn't that I'm so very good at it naturally," he said softly. "But that you have captured my attention so singularly that I cannot help but mark every tiny change in you. I see the way your hands clench in your lap, the way your cheek twitches ever so slightly and how your lips turn down just so. You're troubled, and you don't want to tell me why. But I want to hear it, Celeste. It's the only way we can solve the problem."

"She told me she didn't kill Erasmus," Celeste said. Then she folded her arms and arched a brow. "And I'm sure you will think me the biggest fool...but I *believe* her."

CHAPTER 16

Owen hadn't responded to her declaration, and Celeste shifted in her seat with increasing discomfort. Of course he would think her a fool now. Of course he would push her and her observations aside. She hated it, even if she'd known all along that it was how men treated women. Even ones who pretended respect and kindness always turned out this way in the end.

Still, she'd had to say it, hadn't she? Had to defend Pippa in some way.

She lifted her chin. "My intuition may not be evidence, but I do trust it," she continued. "I know what I saw and heard and felt."

He wrinkled his brow. "Do you think I'm going to argue with you?"

She opened and shut her mouth as she gaped at him. Had she misread his reaction? "Well...yes."

"I have no intention of doing so," he assured her. "Had I no faith in you and your ability to understand and follow your instincts, I would never have asked for your help." He folded his arms, which made his chest flex against his jacket a fraction. She tried not to focus on that. "May I ask some further questions?"

She blinked. "Er, yes. Of course. This is your case, after all."

"What made you believe her?"

She pursed her lips as she replayed every interaction with Pippa since the beginning. Especially the conversation that very morning. "When we spoke of the murder, Pippa was so horrified by the idea. That Erasmus might have suffered in his last moments gave her no pleasure. Unlike me, she loved the man once, that was clear. She mourns him on some level, or what she believed him to once be."

"But she was angry with him," Owen said.

"Very much so," Celeste agreed. "She is good at metering it, but it is there. Angry as she might be at his actions, though, *she* also didn't seem to be bent on harming him for them."

"She had no reason to tell you she wanted to defend someone else he'd harmed. If she were the culprit, I would think she'd try to avoid that at all costs. Perhaps even push blame."

"Yes. She in no way tried to deny her emotions. Or that she might have wished Montgomery came to grief as atonement for his behavior at some point. But when it came to his murder, she was very clear. She would not and could not do something so terrible, Owen."

He was examining her very closely now. As if she were the evidence he had to parse out. Then he nodded. "Sometimes those feelings that come deep within our soul are important. I have certainly put suspects lower on my list because I had a sense they could do no wrong, and vice versa. If you believe Phillipa, I accept that. She must remain on the list, but I will not put all my resources into the effort. There are better paths."

She blinked. "So you...believe me?"

"Of course. I said as much, didn't I?"

She couldn't move for a moment—she was struck silent by that simple acknowledgment of her value as a partner and a person. When was the last time she'd felt such a thing? Years, perhaps. All the way back to when Harriet was her governess, probably, and had told her she was capable of so much more than what she had experienced most of her life.

And now this man sat across from her in a narrow carriage and gifted her with the same belief. The same acknowledgment. She couldn't stop herself from launching herself across the carriage and into his arms. He caught her with a gasp of surprise, but she smothered it with her mouth.

Kissing him was always spectacular. The man knew how to move his mouth against hers, how to break past her barriers, physical or otherwise, and delve so deep she thought she might drown from it. He knew how to worship and arouse and make her feel weak with need and powerful with desire.

He knew how to make her feel appreciated and respected and important, too.

His arms tightened around her, fingers digging into her back as she arched against him, but before they could go any further, the carriage began to slow. She felt it turn, and he went still as he drew away from her.

"I would very much like to finish that later," he murmured, kissing her again, this time much more chaste, before he smoothed a hand over her hair.

"So would I," she agreed as she shuffled back to the opposite side of the carriage just in time for the door to be opened by a servant. The nerves he had helped to quell with the conversation and the kissing returned in full force.

He must have sensed it—of course he would—because he reached out to touch her hand gently. "Are you ready?"

She forced a smile, though she knew it had to look as weak as it felt. "I'm not," she admitted. "But let's go anyway."

He flashed that grin, the dimple in his cheek on full display, before he got out of the carriage and reached back to help her down.

They stared up at the building together. A bookshop, Mattigan's, took up the first floor, and Celeste couldn't help but boggle at the displays she could already see through the windows. Colorful piles of books with expensive gold filigree on their covers, mixed with vases of fresh flowers meant to draw the eye. It was a beautiful shop and one she did long to browse through, even if she could never hope to afford anything within.

The footman who had opened the door for them stepped up. "There is an entrance for Lady Lena's Salon through the bookshop, but Lady Lena and Miss Smith ask that you use the other entrance." He motioned for them to follow and they did, through a little gate to a pretty blue door in the side alley. He opened it for them and indicated the narrow staircase just a few steps inside. "To the top and turn right. The door at the end of the hallway."

"Thank you," Owen said, and clasped Celeste's hand gently as he took the lead up the stairs. She trailed behind him, noting the drawings mounted up the staircase. Beautiful sketches that she knew were in Harriet's hand. Her governess had always loved to draw.

They reached the aforementioned door at the back of a hall, and Owen gave her a glance before he rapped on it. There was scurrying movement from behind and the door opened. Owen stepped aside and Celeste clapped her hand to her mouth.

Harriet Smith stood there, looking just as she had the last time Celeste saw her in person, years and years ago. She had a beautiful round face and sharp eyes that took in every detail about every person she'd ever met.

"Celeste!" she gasped, and suddenly Celeste was being dragged into a tight hug that was so warm and welcoming it brought tears to her eyes.

"Harriet," she murmured, breathing in the familiar scent of rosemary that had always reminded her of the woman before her. "You haven't aged a day!"

"I have," Harriet chuckled as she drew Celeste in with a side glance for Owen. "But you have only grown lovelier. Come in, come in."

She led them to a big room, stylishly decorated. There were bookshelves on every wall, lined with fiction as well as tomes on topics of justice and politics. Paintings were hung beside them, beautiful originals of landscapes and one of Harriet with a gorgeous woman at her side. There were chairs lining the perimeter of the room, as well as the kind of furniture one would expect in a normal parlor.

But this wasn't a normal parlor. Celeste knew immediately this was the place Harriet and Lena held their meetings.

"Oh, it's wonderful," she cooed as she roamed the room, touching the spines of the books.

"Thank you. We have worked hard to make it so," Harriet said with a smile. She turned toward the door they had just entered and that smile broadened even wider.

Celeste turned to see the reason and caught her breath. Harriet's companion in the portrait was passing into the chamber. She had dark, tightly curly hair and flawless tawny skin. Her high cheekbones and full lips reminded Celeste of a painting she'd once seen of Helen of Troy.

"Celeste, may I present Lena Bright. And Lena, this is my dear friend Celeste," Harriet said as Lena stepped to her side. "And I'm sorry, sir, in all the excitement I did not yet ask your name."

Celeste blinked and jerked her gaze back to Owen, who had been quietly observing and making no attempt to insert himself in the conversation. "Oh, my manners. Gracious, Harriet, you will think I forgot everything you ever taught me. This is Mr. Owen Gregory. A...a friend."

"Mr. Gregory," Harriet said, shaking his hand, but Celeste still knew her well enough to see she was taking him in, wondering about him. Judging whatever she saw there on the surface.

"Mr. Gregory," Lena said with a brief smile toward him. Then she turned brown eyes on Celeste. "And dearest Celeste. I cannot believe it has taken so long for us to meet."

She clasped both Celeste's hands with her own and then leaned in to press a kiss to each cheek. Celeste found herself stunned by the pure essence of the woman. It was no wonder she was so popular despite all the marks against her that might make that unlikely.

Celeste had no doubt Lena wound a spell around everyone she came in contact with and there was no escaping, nor even a yearning to do so.

"Sit," Harriet insisted, and pointed toward the settee. "I'll pour the tea."

She and Owen did as they had been asked, taking the settee together as Lena chose one of the chairs across from them. In a few moments, Harriet joined them with tea for all and for a while their party was nothing but pleasant catching up with old friends. Neither woman mentioned Erasmus or the scandal of his death, and Celeste found herself relaxing.

This was what she had missed. What she had loved finding here in London both with Abigail and Pippa, and now with Harriet and Lena. As they spoke, she watched them together. Their love for each other was plain as day and became plainer as they relaxed around Owen. They sometimes completed each other's sentences, and from time to time Lena would rest a hand on Harriet's back or stroke her knuckles.

It seemed so easy for them, and Celeste was happy for Harriet. Her outspoken, intelligent friend hadn't had the simplest life, and Celeste was nothing but pleased to see her settled and contented. Yet it also made her feel other things. A longing to have that same kind of union. And a powerful awareness of the man sitting to her right. The one close enough that Owen, too, could have rested a hand in comfort on her shoulder. Except that wasn't the relationship they had. They'd been lovers once, they were becoming... friends, she supposed she might call it.

But beyond that? There was no certainty.

"And so how did you and Mr. Gregory meet?" Lena asked, and the question dragged Celeste out of her musings.

She glanced at him from the corner of her eye. He had stiffened slightly. "Well," she said. "We...he..."

"We share a few acquaintances," he supplied with a brief glance at her.

He was trying to protect her. And the fact that he would warmed her to her very toes. And yet when she glanced at Harriet and Lena, she didn't feel she needed to hide. She couldn't, at any rate. They might be behaving in a polite manner by not confronting Celeste's situation, but they knew.

Of course they knew. Everyone knew.

"Owen is investigating the death of my..." She trailed off. "I suppose I cannot call him my husband."

Saying the words, not hiding away from them anymore, gave her a strange sense of relief. One that multiplied when Harriet looked at her with the exact same affection and understanding as she ever had. Her friend didn't judge her. But now she realized that she never could have. Celeste felt silly for ever believing she might.

"Oh, Celeste," Harriet said softly. "I am so very sorry."

Celeste shrugged. "You have been kind to avoid the subject, but I know you must be curious about my circumstances."

Lena snorted out a breath and reached for Harriet's hand. She drew it into her own lap and held it there, cupped between hers, as if she could protect the woman she loved. "Curiosity is fine in measure. We only wish to be supportive, not exploitive."

Celeste took that in, let it sink into her skin and her bones and her heart. She looked at Owen again, wondering what he thought of her friends, what he thought of her options. She wanted to touch him, as easily as Lena and Celeste sought support from each other.

Instead, she drew a deep breath. "Very well. It would help to talk about this with people I trust. Let me tell you what happened."

~

Owen knew Celeste's story—he had lived some small part of it with her—so he didn't listen to her words as much as he watched for the reaction of her friends. He wanted her to find support. She had it with Abigail and Pippa, of course, but that was a sisterhood of this pain. Celeste also needed outsiders who would support her, those who wouldn't ask to lean on her but would only give her a place to lean.

But both Miss Smith and Lady Lena were difficult to read, so he had no idea how they would respond as Celeste let out a long sigh. "And so," she said, getting up and crossing to the window to look out on the street below, "*that* is the truth about Erasmus Montgomery and me."

There was a moment where no one moved. Celeste stayed at the window, back to the group, and Miss Smith and Lady Lena were still on their chairs, staring at each other, unspoken communication flowing between them.

But then Miss Smith got to her feet, crossed to Celeste and turned her away from the window. They stared at each other a moment, and the tension all but came off of Celeste in waves. Then Miss Smith embraced her and Owen let out the breath he hadn't realized he'd been holding.

Both women were crying when they parted. Miss Smith wiped at Celeste's tears. "I'm so sorry, love. When you wrote that you were being forced to marry, I hoped it could be a happy union. This...this is not anything I would have wished for you."

Celeste nodded. "I know, I know. But I do not want your pity."

"Pity!" Lady Lena leapt up now and joined the pair. "There is no pity here, my dear, I assure you. I may have just met you, but I have known of you from your letters for many years. If there is one thing that is clear immediately, it is how very strong you are. Despite the unfairness of all of this, you are holding up so very well. And you are not friendless, are you? You are not unprotected."

"Indeed, not," Miss Smith declared. "You will come and stay with us."

Celeste glanced toward Owen, and he held her stare. Whatever she wanted to do, he wished her to see he would support her. Only she could determine her future path, and one where she depended upon Miss Smith and Lady Lena was not so very desperate.

Though he didn't know what it would mean for the two of them.

If Celeste detached herself from the other wives, from the investigation, she might very well be detaching herself from him. And that thought left a very empty hole in his chest, even though he would give her anything in the world to make her happy.

"I appreciate the offer," Celeste said, reaching for Lady Lena's hand so that she now held on to each woman. "And I may yet take you up on it. But for now, I am staying with Abigail and Pippa. Until this is resolved, it is the best place for me to be."

There was no mistaking the hesitation that Miss Smith, especially, showed at that decision. She glanced back at Owen, spearing him with a glance for a long moment before she said, "Lena, my love, why don't you show Celeste around our home? You can explain how the club works, as well, and her membership."

Lady Lena's expression lit up. "Of course!"

"My—my membership?" Celeste repeated.

"Certainly," Miss Smith replied with a shrug. "You are now a member of Lady Lena's Salon."

Though Owen could see the excitement at that idea in Celeste's eyes, her smile fell. "Oh, Harriet, is that wise? Your salon has a certain reputation, everyone knows about it. Do you want to invite in such an infamous person as myself and drag the scandal of my union with Montgomery into this special space you've created?"

"I don't do anything I'm not entirely certain of, Celeste. You ought to remember that about me," Miss Smith said with a stern expression.

That didn't seem to appease Celeste. She worried her hands before her. "I just don't want to hurt your reputation or Lena's after you've worked so hard to build it up."

Lady Lena stepped up and slipped a hand through her arm. "We want you, so stop arguing."

The relief that moved through Celeste was palpable. Miss Smith turned toward him. "And the same invitation is true for Mr. Gregory. If you would be interested."

He inclined his head. "That is very kind, madam. I have always had a great curiosity about the salon and I would be honored to be a part of it, though I am no great intellect."

Celeste snorted, and he was pleased to see her expression was no longer so filled with concern and anxiety. "Do not believe him, Harriet. He is always thinking, thinking, thinking."

Miss Smith nodded slowly. "I can see that about him. Go with Lena now, my dear. I will stay and speak with Mr. Gregory a moment."

Celeste's smile fell and she glanced at him. "Owen?"

"I'm happy to talk to your friend," he said, though he glanced back at Miss Smith and held his gaze there. "Go and enjoy your tour."

Celeste's uncertainty was clear, but so was her excitement as she was swept into the tidal wave that was Lady Lena and led from the room. Owen could hear them giggling and talking all the way down the hall until Miss Smith crossed to the door and shut it with a pointed click, leaving Owen alone with a woman who clearly had opinions about him.

But he wasn't certain if they were good or bad.

They stared at each other for a moment. He made no attempt to read her. After all, he had no duty to do so. He didn't fear what she would do to Celeste either, for it was evident this woman cared deeply for her. But he was no fool. He knew Miss Smith was reading him. Down to the core, to the bone.

It was a somewhat unpleasant sensation and one that made him wonder what the outcome of that judgment would be.

At last Miss Smith stepped closer and spoke words that rocked his very core. "So you are in love with her."

CHAPTER 17

T hat was the last thing Owen had thought Miss Smith would say, and he took a long step back from her as if he could escape those words. Better yet, escape the truth of them. Because they *were* true. Hearing them out loud made them so obvious that he was surprised he hadn't come to this revelation on his own.

Or perhaps he had, with every moment he spent with Celeste, but had pushed those feelings aside. Tried to pretend away his growing love for her because it was so dangerous and fraught. Because it was bound to cause him pain, given the circumstances.

When he didn't answer, Miss Smith tilted her head. "It's impossible not to love her, one way or another. At least to any intelligent person." Her lips thinned as though she was thinking of something unpleasant. "Did you meet her parents when you were coming to collect her in Twiddleport?"

"I did."

She shrugged. "Then you know what she put up with all her life."

"Yes, down to when they forced a marriage with a bigamist on her rather than doing even the slightest due diligence about the man." He clenched his hands at his sides.

She seemed to mark that physical action closely, catalogue it with every other thought she was gathering. The woman would make a wonderful investigator. "Yes. I spent my entire tenure as her governess trying to subvert their selfish disregard for her. Trying to convince them that they should consider her and what she needed in even the smallest way. I was ultimately sacked for it." She shook her head.

"You did very well by her, though, Miss Smith," Owen said. "She is independent-minded and smarter than any other person I've ever known."

"Harriet," Miss Smith said softly. "If you love my Celeste and you are bright enough to see her virtues beyond her pretty face, then you have earned the right to call me Harriet just as she does."

He inclined his head. "Thank you."

"And I know Celeste is all those things you say she is. She always was, and I see her coming into her own now that she is here in London, out from under their thumbs, from under the oppression of that small place and the small minds who live there." She smiled slightly, but then it fell. "But it doesn't change the fact that as a result of her parents' foolishness, she was sheltered."

"I did not see any evidence that she was protected," Owen said.

"Not protected, *sheltered*," Harriet repeated. "And certainly not out of excessive care, but out of a lack of it. They did not show her the world because it had no value to *them*. And now I fear she is not entirely cognizant of what will happen next, after the dust settles on this enormous scandal."

He paced away to the fire and stared into the flames for a moment. "I'll help her."

They both knew what he meant. He wasn't ready to say it out loud yet and she didn't push, but it was clear. He did love Celeste. He wanted a life with her. He knew that as easily as his own name or the street he lived on. He would know it in the darkest corner of the coldest part of the world. He would know it without ever having that emotion returned.

"And can I trust you to do that?" Miss Smith asked.

He faced her. "If she would allow me to."

"And if she won't?" she said slowly, almost carefully, like she was trying to avoid hurting him.

The arrow still landed, though, softly slung or not. A creeping pain in his chest at the idea that for Celeste, their bond was one created merely out of fear of the future. That he was something solid to cling to in a storm, but nothing more. That if he asked her to stay, she would walk away.

All her right. All entirely understandable considering the way she had been controlled her whole life. But God, the idea was painful.

"I would still do everything in my power to see her happy," he said. "Including encouraging her to turn to old friends for a fresh start if they could offer it."

Miss Smith didn't say anything for a moment, just continued to examine him with that careful expression that revealed nothing of what she thought of it all. "Yes," she said at last. "You might at that. Which means you *might* deserve her."

"I don't deserve her," he corrected.

Before she could reply, the door to the salon opened and Celeste and Lena re-entered the room. Their arms were still linked and they were laughing. Owen stared. All the pressure of the last few days was gone from Celeste's face. She was flushed with pure delight and his heart thudded with even more love for her than he had admitted, if only to himself, a moment ago.

"Oh, Owen, the rest of the apartment is charming! They have the sweetest little library," Celeste said as she crossed to him and stared up at him with those shining eyes that took his breath away.

"It is the hazard of living above London's finest bookshop," Lena said as she moved to stand beside Harriet. "Mr. Mattigan is the most delightful enabler of a love for books. Speaking of which, Celeste, I will find that book we were discussing down in the shop and have it sent over to you later today."

Something in Celeste's cheek fluttered and she nodded. "That's very kind. I appreciate it." She glanced up at Owen. "You and I have another engagement, don't we?"

He wrinkled his brow, for they had made no other appointment. But it was clear she wished to speak to him away from the others, so he went along with the ruse. "We do, indeed."

Harriet exchanged a quick glance with Lena before she moved forward and embraced Celeste warmly. "We won't keep you. But I hope you will come back for the Salon and also to have supper with us."

"Oh yes, do!" Lena said, and squeezed Celeste's hand with both of hers. "We would be a jolly foursome!"

"We will," Celeste assured them as they moved as a group to the door where they had met not so very long ago. "I'm so happy to have been able to see you, Harriet, and to meet Lena at last!"

They said their goodbyes and Owen followed Celeste down the stairs back to the entrance where they'd come in. The footman who had greeted them was waiting there, and he ran to fetch their carriage back to the street as Celeste and Owen strolled back to the front of the building.

Owen smiled as Celeste peered in the windows of Mattigan's Bookshop. "We could go in," he offered.

She jumped as if she hadn't expected him to talk, so wrapped up was she in examining the books through the window. "If I go in, we will be in there for hours," she said. "I know myself too well. And I want to talk to *you*."

He didn't understand why she felt this sudden drive to speak to him, but he wasn't about to let it go. "You know," he said, leaning a little closer so they wouldn't be overheard. "You are very beautiful when you are happy. You shine."

Pink suffused her cheeks and she ducked her head for a moment at the compliment. Then she lifted her gaze back to his. "Owen?"

He nodded.

"Do we have time to go back to your home and…finish what we started in the carriage?"

He blinked down into her upturned face. Oh yes, he was definitely in love with this woman. Desperately, completely and irretrievably in love. And he was not going to allow himself to fret over or regret it, just revel in it as long as he could spend time with her.

"Oh yes," he said softly. "We most definitely do."

R ather than his parlor, Owen had escorted Celeste to his bedchamber this time after they arrived at his home. He had stepped out for a moment, to talk to a servant about something, and so she was alone in his room.

It was not a giant chamber, but it was very much...him. With dark wall coloring, a few pretty landscapes on the walls and books stacked on every free surface. She smiled as she perused the titles. Novels and history books and information about everything in between. They spoke of a busy mind always collecting, collecting and then making that information work for him.

Of course there was a huge stack of books next to his bed, and that made her eyes travel there. It was certainly big enough for two, with a soft coverlet that looked like one could be comfortable there for hours.

She very much wanted to do just that. Lock out the real world, the worrying world, the uncertain world, and create a tiny little corner where only she and Owen existed.

She moved to touch the coverlet, drawing her hand over it slowly from the foot of the bed to the head. There were papers stacked on the bedside table, and she turned her head to look at the top one. A list, because of course it was a list. She would have smiled if not for the contents of it.

Abigail's name—and a long string of reasons for her being the murderer.

Celeste's heart sank and her stomach turned. She'd known he kept her friend on his suspect list, but this seemed far more serious a thing. He was narrowing down the people who could have killed Erasmus and his brilliant mind had begun to settle, it seemed.

There were voices in the hall and Celeste stepped away from the list so he wouldn't know she was peeking at it. She very much wanted to bring it up, of course, but what would she say? She had already declared Pippa innocent due to a "feeling" and if she repeated that same mantra with Abigail, who he clearly suspected all the more, she doubted it would land as well.

No, what she needed was more evidence. Something to counter the points she had read in his neat, even hand. And that wasn't something she would find tonight in his bedroom. She moved to the fire and tried to look as innocent as she could when he opened the door.

He stood in the doorway a moment, staring at her. All her thoughts fell away, all her fears vanished. Tonight wasn't about investigations or discussions or anything but the way his gaze fluttered over her. The way his pupils dilated with desire. The way his hands flexed at his sides as if he was desperately fighting for control.

They had been in this place before. He had looked at her with such passion before, she had felt her body respond in kind before. And yet this time it felt different. It felt less fraught and more... impactful to have asked for this pleasure rather than surrendered to it.

"Oh, that will not do," he said softly as he closed and locked the door behind himself.

"What will not do?" she asked, her voice breathy in the quiet.

"That frown," he said. "I will have to find some way to make it go away."

Already she felt herself smiling, even though the dark desire in his eyes made her entire body heavy and ready for what would come next. If he wanted to work at making her even more ready?

Well, she wouldn't argue with the man. He was far more the expert, after all.

He crossed to her in a few long steps and his arms came around her. She breathed in his scent, soap and leather and something that was uniquely this man. She reveled in the warmth and comfort of his arms around her, smoothing her back so gently, so protectively.

"Did you have a good time today?" he whispered.

She stared up into his face, marveling that she was offering herself to him quite shamelessly and yet he was still inquiring after her health and well-being. There was no one in the world like him.

And somehow he wanted her.

"I did," she said with a smile she didn't have to force. "Seeing Harriet again was everything I hadn't dared to hope for. And Lena is wonderful. They are really in love."

"They are," he agreed softly. Wistfully? No, that couldn't be true. "It is a wonderful partnership between them."

She nodded. "I'm so glad Harriet is happy and has found someone who is her equal. And their welcome to me was...I was so pleased."

"Not surprised, though," he said, smoothing a lock of hair away from her face gently.

She leaned forward and rested her head on his shoulder. His arms pulled in tighter and she wrapped her own around his waist. For moment she reveled in the fact that he was just *holding* her and it felt like home.

He felt like home, and she ignored how dangerous that idea was.

"I hoped I wouldn't be treated differently, but my circumstances cannot guarantee that I won't be shunned, even by old friends." She sighed against his shoulder. "I couldn't even blame them if they had gone the route of self-preservation."

He made a rumbling sound in his chest. Displeasure at the thought. But the vibration of him against her was anything but unpleasant. She burrowed even closer to him and let one hand drift lower. Down his waist and over the curve of his backside. When she squeezed, the rumble in his chest was no longer a negative sound.

She lifted her head to watch his face as she squeezed again, this time a little harder. His gaze glinted in the firelight, suddenly much harsher and more intense than she had ever seen. He caught her chin, tilting her face toward his, and then his mouth came down and claimed hers, hard and fast and with so much purpose that her knees went weak.

She opened to him, welcoming him in as she lost track of time and space. She lost track of everything but the sensation of drawing her hands along his body, of him touching her in return, of his mouth colliding with hers, of the taste of him merging with her own flavor. God, how she wanted this man, in a way she had convinced herself she could not feel after her terrible experiences with Erasmus. But here it was and it was intoxicating.

Owen broke his lips from hers, his breath short as he stared down at her. Yes, the expression was still heavy with desire, but there was something else there too. Something...far more powerful. She tilted her head to find it, to identify it. She wanted it to be more than lust. She wanted it to be more than friendship.

She wanted more from this man, even if that was foolhardy and impossible. Even if it would only lead to both their ruin in the end, considering how utterly hazy the future was.

As if he sensed that desire, he spun her around so that her back was to him, cutting off her access to seeing him, watching him. Cutting off any hope she had of seeing what was in his heart. It was...disappointing, far more than it should have been.

But what wasn't disappointing was that he began to unbutton her gown. So she leaned back into him, pushing aside those wild and foolish desires for something she couldn't have. Instead, she focused on what she did have. And hoped it would be enough when all was said and done.

CHAPTER 18

A s Owen unfastened Celeste's gown, he kissed the side of her
neck, sucking hard, then soft, back and forth until she found
herself grinding her bottom against him. She had never realized
how sensitive that spot was, how it sent vibrations of sensation
ricocheting through her with even this simple touch. But it did. She
heard whimpered sounds of pleasure in the air around them. Word-
less pleas for more. They were in her own voice, desperate and
needy.

"More?" he asked, his voice muffled by her flesh against his
tongue.

"All of it," she begged.

He hesitated for a mere flash of a moment, then pushed her
dress forward off her shoulders. His fingers dragged back up the
front of her chemise slowly, hands cupping both her breasts from
behind. He massaged there and she gasped out a helpless breath.
How could every single touch light her up with more intensity than
the last? How could he make her feel all the need and passion and
pleasure she had convinced herself didn't even exist with just the
simplest brush of his hands?

She didn't know the answer, but she knew she didn't want it to end. She pivoted around into his broad chest, lifting her mouth hard into his even as she shoved the gown down her body and impatiently kicked it away. She wanted to feel this man's flesh against her, free of all other impediments. Nothing else would do.

He caught her hips with both hands, his fingers pressing against the flesh through her thin chemise, massaging the curves there. It only made her more desperate, so she pushed his jacket away and then lifted shaking hands to his cravat. She had to open her eyes to unknot it. She was not so experienced in undressing a man to do it by feel alone. She found him watching her as she did so, pale brown eyes locked on hers. Her fingers fumbled in the long swath of fabric.

"Need help?" he asked, smiling, that dimple popping in his cheek. She released the cravat with a sharp inhalation of breath and reached up to trace his lips and then his cheek, smoothing her thumb across that fascinating divot of his dimple as she had longed to do since the first moment he flashed it toward her.

"Yes," she whispered. "Please."

He untied the cravat with a few flicks of his wrist and unwound it just as expertly. But instead of dropping it to the floor to join her dress, he looped it around behind her, catching her in the snare of it and drawing her even closer with the cravat as leverage.

She was trapped and she didn't care. She wanted it. She wanted all of it and more and more and more. She was going to take it, take him, one way or another.

She began to unbutton his shirt as he tugged her hips flush to his with the cravat. She arched against him, her breath coming short and her vision blurring as they ground against each other. He dropped the cravat and cupped her backside with his hands instead, moving her against him, making her forget his half-undone shirt as he backed her toward the bed. Her thighs hit the high edge and he lifted her, depositing her there and wedging himself between her legs.

She locked them around his thighs as he kissed her yet again. The hard length of him was still encased in linen, but when she lifted against him there was no doubt he was very ready for her. And she felt equally ready. Her sex tingled, wet with anticipation of what he would do to her.

She wanted it all and she wanted it now.

He pulled away and stared at her, his expression almost stunned, as if he was understanding something that had eluded him until this moment. Then he pointed at the bed.

"Slide over," he said. "And take that chemise off, please."

She wrinkled her brow but slid to the opposite side of the bed and tugged her chemise off. Then she unbuckled her slippers and dropped them off the bed, as well. She was going to unroll her stockings, but he shook his head. "Not those. I like those, they are very pretty."

She might have answered, but she was too mesmerized with the way he tugged his half-buttoned shirt over his head with one hand. His muscles flexed as he did it, and she licked her lips at the sight of this man undressing for her pleasure.

He shucked off the trousers, kicking them aside, and then he joined her on the bed. She expected him to roll over her, to take her, but instead he slid his pillow down a little, lay flat on his back and said, "Have a seat."

Utterly confused, she stared at him, naked beside her, reclining like some kind of king, waiting for tribute. His cock was at half-mast, hinting at the pleasure he could give, but not yet fully ready.

"Er, where?" she asked, and then motioned to his hips.

He smiled. "Later. But right now..." He patted his mouth.

She swallowed hard. "You want me to sit...on your...face?"

"Most definitely. Because I want to do exactly what I did the last time we did this...only I'm very lazy, as you can see, and I'd like to lay here like this while you writhe above me. So...hop on."

She couldn't help it—shocked as she was, she let out a laugh. How could she not when he was being utterly ridiculous and playful and just...*fun*? Owen was *fun*, and she'd had precious little of that in her life.

"Very well," she said, and scooted over to him. She straddled him but didn't sink fully down, just stared at him. "You're certain I won't hurt you?"

"Very certain," he murmured, his voice no longer playful, but rough as he caught her hips and pulled her down hard against him. She hardly had a moment to adjust to the feel of his mouth and chin and teeth against her before he began to lick. Suck.

She caught her breath and tipped forward, grabbing for the carved headrest with both hands as he stroked his tongue over her clitoris with focused purpose. She began to circle her hips in time, grinding down against him as the pleasure built. He gripped her hips, his fingers digging into her flesh as he pulled her tighter to him, sucking her clitoris hard as she began to jerk with uncontrolled pleasure.

She no longer cared about anything in this world except his mouth on her, his tongue lashing her, drawing orgasm from her like it was effortless. She rode the waves of it, throwing her head back, gasping out his name in the quiet until it felt like she would shatter from it.

Finally, though, the waves subsided and he released her. She collapsed onto her side, sucking in breath, feeling her heartbeat slow at last. She glanced down his body and found he was hard now even though she hadn't touched him.

He followed her gaze and smiled. "I get pleasure from watching and feeling you get pleasure," he explained. "Feeling you flutter on my tongue is the world's best aphrodisiac."

"Hmmm," she murmured as she slid her hand down his stomach, across his hip, and caught him in her hand. She stroked him from base to tip once, twice, and reveled in how his back arched with the same pleasure she had recently experienced. "Would it be the same for me? If I took *you* in my mouth and made *you* quake, would I be overcome with even more desire?"

He licked his lips. "It's a good experiment. Though some ladies do not like the act."

She slid down the bed and glanced up at him as she positioned herself between his legs. "Why don't we see if I do?"

She didn't allow him time to respond, but drew him between her lips. A droplet of his essence eased from the tip of his cock, and she tasted him gingerly. She knew her own intimate flavor thanks to him, but hadn't experienced his. Salty sweet, entirely pleasant. And hearing his moan as she swept her tongue around the head of him was vastly more than just pleasant.

It was power. It was desire. It was everything.

So she dove into the act, learning as she went and reveling in every taste and lick and way she made him twitch. This man was hers, at least for the moment, and she was going to fully use him for as long as he would allow it.

Owen gripped the edge of the coverlet so hard that he thought he might rend the heavy fabric. Christ, but the woman would unman him. Celeste might not have much experience in what she was doing as she took his cock into her mouth, but her instincts were...spot on. She took him deep, she swirled her tongue, she sucked just hard enough that his vision blurred. And she watched him while she did it, reading his reactions, adjusting to them to give him even more pleasure.

He found himself surging up, gently but insistently, taking what she offered, grunting her name as his balls tightened and pleasure arced from his cock through every single nerve ending in his ultra-sensitive body.

He was going to come. He felt it on the edge of happening. And one day, he would let it, he would come with her mouth around him and watch her milk him dry.

But not today. Today he caught her elbows and drew her up his body, mashing his mouth to hers as she settled over him, her wet pussy stroking his cock with as much warmth as her mouth. He reached between them, aligning himself to her with shaking hands. The slippery intensity of her was intoxicating as he thrust into her.

She was so tight, so hot around him, like a glove made to fit him. She barked out a cry against his lips and immediately they moved together, hips grinding in time as if they had been made to do this. For that moment, he believed it. He surrendered to the idea that this woman had been built for him and he for her. To give her pleasure, to take her breath, to make her rock against him with insistent and building desperation.

He *wanted* to believe it, that she was the one for him, that he was the one for her.

Her nails dug into his chest as she sat up, riding him hard and heavy. He cupped her breasts, strumming her nipples with his thumbs as she threw back her head. Her red hair cascaded around her cheeks, her breasts, his fingers.

She came again, her body gripping him so hard that the border between pleasure and pain blurred. Tears streaming down her face, she screamed into the quiet of the room, and he took it all, mesmerized by her pleasure. In love with her surrender. Wanting this all day, all night, every night, forever.

Only when she collapsed forward onto his chest, her breath heaving, did he roll her on to her back. He moved slower then, gentle thrusts as she came down from the high. Her gaze was blurry and soft as she let her hands stroke over his skin. She lifted beneath him, the ocean of desire much calmer now. Much gentler. But still an ocean, still powerful. Control was an illusion in this moment— her body stole it from him as he took her.

The desire that had built when she sucked him rushed back, hard and heavy and tugging him closer and closer to the edge. He pulled out of the heaven of her heat and stroked himself as he came in a blur of powerful sensation and emotion she had inspired and kept inspiring. Then he collapsed over her, her arms folding around him in welcome, their sweat and their breath mingling.

God, how he loved this woman. And he would do anything in his power to keep her safe, to keep her here, to make her his. *Anything.*

~

C eleste had no idea how long she lay in Owen's arms after they made love. It felt like a lifetime, but a blink of an eye at the same time. That was how it was with him. The moment he touched her, everything else faded away and nothing else mattered.

A dangerous proposition. And yet she didn't pull away from it. He was like a magnet in that way. He drew her in and she made no effort to escape from his pull.

"You know there is nothing to fear, don't you?" he whispered, threading his fingers through her hair gently.

She glanced up at him with a laugh. "Isn't there? It seems like there is plenty so far. I am a pariah, the experience today aside. I have no money, I have no prospects. Not to mention there is a murderer on the loose."

When he frowned, she leaned up and kissed him gently. She had thought to mention his suspicions of Abigail, but now she hesitated. What they'd shared had meant so much…she didn't want to spoil it by stirring that pot. She needed more information. She needed to do a little work of her own before she broached that subject, it seemed.

"I'm sorry."

"You, of all people, shouldn't be, Owen," she said. "Today helped. And not just seeing Harriet and Lena. This. You. *You* help."

That seemed to appease him. His harsher expression relaxed, and once again she saw that glimmer of something deeper in his stare. But he hid it again. Hid whatever he felt from her as he drew her back down across his chest. "I hope so. I do try."

"Today I could see a future for the first time in…"

She trailed off as she tried to think of the last time she had allowed herself to think about the future. God's teeth, it had to be years, decades perhaps. Her future had never been her own, thanks to her grasping parents and her feckless husband.

"It's the first future I've seen since even before Erasmus," she admitted at last.

"Good," he said softly.

He continued to comb through her hair with his fingers. The action was so relaxing, and yet she felt his tension. It practically vibrated beneath her. Why, though? Why the shift? Was it her? Was it them? Was it his suspicions when it came to Abigail?

"You *deserve* a future, Celeste."

She lifted her head again and looked down into his face. "I like my present...at present. I like it very much."

He held her stare for what felt like a lifetime before he caught the back of her neck and drew her in. His mouth just brushed hers, not quite a proper kiss and not what she yearned for the moment he drew her close.

He pulled back and that smile flashed across his face once more, this time a bit more wicked. "What do you say about writing a little note to Abigail and Phillipa?"

She smiled back. "And what, pray tell, would this note say?"

"Hmmmm," he teased. "Why don't you say that you'll be joining me for supper?"

"I think that is the best idea you've had yet, Mr. Gregory. Will you get me paper?"

He shook his head. "After. After."

Then he kissed her and her mind emptied of all the questions and problems and fears. Emptied of everything but the intense pleasure this man always created. Some day it would end. But not today.

CHAPTER 19

Celeste hunched over the book open at the table in her chamber, the candlelight fading as she scribbled notes. Her stomach ached as she read over what she'd written, what she had etched out a star next to in the book. Nothing made sense and her heart throbbed.

"Celeste!"

She jumped to her feet at the unexpected interruption and turned to find Pippa just inside her doorway, brow wrinkled and eyes filled with concern.

"Pippa, you scared the life out of me," Celeste said, clutching her hand over her heart.

"I knocked several times and said your name more than once," Pippa said. "But you were entirely engrossed with that book. What is it?"

She moved forward and swept up the tome before Celeste could stop her. "*Harrison's Poisons and Potions,*" Pippa read. "I have had my eye on that one in Abigail's library, as well."

Celeste stared at her. "Abigail's library?" she repeated in confusion. "What are you talking about?"

"I saw this in Abigail's private library a few days ago," Pippa explained. "She and I were talking about it and she claimed it to be a very good source on remedies. She was so convincing, I began to wonder if developing some knowledge in that area would be something worth pursuing."

Celeste's stomach sank at that information and she reached out to take the book from Pippa's hand. "Is Abigail home at present?"

Pippa cocked her head at the question. "I...don't think so. She had something to attend to this morning, she said last night while you were still out with Mr. Gregory."

That was for the best, of course, but it made Celeste feel very uneasy about betraying her friend as she caught Pippa's hand. "Can you...show me that book?"

"You have it," Pippa said. "What is going on? Why do you look so pale and what is the issue with Abigail's book?"

"I will explain in a moment," Celeste promised. "Will you take me to where you saw it?"

Pippa's lips pressed together hard, but she nodded and led Celeste down the hall and into a chamber attached to Abigail's bedroom. It was a small study and there was a row of bookcases beside the fire. Under normal circumstances, Celeste would have cooed and studied the titles, but right now she had to focus.

"Abigail and I had tea here a few days ago when you were out. She told me I was free to come in and take any book I liked at any time," Pippa explained. "And *Poisons and Potions* was right..."

She trailed off as she pulled the same book Celeste was holding from the shelf. She gazed from one copy to another. "I don't understand."

Celeste took the second copy and moved to the escritoire by the window. She set both down on the top with what felt like a very loud thud. "I hadn't known about Abigail's library or her copy. Yesterday at Lady Lena's Salon, we were discussing the topic of poisons and she offered to send me the very same book. I returned so late that I didn't begin looking at it before this morning."

She stared at Abigail's copy of the book. The pages were worn, as if someone had looked at it often.

"Why were you talking about poisons with Lady Lena?" Pippa asked slowly.

Celeste lifted her gaze. "You know why. There is a belief that Erasmus was murdered using arsenic and I wanted to know more about the poison. I wanted to be able to better help Owen in his hunt. And I wanted to know...to know..."

"How he died."

Celeste nodded. "Yes. But I'm confused by what I discovered."

Pippa held out a hand and took the Lena's copy of the book. As she did so, Celeste said, "Page thirty-four."

Pippa turned there without answering and began to skim the passage. She paled as she did so, and Celeste knew why.

"You see," Celeste said. "Arsenic is a known poisoning agent, but it is also in a great many things. The danger of it is usually acciden-tal...or purposeful...poisoning in small doses over time. A slow sickness that is unexplained and takes a victim without anyone understanding what had occurred."

Pippa nodded. "And yet we were led to believe that Ras was poisoned that night, not over a long period."

"Which is why it doesn't make sense. Certainly if the murderer had forced or tricked him into ingesting a large amount of the poison he would have died, but the reaction would have been horrific. There would have been bleeding and vomiting and excre-ment everywhere. His skin would have turned a horrible red."

"None of those things were ever described by Abigail, Mr. Gregory or the Duke of Gilmore, and all of them saw Ras dead on the parlor floor," Pippa breathed.

"They are not details one would leave out," Celeste agreed. "Even to protect us from knowing the terrible truth. And it makes me wonder...what if he *wasn't* poisoned, at least not that way?"

"Why did they believe he was poisoned with arsenic?" Pippa asked.

"I don't know," Celeste said. "Owen told me when he first broke the news and I never asked further. But I think it's time I did."

She shook her head and absently thumbed Abigail's copy of the book to the same page that Pippa was looking at in her own copy. She froze as she reached it. "Pippa...the page about arsenic is torn out in this book."

Pippa set the book in her hand down and rushed to Celeste. "What?"

"It's torn from the book," Celeste whispered. "Though it looks as though there was a note written on the page. The imprint of it is on the next page. Is there a charcoal pencil here?"

Pippa went back to the desk and searched the drawers. "I have one here."

Celeste brought the book to her and they set it down next to her own copy. Pippa drew a deep breath and began to rub the pencil on the indentations on Abigail's copy of the book. "He...deserves..." Pippa read as the words became clear. She dropped the pencil with a gasp.

"*He deserves it*," Celeste read out loud. "Oh God."

"But this makes no sense," Pippa said. "How can the symptoms of an arsenic poisoning not match but then someone...Abigail presumably...leave this note on the page about the poison?"

"I don't know," Celeste admitted. "I cannot believe...well, I do not *want* to believe that Abigail could do such a thing. She has been nothing but kind to me and to you."

"But it is possible," Pippa whispered, tears filling her eyes. "If Abigail somehow knew the truth, if she knew anything at all about Ras's selfish actions..." She shook her head. "Oh, Celeste, what do we do?"

Celeste paced away so that she no longer had to see the jagged words written in the margin of Abigail's copy of the book. "I don't know."

Only that wasn't true. She knew exactly what she had to do. And she also knew what would likely happen once she had done it.

"Celeste," Pippa said.

She turned back. "We must…tell Owen," she said slowly. "We must show him what we've found. He will have a better handle on the next step."

Pippa blinked and a tear slid down her cheek. "He will arrest Abigail," she whispered. "He will see her charged with this murder."

"I don't know," Celeste said. Lied, for she knew that was very likely what he would do. It was his duty, after all. "The particulars still don't make any sense. There might be more to this. Perhaps together we can figure it out."

Pippa nodded slowly. "I would like to come with you."

Celeste caught her breath. "You would?"

"Yes. Abigail is our friend, mine as much as yours. And three heads will be better than one."

"Of course," Celeste said, though she knew having Pippa there would perhaps limit how she could approach Owen. She would have to remain more professional. She would have to appeal to him without including pleas that had to do with her heart or his.

Perhaps that was better, though. Manipulating their relationship did not feel like the right thing to do, even if she wanted to do anything to save Abigail from her potential fate.

"Let us go now," Celeste said. "The sooner we do so, the sooner we can figure this out."

Pippa nodded. "Yes. I'll fetch my wrap. You'll gather both books?"

"Yes," Celeste said, her voice suddenly rough as she stacked the books together.

Pippa said nothing else, but rushed from the room to collect herself. For a moment Celeste stared at the low fire that had begun to go out since the earlier part of the day when Abigail's servants had set it.

Celeste could burn these books. She could burn up the evidence that might hurt her friend and convince Pippa to forget about it. Only it wouldn't help, would it? She knew that Owen had already pointed his attention toward Abigail. Book or not, he would continue to follow that through until he knew the truth.

For the first time, she felt like they were working on opposite sides, and it stung her far more than it ever should have. But there were no choices now. She would have to stand before the man she... the man she loved. Because she did love Owen. Perhaps she had loved him from the beginning when he smiled at her and brought peace into her life that was like nothing she'd ever felt before.

She loved him and she would have to tell him what she knew. And then try to convince him that the evidence proved nothing.

Her stomach turned at the thought. But there was no avoiding it, so she stacked the books, steeled herself as best she could, and went to meet Pippa for their journey to the inevitable.

∾

"You have a caller, Mr. Gregory."

Owen lifted his head from his paperwork. "Who is it, Cookson?" he asked, and found himself hoping it was Celeste. Less than twelve hours since he'd seen her last and he already ached for her.

It was most distracting.

"The Duke of Gilmore, sir," Cookson said.

Owen nodded as he got to his feet and smoothed his jacket. "Very good. Have him join me."

The butler departed and returned a moment later with the duke. Once the formal announcements and bows had been made, Cookson left them and Gilmore reached back to partially close the study door.

"Drink?" Owen asked.

Gilmore shook his head. "No. I'm afraid I'm not here for idle conversation. I've taken the last few days to look through my father's correspondence with Leighton's father, as we discussed in the park."

Owen nodded. "Yes. You were going to look for the name of Montgomery's earlier lover. The one he was parted from as a young man."

"Yes. Though I did find out about a great deal more than just that."

"Regarding Montgomery?" Owen asked with a tilt of his head.

Gilmore's lips thinned with disgust. "Indeed. It seems the late earl often complained about his younger son to my father. Montgomery was always up to his elbows in some scheme or another. Easy money, fast women and empty dreams were the man's driving forces. And he didn't seem to care who he hurt."

Owen sucked in a breath through his teeth. "Well, that bad behavior clearly carried on after his father's death. The kind of man who would so badly use women like Abigail, Phillipa and Celeste doesn't happen in a vacuum."

"That is certainly true." Gilmore's jaw set, his rage barely contained.

"Did you determine the first woman's name, though?" Owen pressed.

"I did," Gilmore said. "Forgive me from straying from the topic. Her name was Rosie Stanton. She worked at the Stag and Serpent, an old tavern in Cheapside that Montgomery used to frequent years ago. He did wish to marry her, it seems, a few years before he was...*forced* to take Abigail as his bride." Gilmore's lips thinned and he muttered, "*Forced*. As if she were some burden to be borne, as if it was her fault that he had what he wanted snatched away."

Owen drew back a little at how angry Gilmore sounded. The situation was wrought, of course, but this rage seemed directed more at the cruelty toward Abigail, despite their apparent dislike for each other. "The ladies have been callously mistreated, yes," he said softly.

Gilmore shook his head. "That is an understatement and we both know it. At any rate, my father encouraged the late earl to nip that desire in the bud, and the lovers were parted."

"Christ," Owen said, pacing away and running a hand through his hair. "A fourth woman. Fifth if you count Montgomery's pursuit of your sister. It seems the man had no limits."

"When were you going to tell me?"

Gilmore and Owen both turned toward the study door. Celeste stood there, Phillipa behind her. But all Owen could look at was Celeste. Her cheeks were pale and her gray-blue eyes were flashing with anger and upset. At him. It was the first time he'd ever seen those dark emotions directed at him.

"I'm so sorry, sir," Cookson said as he eased his way past Celeste with a frown. "I did ask her to wait, but she insisted."

"And very good that I did, for it allowed me a chance to overhear what I assume you never intended to tell me," Celeste said as she entered the room and set a parcel she was carrying on the sideboard. "That there was yet another woman in Erasmus's life."

"Celeste, you don't know that he intended to keep this from you," Phillipa said as she grasped Celeste's arm and squeezed gently. "You accuse without knowing the facts."

"Yes, I was unaware of a great many facts," Celeste said, without removing her gaze from Owen. "When did you intend to tell me about this woman, this Rosie Stanton?"

"Cookson, you may go," Owen said.

The butler looked very pleased at that order and scurried away. Gilmore cleared his throat. "Perhaps I should also depart."

"No," Celeste said, turning her attention to the duke. "Do not trouble yourself, Your Grace. This is not a private conversation."

Owen stepped forward. "Celeste—"

She took an equal step back. "How long have you known about this woman?"

"A few days," he admitted.

Her face crumpled slightly, and for a moment she seemed to struggle to find breath. Her voice wavered as she said, "And you kept me in the dark."

He flinched at the use of those words, identical to what she had confessed was so important to her. "I realize that you feel betrayed," he began, but she shook her head.

"Why didn't you tell me?"

He glanced around the room. Gilmore had become intensely interested in a miniature on his mantel and Phillipa was now pouring herself tea at the sideboard as if it took every ounce of her concentration to do so.

But even if they pretended, this entire conversation was still intimate. It still revealed too much about how close they had become. He shifted with discomfort before he whispered, "Because I didn't want to hurt you."

He hoped that would soften her. That she would see his good motives and accept them. Instead her gaze narrowed all the further. "You were supposed to know that I could handle the truth," she said, her voice shaking. "You were not supposed to protect me with lies like my parents did. Or keep me in the dark like Erasmus."

He flinched a second time at the use of that phrase. It clearly resonated with her, sat heavy in her heart. "I'm not like them and you know it."

"Do I?"

Phillipa stepped up them, cheeks flaming as she caught Celeste's arm. "Dearest, dearest...perhaps we should go. Perhaps we should wait on what we came to share with Mr. Gregory until you are less...less out of sorts."

Celeste still didn't unlock her gaze from Owen's. He supposed she wanted him to feel how angry she was and he did. But the more important emotion that pulsed from every single part of her was hurt. She was hurt by his hiding some of the truth from her. And he hated it, despite the fact that this case was his own. Despite the fact that he might not owe her what she desired, at least not when it came to his role as an investigator.

"There is no need for us to go, Pippa," Celeste said, turning her face at last. "I have nothing more of a personal nature to say. I came here to discuss your case, Mr. Gregory, and I would like to do that."

He pursed his lips. The part of him that loved this woman wanted to take her hand and pull her closer and work out the pain that she felt. The investigator told him this was not the time, nor the place, especially if she had important information to convey.

"What would you like to tell me?" he asked.

She lifted her chin. "Given all this new information about Erasmus's first...love? Should we call that a first love if it comes from a loveless, feckless man? The label makes it easier, doesn't it?"

"Celeste," Phillipa said softly, and took her hand the same way Owen wished he could.

Celeste bent her head. "I'm sorry," she whispered. "Do you continue to consider Abigail your strongest suspect in Erasmus's murder?"

Before Owen could respond, Gilmore stepped away from the fire and crossed half the distance toward them in two long steps. "What?"

Owen ignored the interjection. "Celeste..."

She shrugged. "I saw your notes. The ones on your bedside table."

Phillipa blushed red as a tomato and hustled away again. But not far enough. Owen glared at the intruders to this conversation as he caught Celeste's elbow and dragged her away a little farther. He bent his head close to hers, close enough to kiss, even though he had to wonder if those days were over.

"You are angry," he said. "And I understand where that anger comes from, even if I do not agree that I have betrayed you to the level that you seem to accuse. But Celeste, you cannot come here and...and...blow up my case just because you are upset."

She lifted her gaze to his, and for a moment the anger fell, the pain remained, but he saw all her feelings toward him too. All the desire they had shared, all the tenderness. She swiftly blinked it all away.

"Why not?" she asked, but he noted she kept her voice lower, too. "Truth is better, I think. I've lived so many lies."

He tugged her a little closer, no longer caring what Phillipa or Gilmore thought of it. The proverbial cat was out of the bag anyway thanks to Celeste's declaration of where she had found his list of suspects.

"You have not lived a lie with me," he said, and caught her chin. He tilted it up gently and tried with all his might to show his honor to her. To make her see that he still possessed it. And that he felt so much more for her. But letting her feel it wasn't enough. "Celeste...I..."

Her eyes went wide, as if she knew where he was steering this ship. "Please don't," she said as she stepped away from him. "Not in this moment of all moments. Not when it feels like a way to make me go along."

She turned and walked away, leaving him staring after her. She knew he was going to say he loved her. And she was right, it hadn't been the correct moment to do so. Still, it had been there, poised on his tongue to say. That she walked away felt like someone had driven a fist into his chest and come out with his still-beating heart like it was a prize to be won.

She glanced back at him, and for a moment their eyes met. Despite walking away, her expression was not quite so hard now. The hurt he felt at her denial shifted. Hope bloomed. Right now she was angry and betrayed, right now she was focused on the case before them and saving the life of her friend.

But they would circle back to this. He knew it. And the next time he wanted to tell her he loved her, she would hear it. Only then would he know what she felt in return. And that gave him hope despite the rejection. Hope he would cling to until the time was right.

CHAPTER 20

Celeste fought to rein in some control over her emotions, but her hands were shaking so hard that there was no way the entire room didn't notice it. Her heart throbbed too, blood rushing loud in her ears.

Owen was about to say he loved her. She knew it the same way she knew she would draw her next breath.

She wanted to feel joy. She had finally admitted, if only to herself, that she felt the same for him. That hadn't changed, even if his keeping the fact of this other woman secret hurt her.

Only it wasn't just joy that flooded her. Owen had wanted to say those beautiful words to soothe her. To placate her. As a trick, as a trap. Something to bring her under control, just as her parents had done before. Just as Erasmus had done. Owen did it so she didn't harm the case he cared so much about.

And because of that, she wasn't certain that those unspoken words could be true. Love had always been wielded as a weapon in her life. And the idea that it might happen again terrified her.

"We didn't come here for foolishness," she managed to choke out, and hated how her voice shook like her hands. She looked around, uncertain where she had set her evidence when she entered the room and her whole world had felt like it was burning.

"On the sideboard," Pippa said softly.

Celeste smiled in thanks to her friend and crossed back. They had bound the two books with a ribbon and wrapped them in cloth, and now she unwrapped them before she turned back with one in each hand.

"When Mr. Gregory and I visited Lady Lena's Salon the other day, Lena and I had a conversation about Erasmus's death. She suggested I read up on some varieties of poison in this book." She shook the copy Lena had sent toward Owen.

He stepped forward and her heart fluttered. Yet somehow she stayed cool as he took the book. "*Harrison's Poisons and Potions*," he said, and then held her gaze. "You spoke to Lena about this?"

She shrugged. "Not out of *betrayal* to your case, I assure you."

"I didn't assume it was," he said, and his brow wrinkled. "Celeste, I am happy to know you have friends in this world that you can discuss such painful topics. But I'm not sure what the book means to our investigation. We have already determined that Montgomery died of poisoning."

"How?" Pippa asked.

Owen glanced at Gilmore. "When the duke and I arrived to confront Montgomery, we found him dead on the parlor floor. A label from a bottle was clutched in his hand and it said *arsenic*."

Gilmore shifted. "Terrible thing."

"But why couldn't that be suicide?" Celeste pressed.

Pippa snorted. "Ras would never do that. He thought too highly of himself."

"I tended to agree, having read some of his writings. A man who was so selfish certainly would have written a suicide note absolving himself of his sins and demanding sympathy," Owen said. "Plus the contents of the decanter had been shattered on the ground, a mess made that told me Montgomery had either struggled with the person who poisoned him or realized that he'd been injured and began to react as he died."

Celeste flinched. "Did you read much about arsenic poisoning?"

"I'd encountered an arsenic murder a few years ago," Owen said. "With a similar outcome. A woman had been poisoning her husband bit by bit. The family suspected it and she admitted it immediately."

"But that was a poisoning bit by bit and the book contains the description of how one would die from arsenic poisoning in a large dose," Celeste said. "It would have been messy."

"Death is always messy, Mrs. Montgomery," Gilmore said with a frown.

"But this death would have been *very* messy," Pippa insisted. "You can read the description yourself."

Gilmore took the copy of the book from Owen and read it silently. His eyes widened. "I see."

"Why do you have two copies of the book?" Owen said, picking up the other one.

Pippa shifted and reached for Celeste's hand. They stood together a moment as Owen flipped the pages to the description of arsenic and its uses and results. He glanced up. "Who wrote this? Who wrote *He deserved it?*"

"Abigail," Pippa whispered when Celeste couldn't. "Or at least it was written in her copy of the book."

Gilmore slammed the copy he held down on the table, his eyes dark with stormy emotions. "Bollocks! Abigail might be the most irritating woman in this city, but she couldn't kill a man. She *wouldn't.*"

"We don't believe it either," Celeste assured him, though she was surprised to find an ally in the duke, since one might have assumed his disdain for Abigail would allow him to believe her capable of more, not less. "But Owen feels differently."

"And how was this evidence supposed to change my mind?" Owen asked through what sounded like tightly clenched teeth.

Celeste worried her hands before her. "Don't you think it odd that Abigail would keep such damning evidence right in her personal library? That she would have no issue with Pippa asking to borrow the book at a future time? That she would write a message like that at all?"

"She is too clever," Gilmore said with determination.

Pippa nodded. "I agree."

Owen shook his head. "So you three are using the evidence as evidence against the evidence?"

Celeste pursed her lips. "We're using common sense. The alternative is like something out of a bad play!"

Owen held her gaze for a moment, then turned to the others. "I need another moment with Celeste."

He motioned her toward the window and she followed, her heart throbbing, for she had no idea what he was going to say. He folded his arms across his chest. His lips were pursed and he looked down at her with what was clearly frustration.

"I want you to understand that I hear what you're saying," he began. "And I don't entirely dismiss it. I will look into Rosie Stanton, as well as into the notion that...well, I suppose you are saying that someone is framing Abigail."

Celeste's lips parted. That *was* what she was saying. She just hadn't fully processed that utterly terrifying prospect until that moment. "Y-Yes."

"However," he continued. "I cannot dismiss a suspect just because we all *like* her."

"Owen—"

"I *do* like her," he interrupted. "I do. But the simplest answer is often the right one. So I don't want you to get your hopes up."

"You would destroy her," Celeste whispered, though there was no heat to the accusation. She knew Owen didn't want this any more than she did or Pippa did or, it seemed, Gilmore did.

"I wouldn't desire to." Owen sighed, and now his gaze darted away from her. "Also...I-I don't think it is a good idea if you help me with the investigation anymore."

She stared at him in shock. "What?"

"You have been of great assistance," he said. "I don't say that to placate you—I mean it sincerely. But you are emotionally compromised, Celeste. I suppose you always were, but I was selfish and I wanted you near. I wanted what you knew and I wanted...I wanted *you*. But I shouldn't have let my own...my own feelings keep me from protecting you. I must do it now. It would be dangerous to let you continue."

She could hardly breathe as she gaped at him. His smile was long gone, his dimple faded into his cheek as he frowned and dodged her gaze. She no longer felt that pulsing pull that always charged the air between them. That fact made her question it entirely. Had she misread him entirely? Did the fact that she had never felt truly loved made her mistake any attention as that emotion? At least from his side.

The love she felt for him was real. But now it burned inside of her, more powerful than any grief she'd ever felt. She wanted to run away from that pain, to run away from him.

So she pivoted on her heel and stalked away from him without answering him. Pippa's expression softened in what was dangerously close to pity as Celeste reached her and the duke.

"We have come to deliver the information we meant to," Celeste said. "And Mr. Gregory would like us to go."

"That isn't—" he began.

She held up a hand without looking back at him. "Do not trouble yourself. I understood your meaning completely. Good day, Your Grace," she said with a quick nod for the duke. She slid her arm through Pippa's and made from the door. "Good day, Mr. Gregory."

Pippa called out her own farewells and then staggered after Celeste in the hallway. "Dearest, what is going on?"

Celeste caught her breath in a great gasp as they reached the foyer and Cookson rushed to have their carriage brought around. "He—he doesn't want me. He says I am compromised and can no longer assist him."

Pippa's lips parted. "That doesn't mean he doesn't want you," she whispered.

Celeste ignored that statement as their carriage arrived and they were helped up into the vehicle. They settled in and the carriage moved into the busy streets.

"Celeste," Pippa said.

"I have never been good at...understanding people's hearts," Celeste choked out. "I can often read their motives or guess their next action, but when it comes to how they feel, especially how they feel about me, I do not feel that I have a clear vision."

Pippa tilted her head. "You cannot see that Owen Gregory cares deeply for you? That he is likely in love with you?"

Those words were like arrows and they found their mark in Celeste's heart. But they did not solve the problem at hand, not even in the smallest way.

"He might love me," she whispered. "I have sometimes felt that he did, and I would be lucky to have the heart of such a man."

"He would be lucky to have you," Pippa insisted.

Celeste smiled at the correction and continued, "But I think until this case is resolved I will never be able to parse out what part of him truly loves me and what part is simply bound to me because I am a victim of Erasmus Montgomery. And so we must solve the mystery of what truly happened and why."

"But you said he wished to dismiss you," Pippa said. "And you left. Do you intend to come back and convince him to allow you to continue?"

Celeste froze. She could do that. She certainly had some ideas of how to *convince* him that would be most pleasing to them both.

She blinked and pushed that thought away. "I didn't mean we as in him and me," she said and reached out to take Pippa's hand. "I mean we as in you and me."

"Oh," Pippa breathed, and a thrill lit up in her gaze.

"I would like to visit this woman, Rosie Stanton," Celeste explained. "She is like us, another woman he claimed to love.

Another woman who lost and suffered because of him. I think we would get further with her than Owen could."

Pippa shifted. "But we don't know her, do we? Couldn't she be dangerous? And don't you worry that Owen will be angry that you went behind his back and worked on the situation without him?"

Celeste looked out the window at the passing bustle on the street. She tried not to focus on what Owen might think or say about her further interference.

"If what I do helps end this madness, he will have to accept it," she said. "I will make him accept it. Or...I suppose I will lose him."

Pippa said nothing for what felt like forever. Then she shifted to the side of the carriage where Celeste sat and wrapped an arm around her. Pippa rested her chin on Celeste's shoulder and smiled up at her.

"You said you sometimes don't have a clear vision about how people feel about you," Pippa said. Celeste nodded. "Well, I want you to know that I adore you. You and Abigail have swiftly become two of my very best friends, not something I could have predicted when we all found out what Ras had done."

"Certainly that is true," Celeste laughed, even though her eyes were stinging with tears from the warmth of this woman's friendship toward her.

"If you think it is best that you and I do this, that you and I pursue this to protect Abigail, to end this investigation once and for all...then I am by your side." Pippa shifted. "But do you think we should tell Abigail about what we are doing?"

Celeste worried her lip. The fact was that the scribbled note in the book did implicate Abigail no matter how much Celeste didn't want to believe that she was a murderer. "I think we shouldn't tell her about the book...not yet. If she notices it is gone from her shelf, that is another thing, but until that moment, we leave that be. But as far as Rosie Stanton...we should be in this together, shouldn't we?"

Pippa's shoulders rolled forward in what was plainly relief. "Good. I don't want to keep too many secrets from her. And I think she would be of great help in both determining where this woman is and how to manage her once we find her."

"Then we are in agreement," Celeste said. "And will speak to her as soon as we get home."

Pippa gave her one more squeeze before she moved back to her side of the carriage, and for the rest of the ride, they spoke of anything else but the demanding work about to come. Only the change of subject didn't really help Celeste. She couldn't help but think of Owen. And wonder if her next steps would cement a future life they could have...or push him away forever.

～

Owen pursed his lips as he stood at the window, watching Celeste's carriage ferry her and Phillipa away from his home. When he turned away, he found the Duke of Gilmore watching him intently.

"It's complicated," the duke said.

Owen snorted out a humorless laugh. "It is that, yes."

Gilmore inclined his head. "My apologies. I do hope, though, that the letters from Montgomery's father helped, at least."

"Very much so." Owen struggled to maintain some level of professionalism when all he could do was think of Celeste and the look on her face when she'd walked away from him. It had felt so very permanent. He cleared his throat. "We need to end this. For their sake."

"For ours," Gilmore suggested. "We are all emotionally compromised, I think."

Owen flinched at the use of the same phrase he had said to Celeste. *Compromised.* He was that. It had never happened to him on a case before. It was so very dangerous.

"Well, I do thank you again," Owen said.

Gilmore arched a brow. "You want me to go, and I understand that. But we are not finished, I'm afraid."

"No?" Owen asked, thoughts of Celeste fading a bit at the expression on Gilmore's face. It remained calm, but there was a hint of something dark there. Angry.

"You suspect Abigail," Gilmore said softly. "Now more than ever thanks to this mess about the book."

Owen took a step closer. "Are we going to discuss how *you* are compromised, Your Grace?"

Gilmore's jaw tightened. "I think that would not be wise. For either of us. But I know you count Abigail's understanding of herbs and chemicals as a mark against her. Do you know why she does it?"

Owen shook his head. "I admit I don't."

Gilmore paced away. "Her sister died very young of a fever. She was bled, blistered and forced to vomit regularly. It was a terrible death and Abigail was scarred by witnessing her sister's suffering."

"How do you know that?" Owen asked. "I do not think you and Abigail have the kind of relationship where she would confide such a thing to you."

"No, she would not," Gilmore said. "But I have researched."

Owen arched a brow. "All the wives?"

Gilmore said nothing, but his expression gave him away. Not all the wives. Just the one.

"The reason Abigail has an interest in herbal remedies and tonics is that she wanted to help. To keep anyone else she cared for from ever experiencing the horror her poor sister did. Her interest is admirable and should not be condemned."

"Then what do you make of the note in her copy of the book?" Owen asked. "How do you suggest I explain that?"

Gilmore's lips pursed as he went to the sideboard and flipped through Abigail's copy of the book. He stared at the scrawled message in the margin. "The woman would never lower herself to write to me," Gilmore said. "So I've never seen her handwriting. But I still have deep questions about whether or not she would write something like this. That is my explanation, I recognize it might not be yours."

He set the book down and stood there, staring off into nothing for a moment. "Compromised. What a concept." The duke shook his head. "And now I should go. I have kept you too long."

Owen walked Gilmore to the door and they said their farewells then. He watched the duke ride away on his fine stallion and then returned to his office where he stared at the two books on the sideboard. His mind turned to Celeste. To what he could lose if he couldn't resolve this and as swiftly as possible.

And he thought of what Gilmore had said about Abigail's handwriting.

"He might not know what her handwriting normally looks like," Owen muttered as he snatched up the book. "But I know one man who might."

He could only hope that this new idea might get him closer to the truth. Closer to resolution for him...for Celeste. For all of them.

CHAPTER 21

Abigail was sitting in the parlor reading when Celeste and Pippa returned. When they entered the room, she looked up, smiling at them in greeting. "There you are! When Paisley said you rushed out, I was worried. Where have you been?"

"With Owen and the Duke of Gilmore," Celeste said, trying not to sound as breathless as she felt.

Abigail set her book aside with a pinched expression. "Gilmore. I cannot understand why he would continue to involve himself in this mess. Has he not done enough?"

Celeste pondered for a moment telling Abigail that Gilmore had taken her side in the arguments with Owen, but decided against it. Their cantankerous relationship was not one she could take time to explore at present, and it would mean revealing Owen's doubts about Abigail.

Right now she wanted to focus on something else.

"Have you ever heard of Rosie Stanton?" Celeste asked.

By the way Abigail's cheeks paled and her gaze jerked away, the answer was clear.

Pippa caught Celeste's hand and squeezed as Abigail pushed to her feet and walked across the parlor. As if putting distance between them could make this go away. "Where did you hear that name?" Abigail asked, her voice rough.

"Where did *you*?" Pippa whispered. "Because there is no surprise to you about it, no denial."

Abigail was silent for what felt like a lifetime. Two lifetimes. Long enough that all of Celeste's fears rose up in her chest and roared through her bloodstream. Questions she didn't want to have, suspicions she didn't want to believe.

"I am...not surprised," Abigail said softly. "I knew about her. I knew about all of you."

Celeste pulled her hand from Pippa's and crossed to the fireplace, trying hard to measure her breathing as the shock of that admission rushed through her system.

"How long did you know?" Pippa asked.

Abigail shrugged. "I discovered his duplicity a few months after he married Celeste. I was digging into some financials after a creditor demanded immediate payment and I realized Ras had not been paying his debts. I peeled back the layers of this onion." Her hands began to shake. "This horrible, rotten onion. I discovered all his lies, all his duplicity."

Celeste watched as Abigail bent her head, as tears slid down her cheeks in silent streams. Her friend's pain was palpable, rage and betrayal slashed across her face. It mirrored Celeste's own.

"Why didn't you tell us?" she asked, choking on every word. "If you knew about us, why didn't you tell us the truth then?"

Abigail refused to look at either of them. "I was a coward at first, so shocked by his betrayal that I could scarcely move. If it came out, I would be ruined. We would all be ruined. So I hid. I tried to pretend it wasn't true. I tried to pretend everything would be fine."

"To protect yourself." Pippa's disgust dripped from every word.

"Yes," Abigail gasped out. "At first I could only think of myself. Then as the shock wore off, I began to see the error of my ways, but I was frozen as to what to do. If I told you both, what would have happened? Exactly what *has* happened: destruction and ruination and despair. I was trying to uncover the least horrible way to do so when I realized Ras was courting again."

"Lady Ophelia," Celeste breathed, and the truth of everything came very clear. "You were the one who wrote the anonymous letter to the duke that set Owen's investigation in motion."

"Yes." Abigail shook her head. "Arse though he may be, Gilmore and his sister didn't deserve the hell that would be unleashed on them if Ras succeeded again. I wrote and told him to suspect Ras. I thought he might try to keep it quiet for his sister's sake, that Ras would be stopped or punished, but not revealed. And it all backfired. And he's dead. And it's...my fault."

She sank into the closest chair and put her head in her hands. She wept, not silently like before, but with great heaving sobs that spoke to the weight of what she had carried. The depth of her pain. The guilt of what it had all led to.

"I'm sorry," Abigail whispered at last. "I'm so sorry that my inaction and inability to come to terms with this caused you both so much pain. You have become dear friends to me and I hate myself for what I failed to do."

Celeste came closer and placed a hand on her shoulder. "I can't say that I'm not...upset that you didn't reach out to us sooner."

"We could have put our heads together, just as we have since we met, and worked out what to do," Pippa added. Her pale cheeks were red with emotion now, and she folded her arms across her chest. "Instead of us being mown down so unexpectedly by the news."

"I should have," Abigail said. "If I had known your character, your wonderful personalities, I would have. But I was so afraid of what I would unlock if I reached out. I failed you, and again, I am so sorry."

Celeste could see that Pippa might not be fully ready to accept that apology. She had loved Erasmus, just as Abigail once had. Their betrayals at the hands of that man were very different than her own empty relationship with him.

And that meant she had to take charge now. She was not as emotionally impacted by what had happened, so she could see things more clearly than either of her friends did. And what she saw was that any of Abigail's strange behavior was likely explained by her actions and inactions when it came to Erasmus's bigamy. She hadn't killed him. Celeste knew it deep in her heart. She knew the woman before her, so wracked with guilt, could never harm the man who had ripped her heart out. If she'd wanted to, she would have had plenty of time to do it long before that night in the parlor.

"Abigail, you are Owen's prime suspect in the murder," she burst out.

Abigail jerked her head up. "What?"

"He would be angry at me for telling you, but I think we must *all* be honest now. His focus has landed on you."

"Oh God, I feared that might be true. There are so many reasons to suspect me. And the secrets I've hidden will only make me more the suspicious."

"And that's why we're not going to tell him those secrets," Celeste said, grabbing Abigail's hands with hers and squeezing gently. "Not unless we have to do so. But to save you, we're going to have to determine a way to prove it wasn't you. Perhaps we'll find the true culprit on the way to that, but the most important thing is to make Owen see that you are not the killer."

Pippa stared at Celeste for a moment, then finally looked evenly at Abigail. "I'm angry with you," she said softly. "But I don't want you to be accused of something you didn't do. I agree with Celeste that we must protect you."

Abigail got up and slowly crossed the room to Pippa. When she reached her, she gently touched Pippa's hand. Celeste held her breath as the two locked eyes for a moment. Pippa turned away and Abigail's shoulders rolled forward in defeat.

Pippa walked toward Celeste, her eyes sparkling with tears. "Out with it, then. What do you have in mind, Celeste?"

Celeste nodded. If they could save Abigail, she and Pippa would have some resolution to reach for. "If this Rosie Stanton was Erasmus's first love or first...conquest, it follows that she might have some knowledge about him. Perhaps even a reason to want him dead. I say we determine if she is in London and call on her."

"She is in London," Abigail said, her tone a little flatter now, a little softer. "She returned shortly before you came here, Pippa."

Celeste cocked her head. "And how do you know that?"

"I'd saved a portion of my pin money over the years," Abigail whispered. "And I used it to gather information. Rosie Stanton has a very small house she lets near Lambeth. It isn't the finest neighborhood, but it isn't Seven Dials either."

"We'd be together," Celeste said with a nod. "And we would look out for each other."

"I have a...gun," Pippa whispered. "We will take that."

"Why do you have a gun?" Celeste gasped.

Pippa shrugged. "You never know when you need protection. I came here alone, didn't I? I'll fetch it and then we can make our way."

After she had stepped from the room, Abigail let out her breath in a gasping sigh. "She will never forgive me, will she?"

Celeste crossed the room to wrap an arm around her. Abigail had always felt like such a large presence, so certain of herself and what to do. In this moment she felt small.

"Forgiveness is a tricky thing, isn't it?" she said. "Pippa is hurt now. She can picture paths that never came to be, ways out of this situation that she is currently convinced would have existed if you had only...only...only..."

"I picture them, too," Abigail whispered. "I have since the moment Ras died and the world spun off its axis."

"She's in shock right now," Celeste continued. "But it's obvious you had the best of intentions and that *does* matter."

"Except that the outcome remains the same, no matter my intention: I hurt Pippa. I hurt you. And Ras died perhaps because of what I did and didn't do."

"Ras died because he was a blackguard who flew too close to the sun," Celeste said. "You were a victim of his chicanery, *not* an architect. Give Pippa some time. She will forgive you."

"And what about you?" Abigail asked softly. "Will you forgive me?"

Celeste smiled at her. "I am not like you or Pippa. I was never heartbroken by Erasmus Montgomery's wicked ways. I never loved him."

"But you do love Owen Gregory."

It was a statement, not a question. Celeste bent her head. "I do love him. Very much. I have no idea of our future, but I am happy to have been able to know him and love him as I do, no matter the outcome."

"He'll be angry that you went behind his back to visit this woman, I think. And that you told me I am his main suspect."

Celeste worried her lip. "Perhaps he will. And I grieve that. But just because I love him doesn't mean I must always follow his path. I must do what is right, wholly separate from him and his values and plans. To protect you is right. To confront this woman, just the three of us, to use our collective relationship to a man she cared for at least once, if not still, is the best way. If he cannot forgive me for that, then…"

She swallowed hard. Owen's steady presence had become so very important to her. She feared what her life would be like without it.

"Then?" Abigail whispered.

"Then I suppose our connection was never meant to be more than what it was." Celeste shrugged and tried to feel as nonchalant about it as she pretended to be.

Abigail sighed. "You are risking a great deal for me. For the truth. So I shall be as strong as you are. I'll go call for the carriage and then we shall be off."

She hustled from the room, leaving Celeste alone for a moment. She clenched her hands before her, wishing she could slow their shaking. Slow her racing heart. Slow her growing fears. Thanks to Erasmus, none of them were in a good position. All of them had something to lose.

And for Celeste, losing Owen was not something she could bear to fully contemplate.

~

Owen paced the parlor in the Earl of Leighton's home, clenching his hands in and out of fists as he made turn after turn across the room. He couldn't stop thinking of Celeste.

He had hurt her today. By keeping the truth from her. By denying her a place at his side as he searched out the details. But what else could he do? This situation was about to reach its boiling point and the danger was now far more than physical. Loss and grief and heartache were very likely.

He wanted so much to spare Celeste from those things.

"You are going to wear a path in my carpet."

He jumped and pivoted to face the earl, who was now standing in the doorway watching him. "Forgive me for coming without sending word first."

Leighton's expression grew concerned as his brow furrowed. "Not at all. What is it, Mr. Gregory? Something about my brother's case?"

"Yes. I would like you to accompany me to question a person. Will you do so? I can explain the rest on the ride over."

Leighton stared at him a moment, then nodded. "Of course. Should we take my carriage?"

Owen pursed his lips. "I think the crest might scare off our quarry. I've a rig waiting outside for us."

"Then I will come directly." Leighton motioned toward the door. "Please."

Owen followed him, and as Leighton took his place in the carriage, Owen gave the driver instructions on where to take them.

Once he had taken his own seat and the vehicle had begun to move, Leighton tilted his head. "Tell me then, so I might be prepared."

Owen worried his hands on his lap. "Gilmore is compromised."

"Gilmore? How? Do you suspect my friend of doing this thing to my brother?" Leighton asked, and all the color drained from his face at the thought.

"I don't," Owen said. "I believe him to be innocent. But I also believe he is personally invested in the innocence of my main suspect."

"And who is that?" Leighton breathed.

Owen hesitated. "I hate to say it, but I believe Abigail might be our answer."

Leighton bent his head. "I feared it would be one of the ladies. Christ, poor Abigail."

"You would have pity for the woman who might have stricken your brother down?" Owen asked.

"Of course. My brother was a lout who destroyed everything in his path because of his selfishness. If Abigail snapped and caused him harm, I cannot hold her blameless, but nor am I blind as to why she might have done such a thing. So you think Gilmore has...affection for her? Despite their confrontational relationship?"

"I know he doesn't want her to be guilty," Owen said. "And he will defend her rather than seek the truth if its path leads to her door."

"Fascinating." Leighton shook his head. "I can hardly believe it. So are we going to Abigail's then? Confrontation on your mind?"

"No, Abigail is fine where she is. Gilmore brought me information about Montgomery's first love. The woman you and I discussed a while ago: Rosie Stanton."

"That's right," Leighton said. "Rosie! I knew it was an R name."

"And now that we know it, I think it would be best to speak to her as soon as possible, to see if she has any information regarding the murder." Owen sighed. "Or anything else."

"Why bring me?" Leighton asked. "I hardly knew the woman—I couldn't even recall her name."

"But you did know your brother. It will be easier to have someone with me who can at least attempt to fill in the gaps when it comes to that time in Montgomery's life. And you might also be able to detect if the woman is being honest about her relationship."

"I will try, yes."

They were quiet a moment, and Owen felt how curious Leighton was by his intent stare. "What is it you have to say, my lord?" he asked at last.

"You're a decent fellow," Leighton said softly.

Owen wrinkled his brow. "I try to be, yes."

"And I have come to think of you as a...friend, if that makes any sense," Leighton continued. "You could have been many things when it came to my brother's bad deeds. You have always been discreet, but more importantly, you've been kind. And I've appreciated that as I've attempted to navigate the nightmare Ras left behind."

Owen shifted. "Thank you. I recognize how hard this situation is for everyone involved. Resolution is my only goal, not to create further harm."

"Well, perhaps I can return some of that friendship to you," Leighton said slowly. "You seem...troubled. One must assume that is because of Celeste. Would you like to discuss it?"

Owen sighed. "Not very professional of me, is it? Falling in love with one of the suspects in a case."

"A suspect you dismissed with cause long ago," Leighton said. "And love is a...complicated thing. I know that."

"She's angry with me," Owen mused softly. "Because she doesn't *want* Abigail to be the murderer."

"Nor do any of us."

"No, but I think it is in her nature to try to fix this," Owen said with a shake of his head. "Even if that means destroying everything in her path. That kind of loyalty is admirable. I love her for having it. But I may have to hurt her even more before we're through. And I hate it."

Leighton stared out the window for a moment, apparently lost in his own thoughts. "Let us hope that hurting her, hurting any of them, doesn't come to pass." He cleared his throat. "There is the Stag and Serpent. So we're going to Rosie's old employer."

"She might work there still," Owen said as the carriage stopped and he pushed the door open to exit. "And if not, they may have the address of her residence or next employer."

"A fine notion." They both stared up at the building, and Leighton shrugged. "Decent enough place, I suppose. My brother went to far worse over the years."

Owen led them inside and they took two seats at the bar. They ordered ales, and after they had been delivered, Owen pushed a coin across the table toward the barkeep, a thin man with a scar across his lip.

"Don't suppose you might have any information on someone who once worked here," Owen began.

The barkeep stared at the coin a moment. "What do you want, toff?"

"Rosie Stanton," Owen said. "We're looking for her."

The barkeep sneered as he took the coin. "Rosie don't work here no more."

Leighton leaned closer. "You must have some information about where she lives or might have gone next to work."

The man snorted. "None for you, Your Highness." He turned then and walked away, Owen's coin in his pocket and with no further information.

Owen's heart sank. It wasn't that the reaction was surprising. The bar wasn't for those with uppercrust accents. It was for those who saw enough of those with money and supposed polish all day long in their jobs, in their businesses.

Still, he'd hoped one thing in this God forsaken investigation would be easy. Just this one thing.

They drank their ales in silence. Owen scanned the room, but there was no one else near who looked amenable to conversation. Anyone else who seemed to work here would no longer look at them. The patrons were few and didn't seem any more interested.

"Dead end," Leighton muttered as he set his empty mug aside.

"I'm afraid so," Owen said. "I'll get some of my connections on the hunt for her. But this would have been easier if we had the information now."

Leighton grunted his agreement as they both got up and made their way through the glaring crowd toward the door. They stepped out into the busy streets of Cheapside. Despite the disparaging name, it was a good part of the city. The middle class had homes here, there was bustling trade and even the rich came to visit the shops.

Owen waved for the carriage to be brought back around and as they waited, he sighed in frustration. As the carriage stopped and Leighton began to climb in, Owen felt a tug on his jacket arm. He pivoted to face the person, on guard for a street beggar or sneaky thief. It was a woman who faced him, and from her apron, he thought she might have followed him from the tavern.

"'Scuse me, did I hear you asking about Rosie?"

Owen exchanged a glance with Leighton, who was now leaning out the carriage door to hear what was being said.

"I did," Owen said. "Do you know something about her?"

"For a price," the woman said, holding out a hand with an arch of her brow.

Owen dug into his pocket and drew out another coin. He pressed it into her palm. "Two more if the information seems true."

She flashed him a grin. "Rosie left over a year ago," she said. "Went to Bath to shack up with some lover, I heard."

"Bath," Leighton repeated. "Who was the lover?"

"Some toff like you," the barmaid said with a little flutter of a gaze over Leighton. "Looked a bit like you, even. But you all look the same. She called him a funny name. Rash, Razzle?"

Owen jerked his gaze back to Leighton. The earl's face had lost all color. Owen felt his own doing the same. "Do you know where in Bath?"

"No, but you ought to know she's back now," the woman said with a shrug. "Showed back up a month or so ago and came in to say 'ello to old friends. She lives just outside Lambeth now. Near the smithy there on Colford Road. I visited her a few days ago. Her and her lord and master."

Leighton staggered out of the carriage and nearly deposited himself at her feet. "Wait, you said the man she left London for was with her a few days ago?"

"Aye. Not the babe, though. No explanation for it. Maybe they left 'im with a relative in Bath or some such."

Owen blinked. "They had a child?"

She nodded. "She talked about 'im when I saw her."

"Was the lover's name Erasmus? Ras."

"That's it," the woman said. "Ras. I hardly paid any mind. Handsome fellow. Bit nervous. But tall as you, my lord." She flitted her hand at Leighton. "Same eyes."

"Thank you," Owen said, and pressed three more coins into her palm, rather than the promised two. As she went back into the tavern, he faced Leighton. His heart was throbbing so hard, he almost couldn't hear over the sound. "My lord—"

"She said my brother was alive," Leighton said. His tone was blank and his face deathly pale. "Erasmus is alive."

"He may well be," Owen said. "Somehow. Or she might be lying or mistaken. Either way, we need to get to Rosie Stanton's house right now. Because whatever is happening, it cannot be good."

CHAPTER 22

The house in Lambeth was nice enough. Small, but bright and well kept. Celeste couldn't help but wonder who had paid for these accommodations and think of her own desperate hovel in Twiddleport.

As she followed Abigail and Pippa from the carriage, Abigail said something to her driver and he nodded before he eased the carriage off.

"I asked him to give us some privacy for a little while before he returns to watch for us," Abigail said. "Worst case, we can walk down to the village and find him."

"We might all need some air after this," Pippa said softly as she looked up at the house with a shiver. "Are you ready, ladies?"

Celeste stepped forward to lead the way. "As ready as one can be in these situations. Perhaps she'll turn out to be another friend."

"Yes," Abigail said with a sigh as she followed. "Perhaps."

Her heart throbbing and her hands shaking, Celeste knocked on the door. There was a moment of silence and then movement from within. A woman's voice calling out, "What did you forget, love?" before she threw open the door.

She was a little younger than Celeste, no older than her mid-twenties. She was a beautiful woman with dark hair and eyes the same color as Abigail's. In fact, she looked very much like their friend, and judging from the way Abigail stared, she recognized it too.

But it wasn't Abigail's reaction that shocked Celeste from her silence. It was Pippa's. She pushed forward, her eyes wide. "Rachel?"

The woman behind the door gasped and started to slam it, but Pippa wedged herself in. "Stop, what are you doing here? Where have you been?"

"What's going on?" Abigail asked. "Who is this woman? How do you know her?"

"I knew her as Rachel Simpson," Pippa said, still struggling with the door. She shoved hard and the woman staggered back, allowing them entry into the foyer. "She worked for me back in Bath. Ras insisted I take her on as my maid. She had an affair with Ras that resulted in a child, but right before I came to London, she disappeared. *She* is why I was searching for Ras. But here you are...in a house that is supposed to be for his first lover and...and..."

She trailed off and staggered back. Celeste's stomach flipped, nausea and fear and horror all at once.

"This was a plan, wasn't it?" Celeste whispered. "You...you and Erasmus never parted ways, even when his father tried to separate you. You carried on even when he married Abigail. You knew he was playing Pippa for a fool. You were part of all of this, weren't you?"

Before the woman could answer, the door behind them shut. Celeste pivoted, and her blood ran cold.

Because Erasmus Montgomery was standing there, a gun trained on her and an angry grimace on his face.

"You were always the most clever of this bunch," he said. "I never should have married such a clever woman."

"R-Ras," Pippa breathed, all the color from her cheeks.

Abigail continued to stare, her mouth opening and closing but no sound coming out.

"Good afternoon, wives," he grunted. "God, if this wasn't such a mess, your expressions would be joke."

"You're alive," Celeste choked out.

He arched a brow at her. "Come now, I just called you the clever one. Don't disprove me by stating the patently obvious. Rosie, love, why don't you lead our friends to the parlor? I'll follow behind."

Rosie stared at him a beat, and then she smiled. "Of course, lover. Ladies."

She motioned down the hall, calm as anything, as if she often led the wives of her presumed dead lover into a parlor while he trained a gun on them. Celeste sensed it at her back even when he wasn't touching her.

"Why are you doing this?" she whispered.

He pressed the gun closer now. She felt the barrel against her spine and sucked in a breath through her teeth. "You should have left well fucking enough alone, Celeste," he growled.

She blinked at tears as they entered a small parlor. Rosie glared at the women as she moved to the fireplace and folded her arms. "Sit."

Abigail and Pippa moved to do so, close together on the settee. Celeste planned to join them, but Erasmus caught her arm and yanked her back toward him, hard.

"Except for you," he grunted. "You, my dear, are an insurance policy that neither of my other lovely wives will do something foolishly brave."

"Stop it," Abigail said, glaring up at him. "Don't you hurt her."

"I'm afraid we're past that point now," Erasmus said. "But we can take our time, I think. I assume you all have questions."

"And I'm sure you'll be happy to brag away about what you've done," Pippa hissed.

Erasmus smiled at her. "You changed your hair, Pip. I like it."

"Rot with the devil," Pippa said in return. Celeste gasped at the fire in her friend's eyes. Fire that faded as she met Celeste's gaze. "We're going to get out of this."

She nodded, though she didn't believe Pippa. The gun jabbing her back certainly said otherwise.

"You—you want to monologue, I think," Abigail said. "You were always good at talking and talking. So why don't you do so now? Explain yourself."

He shrugged as he took a seat and dragged Celeste down on his knee. She noticed that Rosie flinched when he did so. Not because of the violence, she didn't think, but because of the intimacy of the action. Perhaps that could be used to their advantage later.

"The only one I ever loved was Rosie," he began.

Both Pippa and Abigail recoiled, though their sadness seemed tempered. This man's actions were killing any faint love that might have remained in the hearts of these remarkable women. His loss, Celeste knew. He didn't. He was too selfish and cruel to know.

"Then why marry me?" Abigail asked. "Why not marry her?"

"We tried," Rosie said with a shake of her head. "His muckworm of a father put a stop to it. Said I wasn't good enough. Said I was looking for a fortune and threatened to take all of his if we went through with it."

Her pain was palpable, real, and had the situation been different, Celeste might have felt for her. The gun in her back and the smirk on Rosie's face tempered that reaction.

"I had to pretend to push her aside," Erasmus continued. "And we convinced my father that I'd seen the end to my foolish notion. I married Abigail and lived two very happy lives."

"More than two," Abigail said softly. "There were other lovers."

"He only wanted you to think that," Rosie said, her face twisting with rage. "There was only ever me."

Abigail held Erasmus's stare evenly. "So you say."

He smirked at her. "One lover, ten lovers, what does it matter? It worked out fine and dandy until my bastard of a brother took the title. He started looking into my dealings. He didn't find Rosie, of course, but other debts and what he liked to judge as foolery. He cut me off." His nostrils flared. "Lord High and Mighty always wanted to do it. Our mums weren't the same, you see. His was buried in the ground hardly a year before our father married mine. If she didn't treat Rhys right, how was it my fault? But he punished me for it."

Pippa shook her head. "If Leighton wished to protect his name and fortune from your machinations, one can see how and why he would do so. Considering you are standing in a parlor with at minimum three wives, a gun in the back of one of them. You sound like a villain from a book, you know. I despise you."

"But you didn't always, did you, Pip?" he said, holding her gaze. "You liked me well enough for a very long time. Practically begged for me every night I was in your bed."

Pippa pushed out a breath of disgust. "And all while the supposed love of your life was below my stairs. What do you think of that, Rachel...*Rosie?*"

Rosie was staring at Erasmus even as she answered Pippa. "I had his heart. His body was something else."

She didn't sound entirely certain of that statement, though, and Celeste caught her breath. Rosie might be the escape route for all of them. *If* they could turn her to their side. That, it seemed, was the next step.

"Still, it wasn't enough," Celeste said. "Because I came a year later. Why?"

"Life is expensive," Erasmus growled, pressing the gun harder. "And you were a way to bridge the gap. Nothing more, Celeste. You know that, don't you?"

"Clearly. You had some affection for Abigail, it seems. And desire for Pippa. Both of them have spoken at length about your time together. How much it meant to them."

Abigail shot her a look, and Celeste slid her eyes toward Rosie. The understanding dawned, and Abigail nodded. "Yes, that is true. We were happy together, weren't we, Ras? Do you remember that afternoon at Bridgely? Your brother had some errand to attend to, and you and I stayed in bed all day making love and talking."

Erasmus stared at her. "I remember."

Pippa had a harder time hiding her disgust, but she seemed to understand what was happening here as well. What Celeste was trying to orchestrate from the increasingly red-faced Rosie. "We had a similar day. Less than a year ago, right around the time Rosie was giving birth, I suppose."

"I've had my fun. Why shouldn't I?" Erasmus said with a shrug. "And I would have had my fun with Ophelia, as well. Extra fun since it would have shattered Gilmore. Toff prick that he was, my brother's 'true' brother. It would have been nice to see him squirm and watch their friendship disintegrate."

Celeste caught her breath. "You...you made a mistake out of emotion."

"Suppose I did," he admitted. "I shouldn't have shit so close to where I lived. Once it was clear the duke was investigating, that the truth would come out, my goose was cooked. I had to think fast. And what better way for a man to start over, to get out, than to die?"

"So you faked your death," Pippa whispered.

"Indeed," Erasmus said with another shrug. As if he hadn't torn the world to shreds.

"How?" Celeste asked.

He smiled and she could see how proud he was of his actions. How smart he thought himself to be. "Found an herb in Abigail's book of potions that slowed the heart, paid off an undertaker to claim I was dead, clutched a label from a bottle of poison. It doesn't take many clues to lead people down the path."

"You bastard," Pippa whispered. "Do you know what you've put your brother through? What you've put us all through?"

"It keeps me from prison." He shrugged.

"But nothing else," Celeste said. "Now that you are in hiding, you cannot have any more money than you did when you got so desperate as to seek out a fourth wife."

"Well, that's where Abigail comes in."

Abigail blinked. "Me?"

"You inserted yourself into this situation," Erasmus said, and he gripped Celeste tighter as he said it, his fingers biting into her skin, bruising as the gun pressed ever harder into her back. She blinked at tears, both those of pain and those of terror. "You told Gilmore, yes?"

"How do you know that?" Abigail asked, her voice shaking.

"I know *everything*, my dear. I always know everything. You blew up my plans, you managed to destroy everything. So *you* are the perfect one to blame for my murder. I believe our intrepid investigator has already turned his sights toward you. The one that Celeste here is spreading her legs for."

Celeste flinched. "Don't talk about him."

"Is he good, Celeste? Does he manage to make you react, you cold, empty harpy? Is he better than me?"

She pivoted to face him as far as he would allow. "He is ten times the man you have ever been on your best day. And he is not a fool."

"Perhaps not," Erasmus said with a half-smile. "But he is a slave to evidence. He has plenty. The book about poisons that Abigail had on her shelf? The message that I deserve it that was written in the pages?"

"What?" Abigail gasped.

"Between that and the fact that Abigail was in the house at the time of my death, I think she'll hang." He shifted his attention to Abigail. "When you do, my brother will find a letter from me, marked to be sent in the event of my untimely death. The one that reveals that I had a child with Rosie. With Abigail swinging from the gallows, with his entire life falling apart around him, he will wish to quiet any whispers about an illegitimate son. He'll offer my sweet, mourning true love a fine settlement. And we will run away happily ever after."

Pippa covered her face. "You *abandoned* that child. Your son. He is why I came here looking for you, looking for Rachel...er, Rosie. *I* have been looking out for him these past few months."

"Very kind of you," Erasmus said with another of those smirks. "And you could have kept him, but now you've all gone and mucked this up right and good. So we're going to have to go with a different plan."

"Ras," Abigail said. "Please…"

"Always liked it when you begged, my dear. That's why I always made you do it," Erasmus said. "But it seems that the discovery of yet another lover has driven you to the brink. You're going to shoot Celeste. And Pippa. In a rage, you know. That rage you hide inside yourself that will finally come out. You'll attempt to kill Rosie, too." He glanced toward her. "I'll shoot an arm, love. Nothing permanent."

"You're going to shoot me?" Rosie gasped.

"I must do so to make it look right." He shook his head. "Think of the future. You survive this vicious attack and my brother will pay you double what he might have otherwise. You and I can go to America, a new life with no other wives. Freedom to do anything. Nothing holding us down."

"Except for your son," Pippa said.

Erasmus glanced at her. "We won't even need him with this new plan. Why take him when we could be truly free?"

"You would abandon our son?" Rosie whispered.

"No one is abandoning anyone."

They all pivoted toward the door, toward the voice there. Celeste knew it before she even looked. Owen stood there, his own weapon trained on Erasmus. With him was the Earl of Leighton, and he stared at his brother, face entirely drained of color.

"What is this, Ras?" he whispered. "What have you done? My God, what have you done?"

CHAPTER 23

Owen could hardly breathe, hardly think, as he stared at Celeste, perched precariously on Erasmus Montgomery's lap with a pistol pressed into her side. And he needed to think. He needed to remain calm even though the woman he loved was threatened.

"Are you hurt?" he asked, never removing his eyes from her, willing her to see that he would protect her.

"No," she whispered. "I'm so sorry, Owen. I'm so sorry."

He shook his head. "None of that."

"Very romantic," Montgomery snapped. "But why don't we get back to the matter at hand? Rhys, you fool. Why couldn't you leave bloody well enough alone?"

"Because I thought you were murdered and I gave a damn about bringing the killer of my only brother to justice," Leighton said, his voice shaking. "And here you are, playing out another game with people's emotions. Like we're all pieces on your bloody chessboard."

"You were always better at that game than I was," Montgomery said.

"But not this one. This game you are expert at," Leighton replied, turning his face in disgust. His gaze landed on Phillipa. "Has he hurt you?"

"No," she whispered, and cast her eyes to the ground.

"I'm also fine, thank you both for asking," Abigail muttered.

"My wife, eh?" Montgomery said. "Tsk, tsk, big brother. That isn't very proper at all."

"Enough of this!" Leighton snapped. "You are going to put that fucking gun down and you are going to answer for what you've done."

"You're not my lord and master. You're barely my brother," Montgomery snapped, and Owen flinched. He was dangerous, and even more so as he became agitated.

Leighton seemed to see the same because he drew in a few breaths. "You must know this is inescapable now." His tone was much gentler. "Please, Ras, let Celeste go, let the others go, and you and I can talk. We'll mitigate the damage, we'll—"

"Will you shut your mouth?" Montgomery drawled. "Bloody fucking hell, shut your mouth. Stop pretending you give a damn about me. Yeah, we need to work this out. But it's on my terms now, *my lord.*"

Owen cleared his throat. "And what are those terms?"

Montgomery shook his head. "I want my money, Rhys. I want the money you stole from me."

"I didn't steal anything. You had access to an inheritance for years, far beyond what Father left for you. I cut you off because you couldn't manage to keep any control over yourself. I stole nothing from you."

"Leighton," Owen said. "Look at Celeste."

Her eyes were squeezed shut, her face entirely white and pinched with pain. Montgomery had jammed the gun so hard against her ribs that Owen was certain she would have a massive bruise. If she survived this.

But no, he couldn't think of an alternative to her survival. Not if he wanted to function.

Leighton cleared his throat. "Please let her go."

"I have leverage with this one," Montgomery said with a flash of a grin toward Owen that made him want to grab the man and strangle the very life out of his body. "And I think I might have some leverage with that one, too." He nudged his head toward Pippa. "Tough luck, Abigail—looks like you don't have a champion."

At the fireplace, Rosie Stanton gave a little cruel laugh.

Montgomery arched a brow at his brother. "Tell me what I want to hear and then I'll give you gentlemen what you want."

"Money," Leighton said softly. "Enough to start your life wherever you want. With your family, Rosie and the..." He cleared his throat. "The child. Assuming you want him."

There was a beat where Montgomery gave no answer, and it was all the answer in the world. Rosie Stanton stepped forward, her hands behind her back as she glared at him. "You would truly abandon our son?"

Montgomery pursed his lips. "He served his purpose if we get what we want, didn't he? Do you really want some screaming brat bogging us down, ruining the fun we'll have?"

"He's my child!" she screeched at the top of her lungs.

Montgomery looked at her with disgust, undisguised and cruel. "Maybe you don't want to come then, eh, girl? Maybe you want to stay behind and face whatever consequences my brother has in mind for your part in this?"

Rosie was silent for a moment, staring at him like she didn't even know him. And then she pulled a pistol from behind her back and trained it on him, on Celeste just as surely. And Owen's heart felt like it was being torn from his chest.

Celeste bit back a yelp as Erasmus yanked her so that Rosie Stanton's gun was only pointed at her. A shield to protect him, just as he'd always been using others to protect himself over the years. They were all victims of it, everyone in this room. Even the woman who could very easily end her life.

"I've been following you for years," Rosie sobbed, the gun shaking in her hand. "Watching you bed woman after woman and tell me it was for our future. Watching you waste everything you got and pretend that it was for me and our son."

"For you," he said. "You ungrateful cow. And now you point a pistol at me? At *me*? The man who has done all this to give you what you wanted?"

"It was never about what I wanted. I lived in your house in Bath and I listened to you bed *her*—" She pointed the hand that didn't hold the gun toward Pippa. "—again and again. I watched you waste all their dowries on your frivolities while you promised it was for me. And you convinced me to bear you a child. I thought it was because you loved me, but...you don't love anyone but yourself, do you?"

"Christ but you run your mouth," Erasmus barked at Rosie, but Celeste blocked him out. She focused instead on Owen. Owen's handsome face, Owen's fear that lit up his beautiful pale brown eyes.

I love you, she mouthed.

Those eyes widened and he swallowed hard. Nodded once. And then looked hard at Erasmus. She glanced up at her once husband. He was so busy screeching at Rosie, berating her, that he had loosened his grip on Celeste a fraction. Owen was practically spelling out to her that this was her chance.

Her only chance.

She drew in a deep breath and then swung her elbow back. She hit Erasmus in the center of his chest and he gasped in surprised pain. She dove out of his arms, flattening on the floor.

Not a moment too soon, because just as she did Rosie shook her head. "You are the worst thing that has ever happened to me."

She fired the gun as Celeste covered her ears and screamed. A weight hit her, and for a moment she thought it was Erasmus, falling over her as he died. But it wasn't. It was Owen, and he was warm and real as he covered her.

There was a deafening silence in the room for what couldn't have been more than a few seconds but felt like a lifetime. Owen rolled away, allowing Celeste to see what had transpired. Abigail was barely rising from the floor in front of the settee. Leighton had grabbed for Pippa and was holding her against his chest, turned away from Erasmus's body.

Dead. This time in reality, if the glazed emptiness of his stare was any indication.

"Miss Stanton," Owen said softy, his voice gentle. He held out a hand. "Give me the gun."

Rosie stared at the dead body, then at the gun in her hand. She let out a keening cry that seemed to tear the room down as she dropped the weapon with a clatter.

"What have I done?" she gasped out. And then she ran from the room.

Leighton released Pippa and took a long step after her. "Wait there!" he called out.

"Go with him," Celeste whispered. "I'm fine. I'm fine."

Owen didn't seem to believe that, but he squeezed her gently and then took off after Leighton and Rosie. Which left the three wives of Erasmus Montgomery to stare at his dead body on the floor.

"Oh, Ras," Abigail said, sinking down on her haunches. She felt for his pulse. After a moment, she shook her head. "He is well and truly gone this time."

Pippa covered her mouth. "I cannot believe it."

Celeste didn't add her voice to their chorus. They had loved the handsome, selfish, cruel man who lay at their feet. Or loved something he had presented to them, something he had offered in order to save himself. But Celeste hadn't. And she felt almost nothing as she looked down at him.

"What he said about how he faked the death...." She shook her head.

Abigail pressed his eyes closed and got to her feet, wiping her eyes with the back of her hand. "He was always...clever, despite himself."

"Yes," Pippa said softly. "Despite himself."

Leighton and Owen returned to the room, panting but long faced. "Rosie is gone. She raced off and we lost her in the crowd." Owen crossed back to Celeste as if he couldn't stand not to be near her. As she wrapped an arm around him, she leaned into him, feeling the steady thud of his heartbeat, the warmth of his presence that somehow made the horrific events of this long day bearable.

Leighton sank to his knees before the body of his brother and stared. "We were never brothers," he whispered. "His mother made certain of it. And yet I feel..."

Pippa stepped toward him, rested her hand on his shoulder. "Rhys," she whispered. His given name, not his title. He glanced up at her, held her stare for a long, charged moment, and then shook his head.

"I would suggest that the ladies leave. Gregory, perhaps you could escort them in Abigail's carriage. I will call for Gilmore and we will...take care of this."

Owen tilted his head. "Take care of it?"

Leighton met his eyes. "I asked you to find out who killed my brother, and now we know the sordid truth."

Celeste stared at this man. Unlike his brother, he had never been anything but decent and kind toward her. She saw his pain, she saw his grief and loss and his strength. She saw all he was that his brother had never been. And she mourned for him.

"I'm so sorry, my lord," she said.

Leighton looked up at her. "You are too kind, Celeste. I do not deserve your apology and I owe you a great many more." He sighed as he pushed to his feet. "I think Erasmus has done enough damage to everyone involved, even the young lady who shot him. If there is anything that men like Gilmore and I know how to do, it is to make things easier for ourselves, to cover up the cracks so the world sees perfection."

"The cracks were not yours to fill," Pippa said softly. "The imperfection never yours."

"But it shares my name. My blood. And it is my responsibility." Leighton glanced at Pippa again and then at Owen. "Let me do it, Mr. Gregory. Let me cover this up. Not to save myself—there is no doing that. The world knows of Erasmus's bigamy and betrayal, and I will spend years regaining the honor he took from our family. But let me cover up the rest for *them*."

Owen looked at Abigail and Pippa. He looked down at Celeste. And he nodded. "I will meet with you later. And you will tell me how to word the report."

Leighton stepped forward and extended a hand. "Thank you, Owen."

"Rhys," Owen said as they shook. Then he led Celeste from the room with Abigail and Pippa trailing behind them. Celeste was numb as they got back into the carriage. Numb as they rode off back to London. Back to a reality she could not see played out before her except in shades of pain.

And she could only hope there would be one light in the distance. One light held by the man who now held her. But it was not guaranteed and she would have to wait to see if it were even possible.

Owen lay in bed, his arms around Celeste. It had been twelve hours since the horrible events in Lambeth. Ten since he had escorted Pippa and Abigail back to their home and brought Celeste to his. They had not spoken. He thought she could not yet. He certainly couldn't find the words to talk about what had happened.

Seeing her with the gun jabbed in her side, hearing Montgomery declare that he would kill her, knowing that bastard meant it...it had ripped a hole in Owen that he doubted would ever be filled. He would wake the rest of his days from that nightmare, sweating in pure terror.

He could only hope that the woman laying beside him right now would still be there during those future nights, future nightmares. That would make the rest almost worthwhile.

She stirred a little and he tightened his arms around her. She was still in her gown. He'd made no attempt to undress her, just let her fall into his bed, weeping until she slept. He'd only removed his own boots, his shirt so he could feel her against his skin. Know she was real and whole.

"Owen?" she said softly, her breath gentle against his bare chest.

She glanced up at him, and he smiled at her. "Sleep. You need to rest."

"What time is it?" she asked, her fingers tracing patterns into his skin.

"After four," he said. "Very early."

"I cannot believe I slept like that," she said. "How could I sleep after what happened?"

"Your body needed to release," he said, smoothing his fingers through her hair the way he loved to when he held her like this. "You needed to turn off the world and recover."

"What will happen now?" she whispered.

He shifted. "Well, Leighton and Gilmore will pay their way into a cover up, I assume. The rumors of a murder will transform to one of a suicide, or if Leighton pays enough, perhaps an accident. Some of the pressure will come off. Not all. But enough that Leighton will at least be able to move again."

"You will be agreeable to that lie?" she asked.

He drew in a long breath. "That isn't an easy question," he said. "And I admit that I have lain here thinking about it all night. Leighton is a decent man, despite his bad relations. And Gilmore is too. I was hired to uncover the truth to their satisfaction, and I did that. Would revealing the desperate truth to the public, to the authorities, do anything positive? Or would it bring ruin?"

"And what about Rosie Stanton?" she whispered.

He held Celeste tighter as a shudder worked through her. "She is running now. Perhaps she'll return for the child she left behind. The son Montgomery wanted to abandon. Leighton will have his say in that, and I think Phillipa, too, since she is involved in his life in some way."

Celeste nodded against his chest. "I suppose that is a bridge to cross in the future."

"It is. Perhaps it is not a bridge you need worry about, except as a friend to the parties involved." Owen leaned down to kiss her forehead.

She was quiet for a moment and he let her be. Enjoyed the presence of her in his life, in his bed, in his arms. But there were things that needed to be said now. Things he refused to avoid.

"You mouthed that you loved me when Montgomery had that gun to your back," he said. "When you thought you would die."

She stiffened against him. "I did," she admitted. "I wasn't sure you understood. I thought you did, but…"

"Oh, I most definitely did."

She lifted her gaze to him. "And what did you think? Be honest with me. It was a moment of great pressure and I don't expect you to pretend that you return my feelings if you don't. We never made promises to each other and I—"

He cupped her jaw and tilted her face up. With a smile, he caught her lips with his and kissed her, first tenderly and then with more passion as she lifted against him with a sigh.

"I love you, Celeste," he whispered against her lips as they broke apart at last. "Not because it was a situation filled with tension, not because I don't want to hurt you, not because I feel an obligation. I have loved you almost since the first moment I saw you. I will love you until the moment I take my last breath. So when you ask what I thought, it was this great, discordant joy in the midst of terror and anguish. But I must ask if your heart still feels the same now that a gun isn't pressed to your flesh."

He held his breath as she sat up and stared at him. "Are you mad? I adore you, Owen Gregory. With all my heart and soul. I love you so very much."

She launched herself into his arms and he caught her, joy filling him in every part of his being. And a longing to be with her that he had tamped down reawakened as he drew her across his body, laid back with her covering him.

"Show me," he murmured against her lips.

CHAPTER 24

When the door to Rosie Stanton's house opened and revealed that Erasmus was alive, Celeste had many thoughts. Chief among them was the sinking dread that she would never be happy again. That the actions of one selfish man would end her life, either by snuffing it out with his gun, or grinding all the good away until there was nothing left.

But as she straddled Owen's hips, her mouth seeking his with urgency, being met so sweetly and passionately, those fears melted away. The future wouldn't be perfect. There were many unanswered questions and doors that would be forever closed because of her bigamist husband.

But one door that was open now was the one that led to Owen. The one that merged their hearts and their bodies and their lives from this day forward.

And because she had almost lost that, she found herself desperate to feel it now. She pushed at her skirts, bunching them around her waist, she fumbled with his front fall and he caught her hand with his, pulling away from her lips to smile up at her.

"We have all the time in the world," he whispered.

She shook her head. "I need this now."

He held her stare and then nodded. With a flick of his wrist, he opened his trousers and let the flap fall away. She licked her lips as she looked at him, hard as steel, as ready as she was. And hers. He was hers, from head to toe. Including this magnificent cock she caught in her hand and stroked once, twice, until his eyes rolled back and he let out a deep, guttural moan.

And it was too much. She leaned forward and brushed the head of him against her lips, stroking him back and forth across the crease.

"Celeste," he grunted, but she didn't allow him to protest or question. She took him into her mouth, swirling her tongue around him, reveling in his taste.

He lifted into her, taking a little more, and she didn't resist. She stroked over him, drawing him to the brink, slowing to take him back. She watched him, loving how he gripped his hands against the coverlet, dug his fingers into her hair to hold her closer.

She gave to him and the tingling between her legs multiplied with his pleasure. Until she knew she would come with just a touch when the moment arrived.

At last he grunted, pushing her mouth from him, dragging her up his body, pulling her over him once more so that his cock slipped into the slit of her drawers and teased her entrance.

"Today I need to feel you," he gasped as he wound his fingers into her hair and tilted her face so she would look at him. "Today I need to love you completely. And tomorrow you can suck me dry."

"Tomorrow and forever, for all of it," she promised.

He thrust hard and fast and filled her to the brim with him. She ground down with a garbled moan, lost in the gorgeous sensation of their joining. Bound by the fact that they would never have to be parted again. That there were no more questions. He loved her, she loved him, and this was everything.

She rolled her hips over him, their kisses growing more and

more heated, more and more desperate as her pleasure mounted. The edge of release was right there, the cusp of madness so close she could feel it. When it came, when *she* came, she threw her head back, slamming her hips to his in the quiet as she said his name over and over, said she loved him over and over. He caught her hips, the tendons in his neck straining as he lifted into her, lifted her off the bed, forced her to ride through her crisis and into his.

She smiled as he cried out and pumped into her, joined fully at last. Then she collapsed onto his chest, their bodies still connected, slick and hot. The silence that followed was perfect. The silence of *knowing*.

But finally he tightened his arms around her and let out a sigh. "You asked me earlier what came next," he said. "And I think I gave you a coward's answer by telling you tales of what everyone else in our lives would do next."

"You want to tell me about us," she said, resting her hands on his chest and her chin against them. "Oh yes, I'd love to hear that."

"I want to marry you, Celeste. Not now if you don't want it. I know you've been given very few choices and haven't had any autonomy, but when you are ready. And in our future I see evenings at Lena and Harriet's salon. I see nights in this bed, doing what we just did, slower and with more licking."

She laughed even though tears had begun to sting her eyes. "And faster?"

"Sometimes faster," he promised. "I see you inserting yourself in every investigation, because I know you. And I see myself needing your input because you make me better at what I do. Better at who I am."

"I would like that," she whispered.

"And I see you exploring whatever you'd like to do or be. Write a book? Paint? Become an accomplished pianoforte player? I want to see you do it all. Whatever you want, whoever you wish to be."

The tears slid down her cheeks now. Joyful and hopeful for the first time in perhaps her whole life. "If you are a soothsayer, Owen

Gregory, I love the future in your eyes. I want all of it. As soon as possible."

"Marry me?" he whispered, brushing his lips to hers.

"Did I not say yes?" she asked. "I thought I had been saying it the first moment you stepped into my parlor. But let me be clearer. Yes. Yes to it all. Yes to you and our future. Just...yes."

EPILOGUE

Two weeks later

Though the room wore black for propriety, for the world had now been convinced that Erasmus Montgomery had died of an unfortunate accident, the party was anything but bleak. The parlor in the little blue house across from Pettyfort Park was bright with a fire and friends gathered to celebrate the recent union of Owen Gregory and Celeste Hendricks no more and Montgomery never quite. But now she was Celeste Gregory, and that was more than enough.

Celeste smiled at Harriet and Lena, already a welcome addition to her circle of friends, fellow wives. Abigail stood with them, chatting intently.

The Duke of Gilmore lingered to the side of the group with Lord Leighton. The two old friends were deep in conversation, as well, though Celeste wasn't certain the topic was as light as whatever the women were engaged in.

Pippa was by herself at the fire, staring into the flames. As Celeste approached her, Pippa jumped. "I'm sorry," she said with a laugh that didn't quite meet those bright green eyes of hers. "I was miles away."

"Understandably," Celeste said, taking her arm.

"It was a beautiful wedding," Pippa said with a sigh. "And you will be truly happy, as you have been these last two weeks while the special license was rushed through. You could not wait a moment more, could you?"

"I couldn't," Celeste said with a laugh. "Both because I am so deliriously in love and also because the longer I waited, the more likely it was that my parents would show up here to put their noses in my future. The rush kept them in Twiddleport, where I hope they will stay."

"I understand that completely." Pippa bent her head.

Celeste wrinkled her brow. "How are you?"

"It's lonely at the Montgomery residence now that you are gone," Pippa admitted. "Abigail and I have each other, of course, but things are still strained. I wish she had told me the truth sooner, and she wishes the same. It's a small wall between us, but a wall nonetheless."

"One you will overcome, I'm sure," Celeste assured her.

Pippa frowned. "It will be harder soon. Though Rosie Stanton has not reappeared, both Leighton and I have concerns about her son's future. We depart for Bath shortly, and I have no idea how long we will remain there, making arrangements for the boy."

Celeste glanced toward Leighton again and found he was watching Pippa, though his eyes darted away when he was caught at it. She had her own questions about those two and what their connection was and could be.

But she kept them to herself. It was a complicated thing, after all, and not one she was ready to push. "You will be of great help to him, I know," Celeste said. "Have Leighton and Gilmore had any information of where Rosie could have gone?"

"There is some indication she might have fled to America. They said something about a ship to Maryland or Lower Canada," Pippa said. "But I do not know whether or not to trust in that." She caught her breath as if to say more, but then she smiled over Celeste's shoulder. "But now here comes your husband. Mr. Gregory, you have yourself a treasure."

Celeste looked back, and her heart skipped as Owen joined them. He wrapped his arm around her waist, and for a moment there was only peace in the world. What a rapturous thing it was, to have a person who could bring such a feeling and with such ease.

"I do, indeed," he said as he pressed a kiss to Celeste's cheek. "A treasure worth more than rubies."

Pippa smiled, though a flicker of sadness sparkled in her eyes. Then she nodded. "I see that Abigail has finished her conversation with Lena and Harriet. I will join her."

She slipped away, and Owen watched her before he glanced at Celeste. "She told you of her and Leighton's plans?"

"Yes. There is a certain longing there, I think."

He was quiet a moment. "I don't think you're wrong. I recognize it as very much like the longing I once felt for you. Do you worry?"

"Only that they are in such a difficult position. I fear they will not let themselves comfort one another, even if that is their mutual desire." She frowned. "I would like them to be happy. Pippa and Abigail deserve the same joy I've found with you."

"Your concern for your friends does you credit." He smiled. "But no one could be as happy as we are."

She laughed. "That may be true. I do love you, you know. With all my heart."

"Then I am truly the luckiest man in the world."

"No, I am the luckiest," she corrected him. "Because I now have a husband in truth and you are well worth anything I went through on the road to you."

EXCERPT OF THE DEFIANT WIFE

THE THREE MRS BOOK 2

Summer 1813

Phillipa Montgomery had expected a great many things in her life, but marrying a bigamist, nearly being murdered by him and then helping one of his other brides ready for her wedding...well, she never would have guessed that one.

Yet here she was, standing in the home of her late...husband? It was easier to just call him husband even though he never really had been.

She was helping adjust the beautiful white feather-and-pearl headpiece in Celeste Montgomery's hair while Abigail Montgomery fastened the pretty sapphire necklace Celeste's future husband had given her, the one that matched her eyes.

"You look so happy," Abigail said, the tightness to her smile mimicking the same emotions Phillipa felt as she looked at her friend

Not because she begrudged Celeste her happiness. No one deserved it more! But just because happiness was a feeling that had fled from Pippa's life years before, thanks to Erasmus Montgomery and his bitter lies, and she was, she could admit, if only to herself...jealous.

"I *am* so happy," Celeste breathed. "I could not have imagined that when Owen knocked on my door not so very long ago and destroyed my world with news of Erasmus's duplicity that I could ever be so happy."

Pippa smiled, and this one felt less tight. Owen Gregory, the investigator hired by Erasmus's brother, Rhys Montgomery, the Earl of Leighton, was the best of men.

Pippa swallowed hard at the thought of the earl. Pushed at things she ought not think when it came to the man.

"I don't think anyone could have imagined *anything* that has happened to us all in recent months," Abigail sighed as she sank onto the settee in the dressing room. "Between finding out our supposed husband had multiple wives, to each being suspected of his murder, to then finding out he wasn't dead after all."

"And then he tried to kill us," Pippa added with a shake of her head. "And now he *is* dead and you are marrying again. It's a whirlwind." Exhaustion overwhelmed her at just the thought of it.

Celeste turned away from the mirror and faced the others. "Yes, all those things are truly terrible. I don't deny it. But I also don't want to forget that what we went through brought us together." She reached out and caught Pippa's hand, then motioned for Abigail to take her other. When she had joined their circle, Celeste smiled through tears. "I'm so lucky to know you both. To call you my friends, as close as sisters despite all the terrible things. So I can't regret any of the worst, as it has brought me so much happiness."

Abigail leaned forward to kiss her cheek. "And it will only bring you more, I think." She glanced at the clock on the mantel. "Gracious, we are almost out of time."

Celeste's cheeks flushed with pleasure. "I can hardly wait."

Pippa smiled at her eagerness and squeezed her hand. "I will go tell the vicar and Mr. Gregory that you are almost ready while Abigail puts on your finishing touches."

"Thank you," Celeste breathed with a smile that rivaled the sun.

Pippa slipped from the warmth of her friend's joy into the hallway and drew a long breath as she pulled the door shut behind herself. Her hands were shaking and she smoothed them along the silky skirt of her gown.

"Phillipa?"

She froze, still facing the shut door. That voice was one she had come to know very well. Too well, truth be told. She swallowed hard, tried to wipe all emotion from her expression and turned.

Rhys Montgomery, Earl of Leighton, stood in the dim light of the hall and her breath caught just as it always caught, from the first moment she met him. He was a beautiful man, there was no denying that. He was tall, very tall, at least a head taller than she was. He had dark hair that swept over his forehead in nothing ever but perfect waves. And blue eyes. The deepest blue she'd ever seen.

He was never mussed, he was never out of place. No, he was too proper for that. Too serious, thanks to the hell his half-brother had unleashed upon them all. Although she thought Rhys...Lord Leighton...had probably always been a thoughtful sort of person.

His perfectly sculpted jawline tightened and those blue eyes flickered over her face. "Are you well, Phillipa?"

Because there were so many Mrs. Montgomerys going around lately, those in the inner circle had taken to calling the women by their first names, at least in private, to reduce confusion. But she would never get used to the way Leighton said *Phillipa*. It rolled over his tongue almost like a caress and made her stomach flip in ways that it most definitely should not.

"I'm fine," she gasped out with a forced smile. "I was just coming to assure the groom that the bride is almost ready for him."

He inclined his head. "And I was sent by said groom to check on the bride."

Her smile became more genuine. "Mr. Gregory is anxious then."

"Very." A flutter of a smile crossed his lips and she swallowed at the sight of it. The man was truly handsome and she had no right to dwell on it so much. For too many reasons.

He cleared his throat. "Actually, I'm glad to have caught you alone. There is something we need to discuss."

Her heart rate ratcheted up a notch and she fought to keep that reaction from her face as she motioned him back up the hall toward the stairs. At least if they were walking side by side, he couldn't look at her so intently. "What is it?"

He paused, like this conversation was uncomfortable. "My brother's son."

Now she stumbled and he reached out to catch her elbow. The briefest of touches, gone the moment she was steady, but she felt it ricochet through her body just like his words did.

The son was not her child, though she had raised him since his mother disappeared. Pippa's former servant, a woman who had turned out to be a long-time lover of Erasmus Montgomery. His true love. They'd had a child, one Erasmus saw as a bargaining chip and who Rosie, the mother, truly loved even if she had made a series of terrible decisions that separated them.

But now Erasmus was dead. Struck down by Rosie, herself, who had promptly run away.

"Kenley," she breathed, trying not to think too hard about those chubby cheeks she adored. She had not seen the boy in weeks, though she regularly heard from the servants who had taken over his care.

Rhys flinched. "He named him...Kenley?" he asked, his voice cracking in a way that revealed emotion he didn't show on his angled face.

"Yes."

He shook his head. "That was our father's given name. Taken from our grandmother's maiden name."

"I...I didn't know. Turns out I didn't know much. But I am sorry for the grief all this has caused."

"I know you are, even if you needn't be."

She lifted her gaze and he held it for a moment. Everything else in the hallway melted away then. All that was left was him as he held her attention, as he made her forget that anything else in the world existed.

She blinked and fought to maintain whatever little dignity she had left. "I appreciate your kindness more than you could know, my lord. When it comes to the child, though, I could make arrangements to return to Bath. Everything will be topsy-turvy because of the wedding, but I'm certain I could be ready the day after tomorrow and be home before the week is out. I could prepare a full report on the boy, and we could find some kind of schedule that would suit you as to his health and well-being."

She expected him to agree and for that to be the end of it. She didn't exactly look forward to a return, but she had always known it was going to happen. She had responsibilities there, of course. She couldn't live in the fantasy land of London forever.

But to her surprise, he shook his head. "No."

Her brow wrinkled. "N-No?" she repeated.

"I need to assess the situation for myself."

She stared at him. "But you...you have so much to attend to here. I know your world has been turned upside down, Rhys..." She shook her head. "Lord Leighton. You cannot possibly spare the time for this."

"He is a child," he said, his gaze holding hers again. "His life and future are the most important matters I have to attend to. I could not focus on the more frivolous resolutions knowing that I had not dealt with this first."

Her lips parted at the passion with which he spoke about a baby he had never even met. Never known the existence of until just two weeks before. "You are truly a decent man."

His jaw tightened and those bright blue eyes flickered over her again. "Not very decent, I assure you." He straightened his perfectly placed jacket with what looked like discomfort and then began to move down the hallway again, forcing her to follow. "Will you accompany me to Bath?" he asked.

Her heart lodged in her throat and she had to swallow hard to have any hope of speaking. "Yes," she squeaked out. "Of course."

"I know you didn't come here with a companion," he said, and his gaze moved straight ahead as they went down the stairs together toward the parlor where friends were gathered for the wedding.

"No, I...it is complicated," she said. "I came here alone."

"Then I will hire someone to attend you on the journey," he said. "For propriety."

She almost laughed at the very idea but held back the unladylike reaction. At the door to the parlor, she stopped and said, "I'm not certain that propriety applies when it comes to me anymore, but anything for your comfort, my lord. I will be ready to return to Bath whenever you need me to be."

"Thank you," he said softly.

She inclined her head and touched the door handle. "We will discuss particulars later, I'm sure."

He nodded and she entered the parlor. He didn't follow, but she felt his stare on her as she walked across the room. Felt it burn into her back like a flame. And knew how careful she had to be, because the warmth of his fire was most definitely off limits to her. For now. For always.

#

Rhys took a long sip of the glass of champagne that had been forced into his hand for the toasts and twitched his nose at the tickle of bubbles it left behind. It was a festive drink and a festive occasion, and he was happy for the couple. He'd begun to consider Owen Gregory a friend, and Celeste—well, now she was Celeste Gregory, not Montgomery—deserved the love she had apparently found.

All the women his brother had destroyed were owed happiness and likely a great deal more.

His gaze flitted across the room toward Phillipa Montgomery.

She stood with Abigail Montgomery and the bride, their heads together in serious conversation. God's teeth but she was beautiful. He never wanted to see it so clearly, but how could one not?

There was just something about the woman. And it wasn't her mop of curly blonde hair that never seemed entirely tamed by whatever pretty style she wore, or the long expanse of neck that made a man want to trace it with his fingertips. It wasn't her green gaze that was filled with intelligence. It wasn't just her lovely figure or her bright smile.

All those things were wonderful, of course. Undeniable in their attraction. But there was something deeper that always made Rhys turn his head when she entered a room. Always made him track her like a hawk.

It was her spark. Despite the terrible situation the woman was in, there was always this light in her. Like a never-ending candle burned in her soul. Her mouth almost always held a little smile, like she knew a secret, even when she was at rest. How he wished he could ferret that secret out. Give her a few more secrets to make her smile like that.

Only...he couldn't. *Ever.* Because she was the widow of his brother. Well, she sort of was, if one ignored the bigamy. He couldn't ignore that, though. It had already destroyed his world. His future. His name.

And so for at least two dozen awful reasons he had to ignore the longing that tightened his chest any time Phillipa entered a room. He had to chastise himself whenever he woke hot and hard because of dreams of her. He had to stop memorizing her scent and the way she tilted her head back when she laughed.

"Leighton." Rhys's best friend, the Duke of Gilmore, stepped up beside him and joined him in looking over the threesome of ladies across the room. Gilmore's sister had been the latest target of Rhys's brother before Erasmus's death. Both the one he faked and the real one. Gilmore had hired Owen Gregory to look into the blackguard pursuing his sister's fortune. And when Erasmus had been presumed murdered, Rhys had hired him in turn to find the culprit.

Complicated, to say the least, but he was pleased that his friendship with Gilmore had not been damaged. He had few enough people he was close to, he didn't want to lose the duke.

"Gilmore," he said, and they clinked their glasses without drinking. Before they could speak, Owen Gregory stepped up to join them. Rhys smiled at him. "It was quite the ceremony. My most sincere wishes for your happiness. Mrs. Gregory is a wonderful woman."

"She is," Gregory said with a happy smile that felt like a punch in Rhys's gut. "I am the luckiest of men."

Rhys let out the air in his lungs. "Will you stay in London?"

"Yes. I intend on taking her away this winter and having her all to myself, but for now I have work to do. So we'll settle into my little home here and practice being newlyweds."

Once more, Rhys's gaze flitted to where it didn't belong: Phillipa.

"And what of you gentlemen? Now that the situation with Montgomery has been resolved, what are your plans?" Gregory asked.

Rhys shook his head. "There is little resolved for me, I fear. Only new problems begun. We can cover up the murder, and I will. My brother was, as far as the law is concerned, a suicide."

Gilmore grunted a sound of displeasure. "And it only took a few bribes and payoffs. Not that I blame you, of course. It was the most palatable story."

Rhys flinched. "None of this is palatable. But the specter of murder or suicide or anything else surrounding his death doesn't change that the world knows what he did before that end. They know about the multiple wives and the debts and the bad acts. There is much to resolve, both the public...and the personal."

Gilmore and Gregory exchanged a glance filled with concern on Rhys's behalf. "Can I help?" Gregory asked.

Rhys felt heat suffuse his neck, creep toward his face at the humiliation. "You've done so much to help already," he said. "And I appreciate your kindness, your counsel and your friendship, both of you. But what is left to manage is something I fear I must do alone."

Gregory looked as though he wanted to argue that point, but before he could his gaze moved toward the three Mrs. Mongomerys. Well, two Mrs. Montgomerys now, and one Mrs. Gregory. There must have been some communication between husband and wife that Rhys couldn't understand because everything in Gregory's demeanor changed. He relaxed, loosened. Rhys envied him for that.

"There will be time enough for maudlin reflection on my destroyed life," Rhys said, giving Gregory a playful shove toward his new wife. "Today is for celebrating. Go to her, as it is obvious you wish to, and don't give another thought to me."

Gregory tossed a grin over his shoulder and then did as he'd been told, moving toward Celeste like a thirsty man toward water. When he was gone, Gilmore sidled close and nudged Rhys with his shoulder.

"What exactly are you left to manage?" Gilmore asked. "I am not fawning over a new bride, so perhaps *I* can be of help."

Rhys sighed. "My first focus must be my nephew." He gulped at the idea. "That child should not suffer for what his parents did, not to themselves, not to each other. So we will go to Bath likely the day after tomorrow and I will see what is best in that situation."

Gilmore arched a brow. "*We*? Who is *we*?" Rhys was quiet for apparently too long because the duke answered his own question. "*We* being you and Phillipa?"

There was something in his tone that made Rhys duck his head. "Don't," he growled.

Gilmore moved to stand in front of him so he could look him in the face and effectively block any attempt at escape. Because his friend knew him so well, damn him.

"I have been your friend for how long?" he asked softly. Gently, even.

Rhys shook his head and refused to meet Gilmore's stare. "I

don't know. Too long. All my life. Long enough for me to tell you that I don't need your opinions."

Gilmore rolled his eyes. "Well, that's never stopped me."

Despite everything, Rhys couldn't help but smile at the quip. He relaxed a fraction. "No, I suppose it hasn't. And since you will do as you like without a thought for me, then go ahead and give them, but know I'll ignore them."

Gilmore snorted but his demeanor quickly became more serious. "Rhys," he began, and Rhys stiffened at the use of his given name. They never called each other by anything but their titles, not since they were in short pants. It gave a gravity to the situation that only piled up on everything else. "She is fascinating."

Rhys wrinkled his brow. He hadn't expected that to be what his friend said. *Fascinating.* Yes, that was the way to describe Phillipa, and a slash of jealousy was his immediate response. One he shoved down as hard and as fast as he could.

"Indeed," he said because Gilmore seemed to be waiting some kind of answer to his statement.

The duke edged a little closer. "But if you are interested in her, and I say *if* even though I know there isn't an if about it…it could be bad."

The first reaction that hit Rhys in the chest was a strong desire to shove Gilmore away from him. Like distance would make what he said less true. That somehow he could erase this moment and pretend it hadn't happened.

But once that sudden and violent sensation passed, a more metered response settled into his chest. Gilmore wasn't wrong. An interest in Phillipa would be…bad. It *was* bad. There was nothing to do but fight it. Deny it to others and to himself until it went away. It had to go away.

He cleared his throat. "I am only interested in making things right for her and for the boy."

Gilmore lifted his brows. "So you say."

Rhys glared at him. "I am!" he snapped, with far more heat than the benign response warranted.

Gilmore raised his hands in surrender. "So you say," he repeated.

Rhys let his hand tighten on the half-full flute of champagne still gripped in his hand and drew a long breath. "And what about you?" he asked.

He noted that Gilmore's gaze slid back across the room to where Abigail Montgomery now stood alone. It flicked over her and his mouth tightened, for everyone knew the two despised each other.

"I am only an interested observer," he grunted. "There is nothing else for me here."

Rhys arched a brow, because he wasn't entirely sure that was true. Then he lifted his glass. "Then we are the same. Nothing of interest for us in the house of cards my brother built. So let us toast to the happy couple."

Gilmore clinked his glass without looking at him. "To the happy couple," he grumbled.

And they both drank without smiling, lost in thoughts of ladies who were out of reach by circumstance, by design, by whatever power made things impossible.

ALSO BY JESS MICHAELS

The Three Mrs

The Unexpected Wife

The Defiant Wife

The Duke's Wife

The Duke's By-Blows

The Love of a Libertine

The Heart of a Hellion

The Matter of a Marquess

The Redemption of a Rogue

The 1797 Club

The Daring Duke

Her Favorite Duke

The Broken Duke

The Silent Duke

The Duke of Nothing

The Undercover Duke

The Duke of Hearts

The Duke Who Lied

The Duke of Desire

The Last Duke

The Scandal Sheet

The Return of Lady Jane

Stealing the Duke

Lady No Says Yes

My Fair Viscount

Guarding the Countess

The House of Pleasure

Seasons

An Affair in Winter

A Spring Deception

One Summer of Surrender

Adored in Autumn

The Wicked Woodleys

Forbidden

Deceived

Tempted

Ruined

Seduced

Fascinated

The Notorious Flynns

The Other Duke

The Scoundrel's Lover

The Widow Wager

No Gentleman for Georgina

A Marquis for Mary

To see a complete listing of Jess Michaels' titles, please visit:

http://www.authorjessmichaels.com/books

ABOUT THE AUTHOR

USA Today Bestselling author Jess Michaels likes geeky stuff, Vanilla Coke Zero, anything coconut, cheese, fluffy cats, smooth cats, any cats, many dogs and people who care about the welfare of their fellow humans. She is lucky enough to be married to her favorite person in the world and lives in the heart of Dallas, TX where she's trying to eat all the amazing food in the city.

When she's not obsessively checking her steps on Fitbit or trying out new flavors of Greek yogurt, she writes historical romances with smoking hot alpha males and sassy ladies who do anything but wait to get what they want. She has written for numerous publishers and is now fully indie and loving every moment of it (well, almost every moment).

Jess loves to hear from fans! So please feel free to contact her at Jess@AuthorJessMichaels.com.

Jess Michaels raffles a gift certificate EVERY month to members of her newsletter, so sign up on her website:
http://www.AuthorJessMichaels.com/

f facebook.com/JessMichaelsBks
🐦 twitter.com/JessMichaelsBks
📷 instagram.com/JessMichaelsBks
BB bookbub.com/authors/jess-michaels

CPSIA information can be obtained
at www.ICGtesting.com
Printed in the USA
BVHW071659100321
602114BV00006B/576